Lost Through a Cottage Window

Mary Caroll

Best Wishes
May Caroll

Trace
BOOKS PUBLISHING

All rights reserved. No part of this book may be reproduced or transmitted in any form or by any means, electronic or mechanical, including photocopying, recording, or by any information storage and retrieval system—except by a reviewer who may quote brief passages in a review to be printed in a magazine, newspaper, or on the Web—without permission in writing from the publisher. For information, please contact Trace Books Publishing, P.O. Box 2193 Loves Park, Illinois 61130-0193.

This is a work of fiction. Names, characters, places and incidents either are a product of the author's imagination or are used fictitiously. Any resemblance to actual persons, living or dead, events, or locations are entirely coincidental.

Copyright © 2007 by Mary Caroll

ISBN-13: 978-0-9791223-0-9
ISBN-10: 0-9791223-0-9

Cover design by Peter Massari

Edited by Kelly Barrales-Saylor

Published by
Trace Books Publishing
P.O. Box 2193 Loves Park, IL 61130-0193

Printed and bound in the United States of America

Acknowledgments

To my husband, Tracy, whom without his support and encouragement this book would never have been placed in a reader's hands. To my children, Josh, Kyra and Kyle, who are three of the finest individuals I've ever had the pleasure of knowing. Thank you for believing in me and for helping me with that big scary thing called a computer. To my sister, Kathy, thank you for wading through all six hundred pages and then having the courage to tackle it again. To my mother, Elaine, thanks for listening and pushing. Jim, thank you for giving me or finding me the answers to all my questions. To Judy, a good neighbor and more importantly, a great teacher, including to my own children, thanks so much for the last-minute read through. While I'm on the subject of teachers, I would like to take this opportunity to thank my high school creative writing teacher, Dr. Marian Hermie, you were the very reason writing a novel became one of my life's goals. Teachers can make such a huge impact on a life, thank you for helping to shape mine.

Chapter One

July 5, 1989

"Marie! Marie!" Daniel's voice was anguished as he yelled up the rocky cliff.

Marie ran from the garden to the edge of the cliff, face ashen, hands in fists. She was afraid to look down into the sandy cove below. The last time she had heard Daniel's voice that urgent was the day they had found their eighteen-year-old daughter in the cove, with not a breath of life left in her. The pain was still so fresh that even twenty-eight years later, it was difficult to look at the beach below and not have that tragedy playing over and over in her mind. Marie focused back to Daniel's voice and forced herself to look down. To her horror, she saw the same scene, only with a different victim.

"Marie, honey, you need to call Doc so he can help me get her up to the house."

"Help get who up to the house?" asked Doc, suddenly appearing.

Marie had felt Doc's presence over her right shoulder, just for an instant, even before he spoke. Doc McNeely was her and Daniel's lifelong friend and neighbor. At seventy years of age, he still practiced medicine. Marie knew the sleepy little

New England village was still having a hard time letting him go into full retirement. Marie respected Doc's opinion and was thankful for his characteristics of being kind, witty, and abounding with wisdom. At the moment, however, his trait of being nosy and on top of every situation was indeed heaven sent. She was glad that whatever had brought Doc over here so quickly, would hopefully work out in favor for this young woman.

"I heard you yelling when I was on my back deck having coffee," explained Doc, shouting down the incline. "What's wrong, Daniel?"

"There's a young woman down here half drowned and injured. I think you and Marie should drive the truck down."

Marie was in her own thoughts, as Doc headed the old Chevy flatbed carefully down the incline. When they reached the bottom, Daniel had the woman carefully pulled up onto the sand, which was already being warmed by the intense morning sunshine. She continued to watch as Daniel walked over and helped Doc take a long wooden board out of the back of the truck, then they all headed toward the woman.

Marie saw first hand now what had caused the urgency in Daniel's voice moments earlier. She was looking at the woman's face, so red and swollen. It was hard to tell if the woman was pretty or plain. Marie saw a bloody gash starting at the woman's eyebrow and ending somewhere in her matted hair. Other areas on the woman's body displayed the same swollen redness, which would later turn into ghastly bruising. Marie also detected how the woman's body was involuntarily quivering. The shade of blue the woman's skin was tinted only confirmed Marie's worries that they needed to get this woman out of the cove and up to the house as fast as they could.

Doc was bending down, checking the woman's injuries.

"Let's slide the board under her very carefully," he ordered. "On the count of three, we'll lift her and walk slowly back to the truck."

Marie, Daniel, and Doc carried the woman carefully back to the truck and gently slid the board with the woman into the back. Marie wrapped a blanket around the woman that had been in the cab of the truck, then she and Doc climbed in the back also. Daniel then started to drive slowly back up the incline.

"Are you okay?" Doc asked.

"Actually, I'm doing better now," Marie answered softly. "It was just such a shock to relive a moment of my life that I've been trying to erase for years. Do you think she'll make it?"

Marie could see Doc was choosing his words carefully.

"I think she's better off than she was a few minutes ago. The head wound bothers me though, not so much the cut, but the swelling around it underneath the skin."

The truck slowed to a stop, as close as Daniel could get it to the front door.

"Same as before," reminded Doc. "On the count of three, we lift her out of the truck and we'll keep moving right into the house."

Marie ran ahead, opening the doors. "We can put her in the bedroom next to the kitchen," she offered, running into the bedroom and turning back the sheets on the bed.

"Daniel, you and I are going to lower the board even with the bed," Doc explained. "Marie, when I tell you to, gently roll her onto the bed. Daniel and I will tilt the board toward the bed to help roll her."

Doc counted to three, and the procedure was done in a few seconds. The woman was lying slightly on her side until Doc gently finished turning her onto her back.

"Daniel," Doc said firmly, "I need you to call for an ambulance and the police. Marie, could you bring me some warm water and clean towels? I need more blankets, too. She's in shock."

Marie and Daniel left the room, but bumped into each other upon reentry.

"The ambulance is on its way," Daniel confirmed. "And so is Dennis."

Marie was glad it was Dennis on call; he was a good sheriff and a good person. Dennis, his wife Susan, and their two children had moved here a few years earlier. Marie loved them all like her own family and she was more than confident in Dennis's ability as an officer of the law.

Marie looked at Doc and noticed his expression contorting from concern to pure anger. Before she could even comment on this change, Doc began speaking in a low, deliberately clear voice. He spoke to no one in particular, but the information flowed from his lips just the same.

"Look at these wounds and bruises," Doc began. "At first I thought they were from crashing around in the surf, but now that I have her cleaned up some, it's obvious these injuries were inflicted on her."

Shocked and confused, Marie stepped closer.

"Here at her jaw," continued Doc, "you can see that if I make a fist and lay it on top of the bruises already forming, under my knuckles is the same pattern already left by someone else's fist. The bruising on the rest of her body looks as though she might have been struck with a pipe or something similar. That same object seems to be what left that gash on her head. On her throat, you can clearly see the finger marks that form a circle around it. She was definitely being choked at some point."

Marie lifted her hands to her own throat, while trying to stretch her mind beyond reasoning.

"It also appears that she was being dragged," continued Doc. "By the open rawness on the back of her legs, and the heels of her feet, sand is still in the wounds. The corners of her mouth are cut open, probably from some sort of gag. And look at the deep cuts and rope burns on her wrists—I would say she was tied up for a long period of time. Those cuts prove she gave it a valiant effort though."

Marie noticed Daniel shaking his head back and forth. She guessed that like herself, Daniel was finding it hard to stomach the list of injuries Doc was compiling.

"I'll have to do the series of tests for a rape victim," Doc continued softly.

A tear slipped down Marie's cheek, as a knock sounded at the door. She watched as Daniel numbly turned to go answer it. At the same moment, Doc looked up from examining the woman.

"Daniel," he stated, "that should be Dennis. But given the circumstances, don't open the door unless you know for sure."

"My thought exactly," nodded Daniel.

Marie was so caught up in the condition of the woman, she hadn't thought of the danger that might still be lurking out there. Real fear gripped in the depths of her soul. She thought, perhaps, the same fear this woman must have felt being forced through her attack. Marie followed Daniel from the room. Anyone capable of doing the horrific damage, as was done to that young woman, was certainly capable of more.

"Daniel! Marie!" a familiar voice called from the outside of the door.

"Dennis," replied Daniel with a sigh, letting the officer in. "Doc felt it was best to bring her up to the house."

"The ambulance is about fifteen minutes behind me." Dennis followed Marie and Daniel into the room by the kitchen. "Dispatch told me what you had reported. My God, I can't believe it—not here."

Marie knew Dennis had never expected to have to do this

kind of job out here. She also knew things like this were exactly the reasons he had quit his job with the bureau in the city, but then things like this were incomprehensible to Marie no matter where they took place.

"She's still unconscious," Doc said, as they all entered the bedroom.

Marie watched several expressions cross Dennis's features, but just as quickly, he regained his composure.

"Was there any identification on her?" asked Dennis, coming to stand next to the bed.

"The clothes she had on were pretty shredded," replied Doc. "Probably from a combination of the attack and being thrashed around in the water all night."

"Crime lab is on its way too," started Dennis. "But Daniel, if you'll take me to where you found her, maybe something will turn up."

"Marie and I will ride in the ambulance with her over to the hospital," offered Doc.

Even as Doc spoke, the shrill of the sirens could be heard in the distance.

"I'll bring Daniel over after we've been down in the cove," Dennis said. "Is that okay with you Daniel?"

"Yes," Daniel replied and opened the door for the paramedics.

They all stood by and watched, as the woman was transferred to a gurney and put into the ambulance. Doc climbed in the back with the woman and one of the paramedics, while Marie rode in front with the driver.

"Ready to take me down?" Dennis asked.

The ambulance once again was blaring in the distance.

"I was out for my morning walk," explained Daniel, walking down the path that led to Doc's house.

Dennis followed the older man.

"It was here." Daniel pointed toward the ground. "When I

started crossing this sandy area, I noticed the sand had these funny markings in it. I would have never noticed just footprints, because we walk up and down here all the time, but these marks, well, you can see why they prodded me to go and look further."

"I can," agreed Dennis. "Especially where these two shallow ruts blend into one. There was definitely more than just an innocent stroll on the beach going on last night. Look at this set of tennis shoe imprints intertwined in the ruts, between the sand being damp last night and the warmth of the sun this morning, those imprints are practically baked in. The tread of the shoe and the sports logo are perfectly clear."

"It almost looks as if the sole of the shoe is just sitting in the sand," agreed Daniel.

"I think the victim must have been unconscious when she was dragged down here. There is no deviation from this one path. That means there wasn't any kind of a struggle going on at this point. It must have been easy enough for whoever did this to have gotten her down here and unceremoniously left her out in the water to die."

"I can't believe Marie, Doc, or I didn't hear anything last night. The only thing I can think of is that it happened during the time we were all at the picnic and fireworks. We got back from the fireworks around eleven o'clock last night. That means that poor woman was down here alone and scared, at least from then until I found her this morning at six-thirty."

"Daniel," said Dennis sympathetically, "you did everything as fast as you could for this woman, without even knowing the situation. You, Doc, and Marie probably saved her life by acting first and asking questions later. Most people would have called the authorities, then stood around until they arrived. You know yourself how long it takes the ambulance to get out this far. She would have been dead by then from the shock alone. You can't change the way it happened any more than she could have stopped this from happening to her. You kept her alive, Daniel, and for that I'm sure she's grateful."

"You're right," nodded Daniel. "At my age I should know this. The 'right now' is what we should be dealing with this moment. Hopefully she'll have many more moments in her life."

"She will," encouraged Dennis. "I want to get a picture of this shoe print, then I'll finish up here and get this cove blocked off for the crime scene specialists. It's going to have to be blocked off for a few days."

"I understand," said Daniel, looking around. "We'll probably be up at the hospital most of the time anyway. She's going to need someone looking out for her."

"That doesn't have to be your job."

"It needs to be someone's," replied Daniel. "I think between myself, Marie, and Doc, we could be pretty good at this."

"Now there's something in this whole mess I have no doubt about. You three will be the best things that woman could have hoped for."

"Come on," said Daniel. "I need to get up to the hospital."

Chapter Two

"Hey, I see by your license plates you're from Illinois," said the stranger, lifting the gas pump and inserting it into his car.

Why did people have to be so nosy? He just wanted to blend into his surroundings, go unnoticed until he could get out and away from this area. Was that too much to ask? His whole life other people were always screwing it up for him. This time even she pushed him too far and now look at the mess he was in.

"We're from Illinois too," continued the stranger. "We're heading home now from vacation. You out here on business or pleasure?"

"A little of both," he grunted, feeling his hands starting to get clammy. Why couldn't this jerk just let him be? Couldn't he tell he wanted nothing to do with small talk? Somebody was sure to put his face with a conversation. He reached in grabbing the purse from the passenger's side seat. As it cleared the window, it seemed to struggle from his angry grasp, throwing itself onto the concrete in an insubordinate gesture. The purse and all of its contents lay strewn at his feet, mocking his very existence.

"That'll cost you," smiled the stranger, bending down to help pick up the objects.

"Leave it alone!"

"I was just trying to give you a hand before your wife sees this mess," replied the stranger, backing off. "I know how women can be about their purses. Most claim they can live out of them."

Finding the wallet was the first item he needed to retrieve. He didn't want any identification waving around like some red flag. Hell, he might as well give this guy his name and be done with it.

His anger began to rise again as he opened her wallet. The money compartment was almost empty and he damn sure wasn't going to start leaving a paper trail with credit cards. The hell with the gas station. The hell with this happy-go-lucky idiot, and the hell with this car. He needed to get rid of it anyway; he was lucky he hadn't been caught with it this far.

Looking back at the car, the decision to destroy it beyond recognition began to form. He would use the remainder of the cash to buy a bus ticket to as close to home as he could get. He took a deep breath and began to feel his sense of calm return. Control, he thought to himself. That's what life was all about, controlling the little things.

"So, do you have far to drive yet tonight?" the stranger was asking.

"No, I'm about done," he replied, civilly.

"Yeah, I think we're going to call it a day soon too. No sense pushing it; that takes all the fun out of it."

"I know what you mean," he said smiling, as he got back in the car and drove off.

Chapter Three

"Daniel," Marie said, "I think she's trying to open her eyes."

Daniel and Marie bent closer to the woman in the hospital bed.

"Dear, can you hear me?" Marie asked soothingly, as she carefully brushed the hair from the woman's eyes. "You're safe now, you are with my husband and me. A friend of ours who is a doctor will be returning in just a minute."

The woman's eyes started to flutter again.

"Daniel," Marie pointed to the window shades. "I think the light is too bright for her. Close the shades and put on that small lamp over in the corner."

Yes, that was better, the woman thought to herself. Her right eye was completely shut, but she was able to open her left one and begin to focus on the people who owned the voices.

"Dear, we're here to help you. My name is Marie and this is my husband, Daniel. He found you in the water in our cove. You've been hurt and you're in a hospital."

"Is she awake?" Doc asked, entering the room with a handful of x-rays.

"Yes," Marie answered. "We've been talking to her for a few seconds now."

"And what is this young lady's name?" Doc asked, checking her IV.

"We hadn't gotten that far yet," replied Marie. "Dear, this is the doctor I was telling you about. His name is Doctor McNeely."

An awkward silence passed and Marie continued. "What is your name?"

The woman's mind was racing now. She had no idea where she was, who these people were, and more importantly, who she was herself. Was she the age of these people standing around her? They couldn't be people she knew; they had introduced themselves and asked for her name. Did she have some sort of illness? Why was she in so much pain? Her body was so hard to move. The woman, Marie, said she had been hurt. She tried to sit up and the incredible pain in her head sent bright lights bursting off behind her eyes.

"Whoa!" Doc said, gently laying his hands on her shoulders, while pressing her carefully back into the pillow. "You can't move around like that. You have a concussion, so you'll need to keep as still as possible for the next few days. You have an IV in your hand, feeding you fluids and pain medication. Your head has been stitched up and, amazingly, according to these x-rays, there are no broken bones. However, there is damage to tendons and ligaments and the bruising on your body is extensive. It will take some time to heal, but I think your prognosis is quite good considering all that you've been through."

Her throat felt as though she were choking when she tried to talk. A burning that was so raw brought tears to her eyes.

"May I have some water, please?" she rasped out.

"Let's try some ice chips and see if you can keep those down. If that stays, we'll try water in a little while."

The woman once again tried to scan her mind, but she just

couldn't piece any of this together. They had told her she was injured, and her body was certainly agreeing with that.

"Was I in a car accident?"

"Do you remember anything?" Doc asked.

She was becoming more frightened, and the woman who introduced herself as Marie came over and held her hand.

"I remember this woman telling me her name was Marie. She also told me you were her husband," she said pointing toward Daniel, "and that your name was Doctor McNeely."

"That's very good," Doc smiled. "Now can you tell us your name?"

After another silent pause, she gave up in defeat. There was no name for her to find, no life for her to claim. Her memories were recent, very recent.

"It's okay, dear," Doc was saying in a fatherly tone. "You've had a nasty blow to your head. Sometimes the brain shuts down for a while, so your body can heal first."

She knew instantly she was going to be sick. The man that was the doctor somehow anticipated it also. He helped her turn her head sideways, while he held some sort of pan under her mouth. The explosion in her head, when she started retching, threw her mind into a deep, dark void that she wondered if she would ever be able to climb out of. She felt the tears streaming from the corners of her eyes, wetting her hair and dampening the pillow she lay on. Then, blessedly, she felt her body starting to pass out.

A few hours later, Marie's, Daniel's, and Doc's vigil of the woman was interrupted by Dennis entering the room with two other detectives.

"I'd prefer we talk out here," Doc said, blocking their entrance and lowering his voice until all but Marie, stepped out into the hallway. "She needs to sleep."

"Daniel, Doc," Dennis said, nodding a greeting. "These are detectives Larson and Williams."

All the men in the hallway shook hands and detective Larson began speaking.

"We got all of the lab work you did. You did a really thorough job, so we won't be needing more from her at this time. We've sent our preliminary stats out over our network, but so far no matches."

"Have you gotten anymore information from her?" asked Detective Williams.

"Actually . . . hopefully, just for the moment," Doc started, "the woman can't seem to remember anything."

"You mean like who did this to her?" asked Williams.

"No, I mean anything," replied Doc. "Her life starts in that hospital room."

"Will she regain her memory anytime soon?!" demanded Larson. "What are we talking about here, a few hours, days, weeks, what?"

Doc hesitated for only a moment. "She's had a hard blow to the head, and it's possible that the swelling is putting pressure on her brain, blocking out the nerve endings that stimulate the part of the brain that houses her memory. I would hope this to be short term for her, but the brain isn't as predictable as a broken bone or a cut to the skin."

The hospital room door opened, and Marie called for Doc. "She's awake again and thirsty, should I call for a nurse?"

"No, I'll come in."

Daniel and Dennis followed, along with the two detectives.

"We need to get more information from her," Detective Larson was saying, but as he entered the room and saw the woman, his voice rose loudly. "Oh my . . ."

"Daniel, get him out of here!" Doc bellowed, cutting off the detective's words.

The woman was confused and frightened. There were too many people in the room that she didn't recognize and that man sounded angry. She thought from the expression on his face that it might be at her. Marie, who had been there every time she woke up, was once again holding her hand. The doctor was asking her a question and she was trying to focus on his voice, but . . .

"Dear, is there anything you remember since the last time we spoke?"

The woman tried going down different corridors in her mind, but she kept coming up with the cold, black emptiness that made her stomach queasy and her mind ache. She felt so lost, so utterly alone. "I'm sorry," she said simply.

Marie squeezed her hand. The woman squeezed back, holding tight to one of the three lifelines she recognized.

"Thanks for all of your help folks," detective Williams bluntly stated, while looking at Doc, Daniel, and Marie. "We'll take it from here."

The woman felt herself starting to quiver. She knew it must be obvious to everyone in the room, but given the choice, if she had one, she certainly didn't want to be put in the care of this rude detective. "Please," she whispered, beseechingly to Doc.

"Well," started Doc, smiling down at her, "since she is my patient, how about if I give the orders around here?"

Detective Williams's mouth opened for speech, but not faster than Doc could continue.

"Actually, I was thinking that in a couple of days, after we've had some complete testing and observation here, we could transfer her back to Daniel and Marie's house. After all, I am a doctor and everything I would need to take care of her with is right next door at my house. It would be no problem to set up a room that could be used as her recovery room, but with a much cheerier atmosphere."

The woman could feel some of the tension leaving her body and she wearily tried to smile.

"Get some rest now, Dear." Doc patted her hand.

Before detective Williams could object to any of this, Doc ushered them out into the hallway, leaving her and Marie behind the closed door.

"Who gave you the right to make that statement to her?" yelled a red-faced Williams.

"It's not a statement," replied Doc calmly. "It's a promise, because after all, I am her doctor. Look, the mind and body are one; she needs to heal them both together. She needs to be cared for with compassion, besides medicine. I just don't see that happening in some sterile hospital."

"I need to talk to her," demanded Larson, who had been waiting outside the door, since Doc had banished him from the room.

"You are not going to badger her for answers when she doesn't have any to give you," Doc stated angrily. "That will only frighten her more and possibly cause an even bigger setback."

"Where do you get off making decisions?" shouted Larson.

"Let's just say I'll be saving the tax payers some money, unless, of course, you want to foot the hospital bill, Detective Larson."

"If she starts talking, you'd better be on that phone immediately," Larson said, angrily walking away with Williams by his side.

"Round one seemed to go in your favor," chuckled Dennis.

Sheepishly, Doc turned to Daniel, "Look, I know we didn't talk about this, I mean, the woman staying at your house and all. Well, I'm trying to say, I'm sorry if I overstepped my bounds."

"I love seeing him squirm," Daniel said, pointing at Doc, but speaking directly to Dennis. "He just thinks he had control of all of this, but did you see Marie's face? She was ready to single-handedly drag those men out by their ears."

Dennis was openly smiling now.

"Marie has never been a violent person," chuckled Doc. "And you know it, Daniel."

"You are obviously not taking into consideration her maternal protectiveness," said Daniel, seriously. "Never cross a lioness when one of her cubs is hurt, and right now, Marie has claimed that woman as one of her own."

"Thanks, Daniel, I just needed to hear you say it," agreed Doc. "I know this sounds crazy, but I feel a strange bond to this woman. Maybe because she's so totally alone at this moment, or maybe because she would be in the same part of her life Julie would have been in, had she lived."

Daniel shook his head sadly.

"I'm sorry, Daniel, I shouldn't have compared them."

"No, it's all right, I've been thinking the same thing for quite some time now. I refuse to let this woman feel she's out there drifting all by herself, with no one in sight to help her."

"I always thought I had accepted Julie's death as best as I could," said Doc. "But now I realize there's always room for more healing. Maybe by helping this woman, we could all heal a little more also."

"It's strange how a moment in time can change our lives," stated Daniel. "Sometimes just for a minute and yet other times for an eternity."

Chapter Four

Doc felt the move by ambulance from the hospital back to Daniel and Marie's house was, for the most part, uneventful. In fact, there were very few moments in the following days that the woman was actually awake. Even in these moments, hardly any words were spoken. The woman was using all of her energy just to heal. Her vital signs were good; however, her face was still so swollen that her features remained distorted. On the right side of her face, the gash and lump had swelled so much that it was forcing her eye to be kept tightly shut. It was impossible to even see her eyelashes on that eye. Her entire body was covered with bruises that were starting to change various shades of purple, green, and blue, making her wounds look even more grotesque. In reality, this was a good sign that the healing process had begun. The woman's good eye began to flutter.

"Good morning," said Marie, smiling. "How are you feeling today?"

"How long have I been here?"

"This is the fourth morning since Daniel found you," explained Doc.

"I'm sorry, please tell me again how I got here? Have we talked about that yet?"

"Actually, we haven't really had a chance to talk about much of anything," Daniel said, gently. "You've been in and out of sleep for most of the last four days."

"Why can't I remember anything?" the woman asked, turning toward Doc. "I have flashes of pictures in my mind, but I'm not sure if they are real or if they even have anything to do with me. There is such an emptiness. It feels like my thoughts are looking for other thoughts, but they're just bouncing around in my head. I do remember all of your names. Do you know mine?"

The woman looked so tortured that Doc hated to tell her no, but a lot of things were going to be hard for her to accept and she had to start sometime.

Doc noticed she was holding her head again and the look of pain was clearly visible on her face. "Do you want me to put some pain medicine in your IV?"

"No, thank you. I want to stay awake and be able to concentrate."

Doc knew in a little while, when all of the medicine had worn completely off, the pain would be unbearable. He also knew she would refuse any more medicine to mask it. Her will to find herself was more important to her than giving in to the pain. Doc once again found himself admiring the strength of this woman he knew nothing about.

"Are you hungry?" asked Marie, giving the woman a warm smile.

"Maybe you can try to eat a little something while we're talking," suggested Doc. "Marie, do you mind getting some clear broth and some Jell-O? We'll start with a clear diet and see how her stomach responds. If she can keep that down, we'll be able to remove the IV."

"I hear a constant sound from outside," the woman said, pointing toward the window. "I heard it every time I woke up. I thought I was dreaming."

"We live by water, on a cliff. You hear the waves breaking against the shore," Doc explained. He waited for a spark of recognition from the woman, but none came. "This is Daniel and Marie's house. I live just down the lane from here. This has been my home for the majority of my life. It's a place that makes me stop and put my life back into perspective." Doc blushed. "Sorry, I get carried away sometimes."

"It's okay," said the woman hurriedly, as if not to offend. "It's just that I can't even imagine what's out there beyond that window. I was just trying to get an idea of where I am and what it looks like."

"If you are feeling better after you've eaten, maybe we can take a walk to that window," smiled Doc. He knew that just crossing the room was going to feel like running a marathon to her. But he also realized that she needed to start having things to associate with, things her mind could begin to grasp and hold on to.

"Here we are, dear." Marie entered the room and set the tray of food down in front of the woman. "Would you like me to help you? You might be a little shaky at first."

"I'd like to try it on my own," the woman said, picking up the spoon.

Doc watched as she began putting her energy into focusing on the spoon. Unfortunately, that also left her looking at her hands. The spoon began to fall, as Doc watched her examine first one, then the other of her hands and arms. He felt helpless, as her eyes sought out his and in a small, pleading voice, the question they had all dreaded floated eerily from her lips.

"What happened to me? Where did I get these bruises?"

"Dear," Marie said, picking up the woman's hand, "do you remember me telling you that Daniel found you at the edge of the water?"

Doc saw the woman nod yes, as she turned and looked at her arms again.

"Did I fall off of something? Did I hit the rocks? Is that why my whole body hurts? Do I look like this everywhere?"

Doc bent down to pick the tray of food up from the bed and place it on a nearby table. Then he gently took her other hand and began: "After we got you out of the water and up here, I began to examine you. It didn't take me long to realize that the wounds on your face and body weren't what I had originally thought either. Dear, someone deliberately did this to you."

"What did they do to me?"

Doc could see that the woman had been petrified to ask, but the need to know was stronger. Taking a moment to clear his throat, he then continued. "From what it appeared to me and the other doctors at the hospital, your wrists were tied together and your mouth had been gagged."

Doc looked at the woman, watching her put her hand to the corners of her mouth. "You were beaten severely over your entire body." Continuing to look into the woman's face, Doc saw the small spark of light that had been there earlier begin to diminish into a cold, empty nothingness. Doc's heart was crying out for her, but he also knew she needed to hear it all so she could begin to deal with the raw pain she must be feeling on the inside. Willing himself to be strong for her, he continued. "We also concluded," he said gently, "because of the bruising and markings on your thighs and other parts of your body, you were raped."

Doc looked to Marie and noticed her eyes starting to mist. He also knew that she too would hold those tears until she reached the privacy of her own room. This woman needed them all to be strong for her and help her to get past this terrible shock.

"Why" was the only word Doc heard the woman choke out.

"Dear, we don't know why—or who. I wish we had more answers for you, but we just don't yet."

Doc watched the woman sitting very still, but he knew inside her brain was moving at the speed of light. He could tell from her facial expression when the never-ending, self-imposed questioning stopped and the wave of embarrassment and self-doubt washed over her, like the waves she had heard tumbling and crashing against the beach.

"May I use the bathroom, please?" the woman asked, sounding desperate.

Doc understood what this woman was really after. She was going to be sick, but he could see the determination in her not to do it in front of any of them again. She needed to gain a little piece of her pride and dignity back. This seemed like a small step, but in truth, it was monumental. Wanting to have her pride was a good sign that she cared about what was going on around her.

"We can help you to the bathroom over there," explained Doc, pointing to a door across the room. "I'll need to take your catheter out first."

"Daniel and I will just step out of the room for a second," Marie said.

"This shouldn't hurt." Doc lifted the sheets back, but he could tell she wasn't hearing a word he was saying, as she was intensely staring at her legs and thighs in disbelief. He knew the bruises would be proof enough for her as to why her body was screaming out in pain. Now, however, he wasn't so sure she would make it to the bathroom in time, but as he was calling Marie and Daniel back into the room, the woman had already sat up and had her legs swung over the side of the bed.

"Whoa," started Doc. "We can't go quite that fast. I need to unplug your IV so we can push it with you. Daniel, can you get on her other side? Okay, let's try this then."

Doc steadied the woman as she rose from the bed. He knew that the incredible pain in her body and head were working hard at keeping her from reaching her goal, but he felt the determination in each step that she took.

"Thank you," she said at the door, putting her hand on the IV unit and pushing it inside with her.

Just as the door closed, Doc could hear the woman getting sick. He knew that the pain, humiliation, and mindlessness that she must be feeling were overwhelming her mind and body.

"No," said Doc, stopping Marie's hand, just before she grasped the doorknob. "It sounds cruel, but as good as our intentions are right now, she needs to do this on her own. She needs to realize she has some control over her own self or she'll become passive and never emerge back into life. We can help her physically and guide her emotionally, but a lot of this has to be done by her. We can't live her life for her. We can only help her find it again."

"It's so hard," cried Marie.

"Yes, it will be hard to watch," agreed Doc. "But it's just like teaching a baby. You know yourself, Marie; you have to let children experience life. They have to learn to use those good and bad experiences on their own to really learn. That's what we have to do for her. We can guide her to do, to become, to understand, and to experience being able to live again. No, not just to live again, but to live with meaning. That will be the challenge, getting her to want to be a part of life again. That's where our guiding will have to be the strongest."

Doc heard silence followed by an anguished gasp from on the other side of the door. He knew Daniel and Marie realized what was happening with the woman as well. She had obviously looked into the mirror and was horrified. Doc could just imagine her putting her hand up to her face, praying that the reflection in the mirror would not mimic her movement, validating the fact that it couldn't possibly be her. Doc had heard when the woman had started crying, but nothing could have prepared him for the tear-stained face and the depth of the beaten look in the woman's eyes as she emerged several minutes later from the bathroom.

"Will my face stay this way?" he heard the woman ask sadly. "Not that I know what it is supposed to look like, but will it look this bad forever?"

"No, no it won't," answered Doc, reassuringly. "I know it looks really bad to you now, but it will mend. It just needs time."

Doc saw the array of emotions washing across the woman's face and he understood how much this was draining her. He doubted she even felt the physical pain, for it was obvious her mind was in a numbing shock.

"We need to get you back to bed, Dear," Marie said.

Doc stood by as the woman took her IV unit and painfully shuffled toward the open window. He held her by her side, as a single tear slid down her cheek. He knew she was physically looking out of the window, but no emotions crossed her face. Still, it was a good sign that she had been curious enough to take the detour. Curiosity could be a strong, yet sometimes overlooked emotion. If she could be curious about this, she would definitely be curious enough to participate in her own life again. Once in bed, Doc watched as pain and exhaustion overtook the woman and she slept.

Chapter Five

The woman awoke, as the shadows of the day were stretching long.

"Dear, you've slept well," said Marie from the woman's bedside. "Do you want to try some broth again?"

The woman felt awkward, as the silence fell heavily in the room. These people were so nice to her, but how was she supposed to fit in here? Realistically, how was she supposed to fit in anywhere?

"You know what, Dear," Marie said more as a statement than as a question, "I'm going to go and get that broth and we're going to see if Doc will be able to take that IV out yet tonight."

After Marie had left, the woman needed to use the bathroom. This time, she was more determined than ever to accomplish this entirely on her own. She got up and unplugged the IV unit from the outlet as she had seen Doctor McNeely do earlier that day. Her body didn't want to have any part of this journey, but her mind centered on pushing away the pain, or at least subduing it long enough to allow her to cross the room.

She leaned heavily on the IV stand when she walked, but she made it. A small sense of accomplishment entered her mind, until the reflection in the mirror brought back all of her feelings of loneliness and embarrassment. She vowed then and there that this would be the last time she would look into a mirror again. After all, it was useless to her anyway. She didn't even recognize the person looking back at her, and it only frightened her to think she never would. She left the bathroom and was drawn to the pink glow pulsating from the window.

"Dear," she heard Marie say, and she turned toward her voice. She was afraid Marie would want her to get back into bed, but lying in bed only gave her time to think and she didn't want to do that anymore. She was emotionally drained from trying to remember. She even found herself welcoming the intense pain that standing up was bringing, because it left no room for the overwhelming disappointment her heart and mind were constantly feeling. Through the fog of her pain and disappointment, she heard Marie's voice again.

"How do you feel about eating your broth on the back deck with me?"

The woman smiled, realizing that Marie had somehow read her thoughts and was offering her a chance to push forward.

"It's really not that far," Marie explained. "You are in the bedroom next to the kitchen and the deck is right off of the kitchen. I could help you, if you feel up to it. Do you want to try?"

"Yes, could I please?" The woman felt as if someone had just handed her an elaborate present. In a way it was—Marie was reaching out to her with the gifts of trust, support, and friendship and she so desperately wanted to start reaching back.

"Okay, good. Let's get you outside first and then I'll come back for the food and some blankets."

The woman let Marie take her elbow, more to guide her than for support, but the steadying hand was a comfort just the same.

"You are doing wonderful, Dear. Do you feel all right? If you're tired, we can stop in the kitchen and sit at the table for a few minutes."

The woman did stop, but she remained standing. She was mesmerized by the view that was surrounding her. The most stunning feature of this large kitchen was that the entire back wall of the house was made of glass. The view was breathtaking! The French doors were open, beckoning her onto the deck beyond. As she crossed the kitchen, she immediately felt the coolness of the ceramic tile. She was equally aware, however, of the warmth of the wood on her bare feet, as she stepped out onto the deck.

"Come sit on this chaise lounge." Marie adjusted the padding on the chair. "While you catch your breath, I'll go and get the food and blankets."

Now that she was alone outside, the woman started to take in all that was surrounding her. Beyond this quaint Victorian deck were the most beautiful flower gardens she could ever have imagined. Some of the gardens were formal and symmetrical, with focal points of fountains, sundials, and gazing balls. Other areas were flowing freely, almost as if the flowers had been there all along. Birdhouses and birdbaths were sporadically placed throughout this charming wildflower area.

Statues of angels graced the gardens and the deck. Wind chimes hung in the gardens as well, for she could hear the tinkling tones of music drifting up toward the house. Beyond all of this, her eyes were drawn to the beautiful blue backdrop of the tranquil water. She relaxed a little and a faint smile touched her lips, as a soft breeze teasingly ruffled her hair.

"What were you thinking about?" she heard Marie ask, as she was stepping back out onto the deck.

The woman was feeling relaxed by the warmth of the fading sun, the scent of the flowers, and the sound of the incessant waves. Her reserve from the last few hours had lapsed and for the first time since she had awoke here, she didn't mind sharing her thoughts.

"I was thinking that an artist must have designed these lovely gardens."

"Well, I'm extremely pleased you like them." Marie blushed. "It has taken me many years to get them this way and I'm still not finished. I'm forever changing things around. My son says I'll never be done. In all honesty, I believe he may be right. I find it extremely relaxing to be out here working. I like nurturing and growing beauty.

"I'd like to think I can accomplish something that others will stop and appreciate or even reflect on. I've never looked at the gardens from the perspective of being art, but I guess that could be one description, thank you."

Marie was so easy to talk to; the woman found herself glad she had come outside.

"This is actually my favorite time of day," continued Marie. "I love to watch the sunset changing the colors in the garden, on the cliffs, and especially out on the water. I love the sea, even though we have had our differences. It can be beautifully calm and blue, like smooth glass, then so green and turbulent that you can almost feel its anger and respect its power. Other times like now though, it will meet a sunset and offer the beauty back to you tenfold in its reflection. It is a constant, rhythmic, heartbeat. It just is. It is life."

The woman understood what Marie was offering her, but she wasn't sure if she was willing or ready to accept this. It wasn't that simple. It couldn't be. As Marie spoke, the woman felt her eyes drawn to this kind-hearted older woman.

"Dear, I know you have a lot of questions about who you are, your past, and about what has happened to you. I don't have the kind of information the detectives might find useful, but I see things in you that make you who you are inside."

"You don't even know me! You don't know if I'm a good or

bad person. Maybe I deserve being like this," the woman said, touching her face. "You've all been so nice to me, but what if I don't deserve it?"

"First of all, no one—and I mean no one—deserves being beaten, raped, and left to die. There is nothing on the face of this earth that could possibly make that all right. It is against God's law and man's law to commit such a horrible act."

"Then if I'm not bad," the woman whimpered, "why did God let this happen to me?"

The woman felt Marie's weathered hand gently wipe away the tears from her cheeks. If only she could wrap herself in Marie's comforting voice.

"Dear, God didn't want this to happen to you. In fact, I'm sure He is feeling your pain and crying with you."

"Then why?"

"I think," Marie answered slowly, "that our lives are a gift from God, just as our souls are. Life is a gift, but it was never meant to be given to us as perfect. We were meant to grow into life by learning, laughing, loving, and, yes, sometimes, facing challenges, sadness, and disappointments. If we didn't have to learn to deal with all of these elements of life, then what would be the sense of living? If you have never known sadness, how could you understand joy? If you have never known hatred, how could you ever feel love?

"Everything in life is a cycle," continued Marie. "Everything has an opposite. I believe it is the same with souls and wills. God gives each of us a will and then leaves it up to us to learn and shape it into the different degrees of how strong we are. You can be very strong and kind with a purpose to your life, or you can allow your will to become weak and let the bad in. If the weakness takes over, people become very unhappy in their own lives, so unhappy they want to lash out and hurt others.

"Good or bad, we are all connected and at some point we must interact. The test comes in dealing with the bad that has happened to us. This is when we find out if we have a good strong soul and if we can come out of these challenges even stronger. I'm not saying it is an easy task."

"How do I know which of those I was?" asked the woman thoughtfully.

"I know it's good," smiled Marie. "I see it in the way you appreciate kindness or the way you are in awe of a sunset, even when I know physically and emotionally you are in great pain. The strength is there in you, Dear, you just have to embrace it. Don't let the person, the evil that has done this to you win. Don't let the weakness start growing in you. That's not who you are. You are much stronger than that.

"You're lost right now, not knowing who you are or where you've come from and we will all help you to find the answers the best we can. But you must also try to be a part of the present. Too many people lose all of their life worrying about the past and the future, when the most important part of life is the moment they are living in. You need to grasp it and hold on tight."

The woman reached over for the tray of food and started drinking the broth. She understood now how Marie's idea of nourishment went far beyond the material aspects. Marie had been providing her with nourishment for her soul, and at that moment, that seemed so much more important.

"Well, Dear, how do you feel about a name?"

The woman knew Marie wasn't trying to be cruel, but the words stabbed at her heart just the same.

"I wish I could remember . . . I just can't."

"Oh dear, I'm sorry. I didn't mean for it to sound that way," empathized Marie. "I meant maybe you could pick a name, something you like. Don't think of it as giving up on finding out about your past, but as a sign of wanting to go on living."

The woman knew in her mind this made sense, but her heart was still hurting. "Maybe you could pick one for me."

"Are you sure? It could be your chance to pick the name you've always really wanted."

"Please, I need you to pick it for me. I don't think I could do it."

The woman watched Marie intensely and didn't miss the smile and small sigh that escaped her lips when Marie breathed out a name.

"Anna, I think. You remind me so much of an Anna."

She could tell the name was special to Marie and for that she felt honored. This kind woman, who hardly even knew her, had just bestowed something so precious to her and that in itself began to make her feel like a person again.

"If you don't like it, we could choose another."

"No," the woman said smiling. "I love it, it sounds like poetry. I only hope I can live up to it."

"Anna, dear," said Marie, "you already have."

"Look!" Anna said, pointing at the sea and the setting sun. It's beautiful!"

The sun was softly kissing the water, just as Marie had described earlier. It appeared to be waiting hesitantly, just above the sea, with all of the brilliant shades of pink, red, orange, and yellow, reflecting majestically in long bands, reaching for the shore.

"The sun wants to share its warmth with the sea," murmured Marie softly. "If you close your eyes, you can almost hear the beauty of their joining. It's a lot like people, Anna, warmth and life are meant to be shared."

Anna reached for Marie's hand, feeling lighter for having shared these precious moments with her.

Chapter Six

"Marie! Marie!"

The two women could hear Daniel and Doc calling.

"Well," Marie chuckled, "should we answer them, or just let them shout their way out onto the deck?"

Anna smiled, "They sound really worried. Maybe we should answer them."

"Oh, all right then. You might want to cover your ears, I'll have to yell loud at those two old coots."

Anna noticed how out of breath Daniel and Doc were after they appeared on the deck.

"What are you doing out here?" Daniel asked.

"We've been very busy since the two of you left," Marie explained. "Anna walked out here, which I might add, she did very well on her own two feet, and we've been admiring nature ever since. She has also done a fabulous job at working on finishing this tray of food."

Under other circumstances, Anna thought the look of astonishment on Daniel and Doc's faces when Marie had referred to her by a name would have been priceless, but the seriousness of her situation wiped out all the traces of humor she might have otherwise felt.

"Oh, and did I forget to mention," prompted Marie, innocently, "we picked a name."

"What do you mean you picked a name?" queried Doc, looking stupefied.

"I mean," continued Marie, "we couldn't just keep calling her 'Dear' forever, although I'm sure I'll continue to use that endearment from time to time. So, we chose a name. Actually, Anna let me do the choosing and she did the accepting."

"I think the name suits you perfectly," smiled Daniel.

Feeling warmed by the sincerity in Daniel's voice, Anna pushed forward timidly. "I was wondering, Doctor McNeely, would it be possible to take this IV out now?"

"Well, Anna, I have two stipulations. First, you have to finish all the juice that is sitting on your tray, and second, you have to start calling me Doc. All my friends call me Doc."

Anna sipped her juice, touched by his acceptance. "I can do both of those things for you, Doc."

"Anna, dear," said Marie, "I know this will be painful, but you should know that Daniel and Doc were over at Doc's house talking to the detectives about your test results that have come back."

"Did you find anything out about me?"

"Your blood type came back O positive," started Doc, "and the rest of your blood work was negative for any infectious diseases. In fact, it showed you to be a very healthy young woman."

"Is there more?" Anna asked eagerly. "Do they know anything more about who I am or how this happened to me?"

"Anna," said Daniel, "no matches have shown up yet through the FBI's computer system, but it may take a while. It might be easier in a couple of weeks, when we can get a better photograph."

Anna knew Daniel was referring to the fact that her face was so unrecognizable. His comment didn't make her angry or upset, because she knew it was the truth. She appreciated his honesty.

"Do you suppose anyone is looking for me? It just doesn't seem as if anyone even knows I am missing."

"Someone knows you are missing, Anna, and someone is missing you," Marie said gently.

Doc cleared his throat and spoke, "How do you feel about getting that IV out?"

"It would feel wonderful." Anna looked up to meet Doc's concerned gaze. She refused to worry him, Marie, or Daniel anymore. She pasted on the best smile her battered face would allow, even though her heart was breaking.

"Then I'll go and get my bag out of your bedroom."

"I was telling Marie how beautiful the gardens were," Anna said, wanting to change the subject.

"Marie works hard at creating beauty," agreed Daniel. "I don't think anyone has ever come here and not gone away with a deeper sense of the beauty of nature."

"Daniel," laughed Marie, "I appreciate the compliment, but I don't think I'm in line for sainthood yet. St. Francis still holds the title of Patron Saint of Nature and Humanity."

"I don't know," said Doc, coming back onto the deck, "you do have a way of making all of us humans appreciate and respect all of our surroundings. I'd be careful, Anna, you won't even know when it's happening. One day you'll wake up and your life will seem so simple and you'll find yourself actually enjoying it. It makes it harder and harder for me to find things to complain about, and that's bad because I'm really good at complaining."

"Don't worry too much," Daniel teased. "You haven't lost your touch."

"I think that would be wonderful," Anna said, feeling the warmth of these three people's friendship spreading to include her.

"Oh, Daniel, we're too late," Doc said, holding his hand over his heart in a comical way. "It's started. I can see Marie's already planted the seed. The best we can do now, is to sit back and watch it grow."

"You two are no good." Marie attempted to sound stern through her laughter. "I have to take care of both of you because nobody else can put up with it."

Anna realized, somewhere in all of this lighthearted bantering, Doc had removed the IV needle without her even noticing it. It was dark now and Marie had lit a few candles, creating a soft, warm glow that seemed to cocoon the four people talking on the deck. Between the soft lighting and the rhythmic sound of the waves, Anna's beaten and bruised body was betraying her and growing tired.

"Anna, how about we call it a night and I help you back to bed?" Marie asked, as if reading her mind.

"I'm enjoying it so much out here though." Anna tried to stifle a yawn.

"I'll tell you what," Doc said, "I need to get some follow-up x-rays of your jaw and head, just for precautionary measures, nothing to worry about. Anyway, I have the equipment to do that over in my office."

"Is your office close by?" asked Anna.

"Doc's house is just on the other side of ours a little ways," explained Daniel. "If you're feeling up to it tomorrow, maybe we could take a slow walk over there. There's a garden bench about halfway if you get tired."

"I would like that. Thank you," Anna said as she started to get up.

"You get some sleep now." Doc rose with Anna to help her walk back to her room. "Don't worry about getting up early. Sleep as long as your body needs it. I'm supposed to be retired now, so whenever you feel like it, get up, have some breakfast, and Daniel will help you walk over."

They had made it back to Anna's room and as she sat down on the bed, she stared down at the nightgown and robe she had on. What was she to do about clothes tomorrow, and the next day and the next? She was too embarrassed to ask.

"You know, Anna," Marie started knowingly, "I have some clothes . . . I know they won't be stylish, given the fact they're over twenty years old, but they are in good shape and my daughter was about your size. I think they might be a good fit temporarily, until we can go shopping."

"I don't want to impose."

"Nonsense! It's no imposition," continued Marie. "Everything has a purpose. I saved those clothes all these years for a reason, and now I couldn't be happier that I did."

Anna knew in her heart she would have been in total darkness and despair if not for Marie, Daniel, and Doc. One by one, they all said goodnight to her. Even with her eyes closed now, Anna felt Marie's light kiss grace her forehead.

"May angels hold you while you sleep, Anna," Marie whispered.

"That's beautiful," said Anna, as she drifted into sleep.

Daniel, Marie, and Doc softly walked out of the room.

"Okay," said Marie when the three of them were back outside on the deck again. "You told Anna her tests came back negative, but you were keeping something else from her. She might not have noticed, but I've known both of you too long, not to know when you are stepping around something."

"The good news we gave her was true," Doc started. "The bad news is that the samples we took for rape were inconclusive, just as I suspected they would be, because of the amount of time she was in the water. The FBI really has nothing to go on now, except the shoe imprint and a tire marking found on the lane up here. The best we can hope for is that she remembers something or someone else saw something unusual. So far, no one's come forward with any kind of information, so we wait."

"I'm not sure if I want her to remember the assault," said Marie sadly. "Maybe that in her condition her lack of memory has been a blessing instead of a side effect of the concussion."

"Marie," said Daniel, "that may be true, but in the meantime, we need to build her strong in case the day comes when she does have to face it."

"I know, Daniel. It's just that I dread that day."

"Imagine how she must feel about it," Doc added. "That's why we need to show her how to go on, especially with her head held high." Doc stood up. "I'm going to sleep at my house tonight. If you need me, don't hesitate to call. If I don't hear from you, I'll see you tomorrow at my house with Anna, Daniel. If she doesn't feel up to it, come and get me. I don't want to push her."

"I think it's more the case of her pushing herself," commented Marie. "I see a drive in her that might be hard to slow down."

"Kind of reminds me of someone else we know, doesn't it?" Doc winked at Daniel on his way out.

Chapter Seven

Daniel woke to Marie shaking his arm and calling his name frantically.

"Daniel! Daniel! Someone's in the house!"

Daniel, still groggy from sleep, was taking a second to process this information, but when his brain came to attention, he bolted from the bed and out of the bedroom. How could he have been so stupid? They should have been more careful with Anna. Maybe the person who did this to her was right here, right now in the room that she slept in. Daniel hoped Marie had the notion to call 911. Creeping down the stairs, he could hear movement in the kitchen.

He looked around for a weapon. The only thing close at hand was one of Marie's antique walking sticks. He'd hoped Marie wouldn't be upset if he used one, as she had spent years collecting them, but he also knew she would agree it was going to a much better use right at the moment.

Daniel hoisted the stick over his shoulder like a batter getting ready for a pitch. He then jumped into the kitchen ready to do battle. Coming face to face with Anna, he realized in that second, her surprise was equally as great. The coffee basket she was holding in her hand seemed to drop in slow motion, spilling ground coffee everywhere onto the ceramic floor.

"Anna, I'm so sorry."

"No, I'm sorry," Anna quickly apologized. "I should have asked first. I was trying to do something nice for you and Marie. I'm sorry I was being too familiar."

"Nonsense, dear," said Marie, entering the kitchen. "We want you to feel at home here. Daniel's just a little jumpy in the morning before his first cup of coffee."

Daniel knew his mouth must have been hanging open. After all, who had awakened him with visions of intruders and burglars? He saw Marie wink at Anna and felt ridiculous, but then Anna began to laugh. Her laughter was so infectious; in seconds, he and Marie had joined in.

As the three of them stood in the kitchen in their pajamas, Dennis came barging through the French doors as if the hounds of hell were hot on his heels. Outside, Daniel could hear the sirens from Dennis's squad car still screeching. The icing on the cake, however, was a second later when Doc came running in, still in his pajamas and robe. The scene reminded Daniel of something straight from a vaudeville production. Through his laughter, he heard Marie starting to speak, while trying not to laugh.

"As you can see, we've invited you all over for morning coffee."

"Darn it, Marie," said Dennis. "What's going on?"

Daniel looked over at Doc, who was still trying to catch his breath. He knew they were all going to get a piece of Doc's mind for scaring the life out of him.

"You three couldn't find a better way to start your day?" Doc grumbled. "Did anyone ever think of breakfast or a shower? I know I always find that a refreshing start."

Daniel knew Doc was capable of sarcasm for hours on end. He figured he had better put an end to this fiasco before Dennis threw them all in jail for disturbing the peace and Doc had a heart attack on the kitchen floor.

"Dennis, I see my wife had the opportunity to call you." Marie at least had the decency to blush, thought Daniel. "We're really sorry to both of you. It's just that we heard a noise and assumed someone had broken in."

"It's my fault," said Anna. Daniel could tell Anna was worried she had gotten them all in trouble, but before he could explain to her Dennis was not only a policeman, but also a good friend, she continued. "I shouldn't have been wandering around the house."

"Anna, I told you before that's just nonsense," Marie scolded, taking Anna by the shoulders and sitting her down at the table. "It just didn't dawn on us that it could be you. We thought it would be hard for you to get up by yourself, but here you are, running around making coffee. That's just about the nicest thing I could have hoped for today."

Daniel knew that Doc knew better than to continue arguing when Marie was having her say. He watched as Doc sat himself at the table and turned to Dennis.

"Dennis," stated Doc, "sit down and have a cup of coffee and I'll introduce you to Anna."

Now that all of the confusion was dying down, Daniel looked at Anna and realized how embarrassed she was feeling at this moment. He could tell she was mortified by her appearance, and when Dennis stuck out his hand to shake hers, Anna kept her head down and softly whispered, "It's nice to meet you." A moment ago she had been enjoying herself in the kitchen, but now, Daniel noted, she couldn't wait to retreat to the safety of her bedroom. Daniel watched, as she stood up and painfully started to limp out of the room.

"Are you all right, dear?" Marie asked, following Anna down the hallway.

"I'm fine," Anna stammered. "I think, if I may, I would like to take a shower."

"Anna, remember, there's no asking to do things around here," said Marie.

"Thank you," replied Anna, giving Marie a gentle hug.

Daniel knew that embrace would mean everything to Marie. It was the sun rising, the stars shining, the smell of flowers, and the softness of rain. It was acceptance, letting yourself be wanted and wanting to be a part of something; like being part of a family. After all, families were made up of people who cared for one another. As far as Daniel could tell, Anna fit into that category nicely.

"I put some shampoo and scented soaps in your shower," said Marie. "And there are more toiletries in the drawers and under the sink. I washed some of the clothes we talked about last night, so while you are showering, I'll throw them in the dryer.

"You just take your time and relax," added Marie. "There's no rush. The clothes need to dry and Doc doesn't look like he'll be ready anytime soon. When you're done, we'll talk about breakfast again. Would you like me to bring you a cup of coffee before you get in the shower?"

"Actually, I don't drink coffee. I was just making it for you and Daniel," Anna confessed shyly, as she entered her bedroom.

"That's even more precious," laughed Marie, as she walked back into the kitchen.

"Well," asked Daniel now that Anna had entered her bedroom, "is she all right?"

"For everything she's gone through, I think she is doing remarkably well," answered Marie.

"She is," agreed Doc. "But we can't expect every day and every minute to be good ones. There will be many difficult moments. Even though my heart was jumping out of my chest when I ran into your kitchen this morning, I must say hearing Anna laugh was quite reassuring. After all she's been through, the fact that she can still see humor in life will work to her advantage. It will create a balance between the depressive pitfalls she will find herself in at times. We can't let our guard down, for there will be deep wells of darkness for her. I can see at times she's already begun to experience them, but tries hard not to let us see this."

Daniel noticed Dennis trying to sit and listen respectively, but his fidgety confusion finally won over.

"So when did she remember her name?" Dennis demanded. "You said when we met with the detectives yesterday that there had been no new progress."

She doesn't remember anything," Daniel replied. "Marie named her."

"How did you find out her name?" Dennis asked, looking even more confused.

"Good heavens, dear," said Marie calmly. "You're making this much too complicated. Everyone has to have a name, so we picked one temporarily, you might say."

"Alright, I see what you're saying," Dennis nodded. "I'm going to have to pass this along to the detectives. We don't want them to think we're holding out on them. Which reminds me, detectives Williams and Larson will be leaving today. Another agent, however, will be coming in, trying to dig up more information. He and I worked together in the city. He's a good guy and good at what he does.

"His main job will be to protect the woman . . . Anna. The FBI wants to keep it just between law enforcement agencies, in case her assailant realizes she's not dead and tries to come back to finish what he'd started. That's why the push to find Anna's identity hasn't been made public."

"That's a horrible thought." Marie covered her mouth with her fist.

"I agree," said Dennis. "But unfortunately, those are the facts."

"I think telling Anna all of this could be more than she could handle right now," Doc warned.

Daniel knew everyone trusted Doc's opinion, so it didn't surprise him when Dennis agreed.

"Then between this agent, myself, and you guys, we'll just have to make sure someone is with her at all times."

"We'll have to do it discreetly," said Daniel, "so she can have some normalcy to her life."

After Dennis left, Doc stood to leave also.

"I'll send muffins over with Daniel and Anna." Marie turned to start the oven.

"What would I do without you feeding me?" Doc chuckled and headed for his house.

Marie left the kitchen to put the clothes in the dryer.

Daniel walked upstairs and returned dressed for the day. He decided to pull his waffle iron out and create a feast. Making waffles always seemed like too much work for just Marie, Doc, and himself anymore, so he only made them on the rare occasions when the grandkids got a chance to visit. Today, however, it didn't seem like much work at all. By the time Marie had come back into the kitchen, Daniel had the waffle batter made and the bacon frying on the griddle.

"I'm impressed, Daniel," she smiled, pushing the muffin tin into the warm oven.

A little while later, Anna walked into the kitchen looking like a ray of sunshine. She still had her battered face, but even that seemed less shocking. Her shoulder-length hair was softened by streaks of sun-kissed highlights, which had gone unnoticed before when her hair was matted and bloodied.

Even the clothes—outdated as they were—seemed fresh and new. Julie had been slightly taller, so the skirt skimmed Anna's ankles, but overall Daniel thought they were a pretty good fit.

"Anna, I can't believe how nice you look in those clothes,"

complimented Marie, voicing Daniel's opinion as well. "What a creative job you've done on refreshing that look."

Not knowing one inkling about woman's clothing, Daniel turned the subject back to breakfast. "Who's hungry?"

"It smells wonderful," Anna smiled, sitting down to her first solid meal.

When they were done eating, Marie got up to clear the table. Anna rose to help, but Marie would not hear of it.

"I appreciate you wanting to help, Anna, but today is your first day up and dressed. Save your energy for your walk with Daniel over to Doc's. Speaking of walking, I have a pair of sandals that I think just might fit you."

"How are you feeling?" asked Daniel.

"I'm good," Anna replied.

Daniel knew "good" was an overstatement, just from the stiffness in Anna's movements. He wanted to allow her this accomplishment, however, because he could sense how badly she needed it. After Marie had walked back into the kitchen and Anna had gingerly put the sandals on, Daniel slowly led Anna to the front of the house and opened the door.

"It's beautiful!" sighed Anna.

Daniel knew Anna was dazzled by the view. He saw it every day and to him, it still felt like looking at a three-dimensional painting, with the doorway acting as a frame. They stepped out onto the large wraparound porch, with its tri-colored spindles and circular columns that were flanked by wooden gingerbread accents. There was a wicker table and chairs that, on occasion, he, Marie, and Doc would have lunch at. On the other side of the porch, four white wooden rocking chairs were swaying slightly in the gentle breeze. Plants of all kinds were everywhere, hanging in planters and in window boxes. Wisteria climbed up one of the porch columns and beyond the porch, roses and daisies danced in the morning sun. Flowers blended together, creating a fragrance of earth, sweetness, and purity.

"All of the elements are here," Daniel said, turning his face toward the sapphire blue sky. "The air, the earth, the sun, the rain . . . Marie just has a real knack for organizing them to show off all of their distinct personalities."

Daniel stood quietly and waited for Anna's lead.

"I'm sorry I'm taking so long," Anna said, smiling at Daniel.

"Don't be. We've got all day. Besides, I find myself doing the very same thing every time I walk out here."

They were on the crushed gravel of the road now and Daniel was explaining to Anna that if they were looking at this from the sea, the coast would look like a giant horseshoe, with his and Marie's house sitting in the middle of the curve.

"Doc's house is this way," Daniel continued, pointing up the road.

He watched as Anna followed his finger toward Doc's house, but she then turned in the other direction to collect her bearings. He noticed when her eye caught sight of the small cottage with the overgrown weeds and flowers. He could tell she was intrigued by it, but she turned back around to continue their walk to Doc's. It was obvious Anna was still in considerable pain, so Daniel made sure to set an easy pace.

At the halfway point at the bench, Daniel watched Anna stop to look out over the sea. He witnessed a small smile as she watched the movement of the waves and her eyes followed them to the shoreline. Then time seemed to split wide open and become warped.

"Anna! Anna!" Daniel shouted, frightened at what he was witnessing. He lowered Anna down onto the bench, worried she might pass out. Her body was shaking and cold to his touch. She was holding—almost squeezing—her hands to her head.

"Anna!" Daniel called again, as he watched flashes of pain cross her eyes, each one leaving her more exhausted and drained. He knew as he watched her put her hand to her face and feel her hot tears that she hadn't even known she'd been crying.

"Are you okay? Do you hurt somewhere?"

"I'm okay now." Anna sounded dazed. "I just got a bit of a headache for a second. I'm fine really."

With all of the concern for Anna, Daniel hadn't even realized Doc had joined them.

"I can get my car," Doc offered.

"No, really, I'm fine," begged Anna.

Daniel was thankful when they made it to Doc's house with no further incidents. Doc took Anna into the part of the house that was his medical office, while Daniel went to find coffee for his overly shaken-up nerves.

"Well, Anna," Doc said, holding up the last x-ray, "the joint by your jaw is in better shape than I had originally thought. Your other injuries look good also. That's not to say your body still doesn't need time to heal. We don't want to damage it further. I'll be sending this new batch of x-rays on to the hospital. I would like a couple of my colleagues to give me their opinions."

"Thank you, Doc, I can't tell you how much I appreciate all you've done for me. About payment . . ."

"Anna, I don't want to hear one word about payment. Let us help you. Life's a circle, Anna. People have helped me in my life and now I get the opportunity to help you. Someday you will help someone, although I have a feeling you already have. Accept our help, Anna. A simple thank you is certainly enough."

"Thank you," Anna said humbly.

"Good then," Doc said clearing his throat. "Now can you tell me what just happened outside?"

"I'm not sure." Anna crossed the room to the open window. "I was looking at the water, but when I looked at the beach in the cove, my head started hurting and pictures were flashing in my mind. I couldn't make out the images though."

"Anna, if Daniel, Marie, or I thought we could take away all of this confusion and pain for you, we would. It's a hard lesson we all have to learn, but if you want to go on, Anna, don't shy away from your fears. Face them. Only you can conquer them and take your life back."

"I'm scared."

"I know you are. I'm not saying it's going to be easy. At times you will be so scared you'll want to run, but where will you run to that will make this all go away? At times, you will be so sad that you'll want to cry for hours. Crying is healthy, Anna, but don't let that crying last a lifetime. You are the one who has to go through this, but you don't have to walk alone. You have us, Anna—you have friends. You can do this and we can help you."

Daniel knocked on the door and stepped into the office, witnessing Anna's body being racked by sobs and Doc holding her in his fatherly embrace. Daniel hadn't meant to, but he had overheard some of the tortured conversation from the other side of the door.

"Anna," Doc began, as Daniel handed her a tissue, "you need to rest now. I think that's part of your frustration. It's hard to concentrate mentally when you are in such enormous physical pain. I promise you though, the tiredness and confusion will get better as your body heals."

"Do you really think I'll get my memory back soon?" asked a hopeful Anna.

"I can't predict when or even how much you'll remember," said Doc. "But I do know that whatever you remember, you'll need to stand up to it and stand tall."

Daniel followed as Doc helped Anna up and out of the chair, leading her out of the room. They walked through the offices and into the part of the building that was Doc's home. It had a cozy ruggedness about it with a nautical theme flowing throughout. Once again, Daniel followed as Doc led Anna outside and onto the deck that circled the entire perimeter of his house. A sail billowed from the roof of the house to the porch railing, where it was fastened down by sailors' knots. This section had been designed to look as if a person was on the deck of a real sailboat, but its primary function was to provide shade from the intense afternoon sun.

"Everything okay?" Daniel asked finally.

"The x-rays look good," informed Doc. "She'll be out running laps around you during your morning walks."

"At least I'm up in the morning," Daniel snapped, taking the bait.

"Daniel, I'm retired now, morning doesn't have to start with the roosters. There's nothing wrong with eight o'clock."

"You've missed half the day by—"

Daniel paused mid-sentence when he saw Doc put his finger to his lip, in a shushing motion. When he followed Doc's gaze down, he saw Anna had fallen asleep, curled up in the lounge chair under the sail.

"Well," murmured Daniel, still grumpy, but smiling, "don't just stand there, go get her a pillow and a blanket."

"I was just going to do that. You know what, Daniel? You're starting to sound an awful lot like Marie."

"Good," replied Daniel in a huff. "You know we both could learn a thing or two from her, as if we haven't already."

Daniel headed for the door. "I'm going to get Marie and bring some food back for lunch. I left the muffins on your kitchen counter. You can snack on those until we get back."

Doc quickly left to get some blankets as Daniel set off to get Marie. Anna turned in her sleep, where she stayed for the rest of the afternoon and on into early evening.

Chapter Eight

Dennis stood on his porch as he watched Erik pull up to the house. Erik had been his partner on the force when Dennis had lived in the city. Erik was still the best friend Dennis had ever known. Their wives had also been friends, until a year ago, when a drunk driver killed Erik's wife and twelve-year-old daughter. Since that time, Dennis had tried to get Erik out here, but Erik had thrown himself hard into his work, as if that would cure the pain of his loss.

Erik was a good detective, the kind that always got the bad guy, but lately Erik was taking too many chances with his own life. Dennis had requested that Erik be the agent who replaced Larson and Williams and, by some miracle, his request had been accepted.

Erik probably resented being sent out here, to what he probably viewed as no-man's land, but if Erik couldn't slow himself down to heal, then Dennis intended to intervene on his behalf. That's what friends are for, isn't it? Just as long as Erik never found out who had been pulling the strings.

"Hey, how you doin', partner?" Dennis asked, shaking Erik's hand as he stepped onto the porch.

"Great, couldn't be better. Where exactly are we anyway?"

Dennis knew Erik couldn't imagine him living out here,

especially since Dennis, like Erik, thrived on getting the "bad guys" off the streets.

"Remind me, Dennis, why was it you had to drop everything and fall off the face of the earth?"

"Inner peace, man," Dennis replied, laughing. But in truth, that was exactly what he had needed to find. "Come on, Susan and the kids are inside."

Dennis saw a look of raw pain cross Erik's face. He knew this family scene was going to be difficult for Erik and maybe that was part of the reason Erik never came around anymore. It would force Erik to confront something that no longer existed in his own life.

"Hey, Susan," said Erik, bending down to kiss her on the cheek. "Where's Brandon and Katie?"

No sooner had Erik mentioned the names of Dennis's two children than screams of joy and the sound of running feet came tumbling into the room.

"Whoa, guys!" Erik grabbed both kids as they jumped on him. "I left the presents in the car."

Dennis knew presents were the furthest thing from Brandon and Katie's minds. To them, Erik was family. On him had been bestowed the title of "uncle." They loved him, missed him, and were ecstatic he was finally there.

"Where have you been?" Katie pouted in her four-year-old, little voice.

"He's been busy," said Brandon, defending Erik and trying to seem much older and mature at six.

"Not so busy that I couldn't find just the right present for both of you," Erik announced, pointing outside to his car. "Why don't you two run out and grab those boxes out of the front seat?"

Dennis watched both of his children race out the door and then he turned back toward Erik.

"So how was the drive out here?"

"Real exciting," drawled Erik. "Nothin' but land, sea, and a bunch of cows."

"I hope you don't have an aversion to cows," laughed Susan. "Or you might want to eat somewhere else tonight."

"Susan," said a forlorn looking Erik, "I've been dreaming this whole trip about one of your pot roasts, with potatoes and carrots cooked to perfection."

"Today's your lucky day then, because that's exactly the kind of grub we'll be serving up," laughed Susan, mimicking Erik's earlier cowboy drawl.

"Mommy!" Katie squealed, entering the room with Brandon. "Look what Uncle Erik gave me!"

Dennis quickly scanned the boxes, noting they both appeared to have "Rollerblade" written on them.

"Erik," Susan said calmly, "let me draw you a map to the nearest hospital, since you'll be the one taking the first child who breaks a leg."

"Look Susan," Erik said while rummaging through the boxes, "they come with knee pads, elbow pads, wrist guards, and helmets."

"My point exactly." Susan tapped her foot. "How safe can it be if you have to wear a suit of armor just to play?"

Using their last trick to wear down Susan's defenses, Erik, Brandon, and Katie went all out with the puppy dog eyes. It must have worked because Dennis could see when Susan was beginning to feel outnumbered.

"All right, Brandon and Katie, let's get you suited up, and we can try these out in the garage," surrendered Susan.

Dennis was glad for the time alone with Erik. It would give him time to fill Erik in on the case and maybe even time to convince Erik to come live in this town and work together again. The town was short one officer and though it was a long shot, Dennis was hoping Erik would accept the position.

"Do you want me to fill you in?" Dennis asked, pulling the file from his briefcase.

"I read up on it from Williams and Larson's files and I also had a chance to look at the test results that have been done. There's such little information and evidence to go by, it's as if she fell out of the sky one day. Her description doesn't even seem to match any newly reported missing persons."

"True, but she's been beaten up pretty badly. I could see where she might be hard to recognize from the photos."

"Do you really believe that?" Erik asked, holding up a picture of the battered woman's face. "Elaine's features were not her own either after the accident, but when I had to identify her at the morgue, I knew it was her. I'd wished to God that it wasn't, but all that wishing didn't change things."

"Has it been hard to go on?" Dennis asked simply. He watched, saddened as his friend tried to form words.

"Every single breath I take feels like fire. I know I have to breathe to live, but sometimes it hurts so much that I find myself holding my breath until my lungs give in to the need. The loneliness and emptiness are so deafening that I put loud music on just to drown it out. I don't know when I eat or sleep. Every minute, every second, feels exactly the same to me—plain."

Dennis knew for sure now that he had made the right decision by having Erik assigned here, where people cared for him. Hopefully, it would be for good; but if he couldn't stay, maybe the time here would help him to heal and cope with the way his life had unfolded.

"Sorry, Dennis, I didn't mean to sidetrack our conversation."

"Erik, you're my friend, you're like a brother to me. You can talk to Susan or me anytime, about anything. We've always been there for each other, don't pull away now."

There was a silent nod between them that formed a bond stronger than any words could express.

"As I was saying," started Erik again, "I know because of the danger to her life, we can't go to the media for help, but it doesn't seem that anyone has even reported her missing."

"Unless we have some major breakthrough," agreed Dennis, "we're not going to know who she is until her memory comes back."

"That's another thing, do you really believe she has no memories, or is she trying to hide something?"

Erik had not met the woman in person, but Dennis was sure that if he had, he would instantly see the pain and frustration this situation was causing her. He'd be interested to get Erik's opinion after the two had met.

"I've only directly talked to her once," admitted Dennis. "But I feel, unfortunately for her, that her condition is all too real. Marie, Daniel, and Doc keep me apprised of any changes. They've started calling her Anna."

"Is that name something she recognizes?"

"No," Dennis replied. "In fact, Marie gave her the name and it is very significant to Marie."

"I can figure out Doc I think, as in Doctor McNeely, who did the preliminary tests and wrote up the medical reports."

"You're on the right track detective," Dennis said, with a lopsided grin.

"Then who are Daniel and Marie?"

"Now there's a question that can only be answered by meeting them," Dennis said, shaking his head in thought. "Tomorrow you'll get your chance."

Chapter Nine

"Good morning," greeted Daniel, entering the kitchen.

"Good morning to you," Anna replied, handing Daniel a cup of coffee.

"What are you two hungry for?" Marie asked, joining them.

"Don't make a lot for me," said Anna. "In fact, just a glass of juice would be fine."

"Nonsense, dear, we have to keep your strength up. At least a muffin and some fruit."

"When we're done eating," Daniel spoke between bites of food, "we can go exploring."

"I would like that," answered an anxious Anna, popping the last bite of muffin into her mouth, while putting her plate into the sink.

"Not too far," Marie warned both of them.

"I was just going to walk Anna around the back gardens, dear." Daniel gave Marie a kiss before walking out the door.

Anna followed Daniel out into the fantasy world that Marie had created after years of hard work. They followed the slate path that wound in and out of the flowerbeds, like the one in the front of the house. Being in the center of these gardens was a wonder to behold. Surprises were to be found in each flowerbed. One grouping of flowers was devoted entirely to attracting butterflies, complete with the butterfly homes to protect them. Another area had a fairy garden, where little furniture and trinkets sat on a large piece of marble.

"'Tis for the wee folk in the area," explained Daniel, using an Irish brogue.

"They must be very happy here," smiled Anna, as they wandered out to the gardens that ended on the cliff's edge, never noticing the squad car that had pulled up to the house.

"Dennis," Marie said, looking through the screen door, "don't just stand there, come in and have some coffee. We actually got it made this morning without your help."

Dennis began to enter the house. "Marie, I want to introduce you to the agent—"

"Marie!" Doc was shouting while rushing in. "Dennis, what are you doing here? That's two days in a row now that I've had to run all the way over here. You're gonna kill me yet this week!"

"That's just because you're the nosiest neighbor I've ever met," Dennis laughed. "Do you ever stay home?"

"Why?" Doc grumped, as Marie handed him a cup of coffee. "The food's better here."

"Agreed." Dennis smiled as he took the mug Marie was offering. "I was just saying that this is the agent who will be taking over the investigation and helping to keep a protective eye on Anna. He's also a good friend of mine, so go easy on him, Doc."

"You might as well give me a first name," said Doc, while surveying Erik. "If that's all right with you? I'm too old to be able to remember last ones too."

Erik could sense this man was sharp as a whip, with a memory to match, so Erik figured he must have passed some sort of test Doc had just run him through to be on a first-name basis. Even so, it gnawed at Erik, not knowing what he had just been tested on.

"I'm Erik," he said, extending his hand to Doc.

"My husband Daniel is out walking with Anna." Marie pointed out toward the gardens.

"Daniel is the other pea in the pod." Dennis grinned.

"You remember we golf next week," Doc was saying. "I'll show you no mercy for that comment. Do you golf, Erik?"

Erik nodded his head yes.

"Good," continued Doc. "We'll see you next week on the course too. We've been looking for a fourth."

Erik realized he should have been upset that he had just been told to be there and not asked, but instead, he felt it to be almost an honor. "Yes sir," was all he could think of to say.

"Doc," said Dennis, "I was mentioning to Erik that you've agreed to let the department rent your cottage, so Erik could have a place of his own while he was here."

Doc, Dennis, and Erik, stepped out onto the back deck. Erik followed Doc's finger as Doc pointed to the right hand side of the land that formed the cove.

"See that first cottage over there?" Doc asked, and then paused.

Surely not, Erik thought to himself. It was hideously overgrown with a repair list the length of his own accomplished police arrest record and he had received numerous medals for it being outstanding.

"Okay, not that one," admitted Doc. "The one right after that one."

"That's great!" Erik said, relief echoing in his voice. "Thanks."

"The family that's in it right now will be out by the end of the week. The family that was supposed to have been in it until the end of summer cancelled. One of their kids came down with chicken pox or something. Anyway, it will be all yours in a couple of days."

"I don't mean to seem rude," Erik abruptly changed the subject, "but I really should meet the woman I'll be protecting."

"Now that's a touchy subject," Doc said slowly.

"How so?" Erik asked, raising an eyebrow.

"It's just that, she doesn't know you or anyone is here to protect her," Dennis began. "Doc, Daniel, and Marie feel it's best not to scare her more by worrying someone still might be out there looking to hurt her."

"But that's probably exactly what's happening," Erik said stubbornly. "I think she has a right to know, so she can be prepared." Erik noticed Marie join them on the deck.

"I think Doc has finally met his match, Dennis," said Marie.

"I think it's time for you to meet Anna," Doc said pointedly. "Maybe then you'll understand how vulnerable she is emotionally. I trust you're used to making good, sound decisions?"

Erik couldn't remember the last time he was so subtly reprimanded. He thought that perhaps it had been by his father years ago. Now, most people were too intimidated by his controlling attitude to cross him, even if he was wrong—which he hardly ever was. In that instant, he found himself liking and respecting Doc all the more, even if Doc was wrong on this matter.

"All right," Erik relented. "I won't say anything until I get a good feel on the situation."

"That's all I ask," Doc said simply.

"Dennis, let's you and I stroll out to the garden and say hello to Anna and Daniel," said Marie, sweetly. "Do you two care to join us?"

Erik knew Marie had just intentionally broken up the stare down that was going on between Doc and himself. Once again, Erik was feeling as if he were six years old and being gently, but firmly put in his place. At least this time though he didn't share the shame alone. Doc was an equal partner in this crime and that gave Erik some consolation.

"You'll realize soon enough, Erik," said a blushing Doc, "Marie is here to keep us all in line. Isn't that right, Dennis?"

"It's true," agreed Dennis.

Erik walked through the gardens, a man on a mission, eyes straight ahead, shoulders back, taking the quickest path he could to reach his target. He knew he was missing everything around him, but he was completely fixated on the objective. That was the same way he lived his life, missing the people and things around him worth taking the time to enjoy. He was beyond a healthy focus of goals. In fact, some people would say he had jumped right up to obsessed. The problem with obsession is that it leaves no room for anything else. It just takes over until it consumes and owns both you and your soul.

"Erik, dear," said Marie, sounding suddenly feeble, "would you mind if I took your arm, so I don't slip on these dew-covered rocks?"

"Not at all." Erik offered Marie his arm, but felt very awkward.

"What is she up to?" Dennis whispered to Doc. "She works in these gardens all the time. She has more energy than most twenty-year-olds."

Erik thought he saw Marie wink at Dennis and Doc, but he couldn't be sure. He definitely heard the laughter from the two men behind him and wondered what it was they found so amusing. Then Marie started talking to him as they walked. Erik found himself being drawn into a conversation about flowers and bird feeders, both subjects he knew nothing about. When Marie stopped to show him a plant, Erik would look and listen to her out of respect, but all the time his body was straining to get to the end of the path where he could barely make out the silhouettes of a man and a woman.

Patience was never a good virtue for him, so it took every ounce of energy he had to slow down and, at times, stand still.

Eventually, they became close enough that Erik could clearly see the woman everyone was calling Anna. She had on light green pants that came to her calves, a sleeveless matching shirt, and sandals. He watched her turn from the white caps out on the water, as her attention was drawn to the overgrown cottage by a flock of seagulls that had landed on the cottage roof. Her sun-streaked hair was shoulder length and billowing in front of her face. Erik thought he caught the hint of a smile between the wisps of her hair, as she continued to gaze at the cottage. Two steps closer brought Erik to the sheer reality of her situation that crashed down on him like the surf. He could see the nasty bruises and abrasions covering most of her arms and the calves of her legs. Her wrists were bandaged with white gauze that stood out eerily against the backdrop of the blue sea and sky. The thought crossed his mind on how painful it must be for her to be standing, let alone walking around.

"Anna, dear," Marie said gently.

Erik watched as the woman turned and smiled at Marie. Thank God that the years of seeing abuse had taught him not to reveal emotions when looking at a victim. The horror of what you see reflects back to them in your facial expressions and actions.

He watched Anna's head lower instantly when she had realized others were here and he recognized it for what it was, embarrassment. Erik had read it all in that one look before she had lowered her eyes. She was embarrassed by the assault, by what she looked like, and the lack of knowing her own life. She was blaming herself, wondering if she deserved it, or if she could have tried harder to prevent it. Erik saw it in every painful move she made, as clearly as if she had spoken the words aloud.

Why was it that the slime of the earth could always make their victims feel this way? This is what made him the angriest in his job. This is what made him angry for her. She didn't have the strength or confidence to be angry for herself yet, so Erik would have to do this for her.

"Anna," Dennis motioned toward the agent, "this is Erik—"

"I'm here to help Dennis," Erik interrupted, while extending his hand out to Anna.

"We're short an officer down at the station," Dennis picked up. "And we're hoping Erik here will take the job."

With his hand still extended, Erik looked at Dennis, thinking his last statement sounded all too real. He noted Doc had that smug, "I told you so" look written all over his face, but what really infuriated Erik the most was the tight little protective circle they had all formed around Anna, leaving him on the outside. They all had another thing coming, though. This was his job to protect her and they were all welcome to help, but they had better darn well open up that circle to include him.

"It's nice to meet you." Anna kept her head down while shaking Erik's hand.

Erik could tell Anna was mortified that yet another person saw her looking like this and knew of her circumstances, but he had to give her a lot of credit for standing her ground and accepting his handshake.

"It's nice to meet you, too," Erik said, softening his voice.

"I'm kind of tired," Anna said to no one in particular. "I think I'll go back to the house."

"I'll go back with you, dear," offered Marie.

Erik watched Marie hold up her hand behind Anna's back, in a motion for the others not to follow.

When Anna and Marie were some distance away, Doc began. "I see you had a change of heart, Erik."

"She doesn't need that right now," said Erik, still thinking about the hurt he saw in Anna's eyes.

"Fine," said Doc.

"Fine!" replied Erik almost shouting.

"Daniel," said Doc, winking, "let me introduce you to Erik. He's our fourth in golf."

Erik noted the twinkle in Doc's eye.

"And Erik," continued Doc, "this is Daniel, the other pea in the pod."

Chapter Ten

Doc, Daniel, and Marie had been sitting in the kitchen for the last four hours, listening to the clock in the hallway tick away. Dennis and Erik had long since left.

"She's not resting you know," Marie said, wringing her hands. "She needs to come out and eat something."

"Well, it's time I go in there and drag her out," said Doc roughly, but only because he was worried.

"Try to be at least a little tactful," Marie requested, as Doc rose from his chair.

"Ye of little faith," Doc said, smiling at both Daniel and Marie. "Who was it that gave me that swift kick in the behind when my Rosy died?"

Doc watched Marie gently shake her head in understanding.

"If I've never said thank you," stammered Doc, "well, the point is, I would have never found my way back amongst the living had you two not been there for me. Let's not give Anna that much time to fall deeper into herself. The climb out of that abyss will be that much harder. She has to start confronting and talking about the reality of what happened to her. The physical pain has kept her mind temporarily busy, but I think we can all see as she is healing that the emotional pain is seeping in. As hard as it will be for her, she needs to start talking about it, make it real, or she'll never be able to conquer it."

"Point taken," Daniel sadly agreed.

"You two just relax and start something for lunch," said Doc. "Anna will need something to eat after we've talked."

"Good luck," Marie whispered, as Doc began knocking on Anna's door.

"Anna, it's Doc." He paused. He knew she probably felt she didn't have the energy to face anyone. She probably just wanted to be left alone, to not have to think or feel, but to become as numb as falling into a frozen pond on a cold winter's day. Her world was gray right now, but Doc was just as determined to show her the brilliance of color, even if it meant wading through all those shades of depression with her.

"Anna, I need to come in to change the bandages on your wrists and to check your eye."

"Can't we do it later?" Anna's feeble voice floated from the other side of the door.

"I need to leave in a few minutes for another appointment, so I'd prefer to do it now." Doc knew he was playing on her kindness, as she wouldn't want him to change his plans for her, but if it took a little white lie to get her to open the door, so be it. He watched as the door opened and Anna quickly wiped the tears from her cheeks.

"Good," he said, moving across the room to where he had left the sterile gauze and the tape. "Why don't you sit across from me, Anna, and we'll start with your right wrist."

The silence in the room was so great; Doc could hear every click of the scissors he was using to cut off the gauze. When the wrappings had fallen away, Doc noticed the scabs that were forming where the rope burns had been.

"There, see, Anna, you're beginning to heal. Everything

looks good. There's no redness or warmth signifying infection. I think we'll be able to leave the gauze off completely in a couple of days."

Doc finished rewrapping both of Anna's wrists, then looked to her face. He gently held his left hand under her chin so he could carefully move her face into different positions.

"I definitely see improvement now that your eye is open almost all of the way. How are you seeing out of it?"

"I guess okay. I hadn't really thought about it."

"Well, let's try this." Doc put his hand over Anna's good eye. "Now how do you see out of it?"

He watched as Anna looked around the room for a minute.

"It seems clear when I look at an object. It's just that after a while, it hurts to stay focused."

"The fact that you can focus even for a small amount of time is a good sign. The amount that you can stay focused without pain will increase every day as the swelling continues to go down. As you look in the mirror, don't be concerned that the white part of your eye is so red. Your eye is bruised the same as your skin, only in the eye, it stays red until all the blood dissipates. This can sometimes take a couple of months, so don't be alarmed by it."

"I've only looked in the mirror once, the first day I was up," said Anna, touching her face and turning away from Doc. "I swore then I would never look again."

Doc knew that no matter how healed Anna's face became, she would never be happy at what she saw. What had happened to Anna was ugly and cruel beyond reason, not because of Anna, but because of the monster that did this to her. He had to make her see that and put the blame where it belonged.

"Anna," Doc continued gently, "have you remembered anything else since your headache yesterday?"

Doc thought maybe because he had caught her off guard

and she was so frustrated that her next words came across a little impatient.

"What is it you would like me to tell you that I haven't asked myself? Am I married? Do I have children? Am I someone's daughter or sister? Why did someone want to kill me? Why hasn't anyone found me? Do you know, Doc? Because I've been trying every waking minute to figure out where I belong!"

Anna's hands came to her face and she began to cry. It was a start, Doc thought. At least now it gave him some insight as to what she'd been experiencing and thinking about these last few days. Doc took Anna's hand gently and let her cry for a few minutes.

"Anna," he began, looking into the depths of her eyes, "I can't tell you who you are or where you are from. What I can tell you though, is where you're headed, because I've been there myself."

Doc watched as Anna's eyes begged for answers.

"I grew up around here," Doc began again. "Then I left to go to college and med school. In my first year of internship, I got married to a wonderful woman named Rose. Eventually, when my internship was up, we moved back here to open up my practice. We built the house that I live in now, with the clinic being a part of it, so I could be close to home when our children were born. Rose wanted children in the worst way. She always said half a dozen was the perfect number. As the years passed, being blessed with even one child wasn't meant to be, but Rose never complained.

"Daniel and Marie have always been friends and even though they moved away, we saw them on holidays and when Marie would spend summers here at her cottage. When Michael and Julie were born, it was only natural that they became the light of Rose's and my life also. We became their second set of parents. Then when Marie moved back here permanently with the kids, our bond became even stronger.

"I was so pleased when Michael graduated and told me he was going on to become a doctor. A couple of years later, Michael was in college doing well and Julie had just graduated high school. Julie had her whole life planned out. She couldn't wait for the fall, when she would be off to college to become a teacher. She was ready to 'make a difference and change the world.'"

Suddenly, Doc felt old and tired.

"Julie never made it to college. She drowned that summer in the cove," Doc continued, sadly shaking his head. "She was saving the life of a nine-year-old child. The pain was so great for everyone. Daniel, Marie, Rose, and I just sort of walked around in a foggy daze . . . each into our own thoughts, selfishly forgetting to comfort one another.

"About four months after we buried Julie Anna, Marie gathered us all together. I noticed for the first time Marie's weight had dropped to an unhealthy amount and the dark smudges under her eyes spoke volumes of her nights without sleep.

"Even though I could see she was physically in trouble, I noticed a light, a shine, a hope, in her eyes that I had been unwilling to put into my own.

"Marie went on to say that she had come to realize that Julie's death was not without purpose. That if she continued to mourn Julie's death as senseless and useless, then the very essence of the act of kindness Julie had performed by saving that little boy would be lost forever. Marie had said that one life was no more or less important than another's.

"Humans' lives are all joined, Marie had explained, and nothing happens by coincidence, but rather with a purpose. Julie even in her tender years had understood this. She had lifted up a scared little boy and now she could go home. Not to a home where we could all physically be with her, but to a place where Julie could expand her horizons and bask in the beauty of a light so bright, the beauty sparkles and dazzles your senses. A warmth so deep, it can only be the most loving hand holding yours for all eternity. This is where our loved ones are, we just need to find the patience so we can one day join them in this incredible journey."

"I'm so sorry." Anna reached over to take Doc's hand. "I'm feeling sorry for myself for loosing my memories of my life, while all of you have lost irreplaceable parts of your lives."

"Oh Anna," Doc said gently, "I didn't tell you this to make you feel guilty or ashamed. I told you this so you could see there are torn lives out there everywhere. No one tragedy is worse or better than another's. They all require healing with faith to mend them back together. God won't supply your wants, Anna, but he will supply your needs."

"He has already supplied me with a generous need," Anna said, giving Doc a quick hug. "He gave me kind friends who won't allow me to wallow in self-pity."

Doc was so flustered; he nearly fell off his chair.

"Anna, Marie's been fretting about you not eating anything, so what do you say we go and see what's in the kitchen?"

"Can I ask you a question first?"

"Of course."

"You called Julie another name when you were talking earlier," Anna hesitated timidly.

Doc had seen the recognition in Anna's eyes earlier in their conversation.

"Her middle name was Anna," explained Doc. "Julie always said she could tell when she was in trouble, because we would call her by her first and middle name. The name fit her so well, though, that more times than not, it was how we all addressed her."

Doc watched Anna process the name lent to her.

"Thank you, I'll try to live up to it."

"Anna, you don't have to live up to anything. A name

doesn't make a person. It's what's inside you that measures your worth. It just so happens we see a lot of worth in you. We just have to get you to see it now."

Doc knew it was awkward for Anna to accept a compliment, so he didn't mind that she quickly changed the subject.

"Weren't you supposed to be going somewhere, Doc?"

"What do you mean?"

"I thought when you came in here you said you had to change my bandages now because you had another appointment."

Doc knew he'd been caught, just as he knew Anna was glad she had been tricked into letting him in.

"Let's go eat," Doc laughed. "My other appointment can wait."

Chapter Eleven

The next week fell into a routine of sorts, with Daniel and Doc taking Anna for walks in the mornings and Marie working in the garden with her in the afternoons. Marie noted that the morning walks were the hardest on Anna, for Anna had felt that the cove held the key to her memories. She was feeling depressed that she was unable to move beyond the edge of the incline. Anna would remain shaking at the top, until eventually she would turn around and walk back to Daniel's and Doc's words of encouragement.

As draining and hard as the morning walks were for Anna, however, Marie knew the opposite was true when they were together working in the garden. Anna loved the physical labor. She had a healthy look about her from the sun, even though Doc had insisted she slather herself up with sunscreen, especially where the cuts and rope burns were. Doc didn't want the new tender skin to burn and leave scars.

Marie had felt it was so easy to talk to Anna; in fact, it seemed more of a rhythm than a conversation. They talked about many things, including Doc's wife and Marie's best friend, Rose, who had passed away tragically of breast cancer. Anna had been so generous with her compassion it still brought tears to Marie's eyes. Anna had told Marie that she believed in her theory that everything happened for a reason, a purpose. Anna had felt that for as painful as everything was that had happened to her, she realized if it hadn't, she would probably never have meet Marie, Daniel, and Doc. Anna had said that if it had been a choice of going through life and never having their friendship, she had known, without hesitation, she would choose them at any cost.

Looking at Anna now, standing there gazing at the overgrown cottage, Marie watched several emotions pass over Anna.

"Dear," Marie said, studying Anna's face, "I've been noticing the swelling on your face and body has gone down considerably. You can hardly see where your injuries were. Have you looked in a mirror lately?"

Marie knew that Anna hadn't, for when she had been in Anna's bathroom to change the towels, she had retrieved one of them that had been purposely draped across the mirror. Marie now hoped that by pointing out her progress in healing, Anna would have the courage to remove that towel herself for good.

"I see you're interested in the cottage," Marie said, changing the subject. "I've watched you gazing at it all week."

"It seems like something out of a pleasant dream. I would love to go over and see it up close. Do you think the owner would mind?"

"I think I could arrange that," Marie replied, smiling mischievously. "Of course, that is, if you don't mind following the owner over there." Marie began to walk toward the cottage.

"That's your cottage? Doc had said you used to bring your children back here, but I didn't realize it was this one. That's why it looks so quaint."

Marie felt a twinge of embarrassment because of the way the cottage and grounds looked at the moment. At one time, Marie had loved the cottage. It had been her home. Even after she had bought the main house and turned it into a bed and breakfast, she had kept the cottage up and tended its gardens. Julie also loved the cottage, and mother and daughter spent a lot of time in it discussing poetry, boy problems, and the future. It had been their place to come to and bond.

When Julie had died, the cottage that had been so dear to Marie became almost as dreaded. Eventually, Marie took the furniture out and closed it up, letting the cottage and the grounds become as abandoned as her heart felt. Daniel and Doc occasionally checked on things, but for the most part, her beloved cottage sat silently alone.

Marie had been so deep in thought that she hadn't realized they had made the walk over here and were now standing in front of the entrance arbor. Looking at the cottage, Marie was saddened by the loneliness she saw from the neglect that had been forced upon it. Marie thought of Anna standing next to her and she knew instantly that Anna needed the cottage as much as the cottage needed Anna.

"I have an idea, Anna," Marie said, starting up the path. "You can say no if you want to, but since I'm getting too old to work both gardens . . . What I'm trying to say is, maybe you would like tending to the gardens over here."

"I would love to do this! When can I start?"

Seeing Anna's face, Marie knew she had made a good decision and she, too, was getting caught up in Anna's excitement.

"I think you should wait at least until tomorrow," Marie chuckled. "It's late already today and besides, you've done enough work for one day. Doc will have both of our heads on a platter if you are overworked, so you have to promise me you'll take it easy over here. This cottage and these gardens have been here for a long time. You don't have to try and fix everything in one day."

"I promise," pledged Anna.

Marie laughed as she watched Anna crossing her heart with her finger as if she were a child.

"Good," said Marie, linking her arm in Anna's and walking back to the main house. "Now I want you to feel free to do whatever you'd like with the gardens. Anything you want from the garden shed up by the house, feel free to take and use over there."

"What if I mess it up?"

"I have all the confidence in the world in you, dear. You'll do splendidly," encouraged Marie.

When Marie and Anna entered the kitchen, Doc and Daniel jumped to their feet looking anxious.

"Where have you two been?" Daniel demanded.

"Well," added Doc, "where have you been? We've been yelling around here like idiots with no one answering."

"If you would have looked around, instead of only beyond your noses," Marie scolded the two overgrown boys, "maybe you would have seen us over at the cottage."

Marie knew that last statement wasn't entirely fair, especially since she was the one who had shut out the cottage all those years ago. This afternoon, standing there with Anna, she realized the hurt had not been within the presence of the cottage, but within the depths of her heart. That span of time was lost to her forever now, but from here on out, she would make peace with the cottage and help Anna find that same warmth and comfort she knew the cottage held.

"Marie said I could start fixing up the gardens over there," Anna announced, pointing toward the cottage.

"You've got to be kidding me," Daniel said, raising his voice. "Marie, it's been years since anyone's done any kind of work over there. Do you know how difficult this job will be?"

"Yes, Daniel," Marie calmly replied.

"Doc," pleaded Daniel, "help me out on this one."

"Sorry Daniel, I have to agree with Marie here. If Anna

feels up to it, I think it will help her regain her physical strength."

"Please," Anna begged, reaching for Daniel's hand.

Marie was once again reminded of the similarities between Julie and Anna. There was an inner determination in Julie that Anna seemed to possess as well and just as with Julie, Daniel didn't stand a chance against her pleas.

"Oh all right," Daniel said, smiling at only Anna.

"Now that that's settled, I'll start supper." Marie reached for a casserole dish.

"I'll help," added Anna.

"What's for supper?" Doc asked.

"Nothing for a traitor like you," grumbled Daniel. "Unless you help me take some garden tools over to the cottage."

"I can get that stuff tomorrow," Anna offered.

"We're just going to throw some shovels and rakes in a wheelbarrow and turn the water back on over there," Daniel said as he walked out the door with Doc in tow. "Believe me, you'll still have plenty to do."

Marie looked at Anna and smiled. Outside they could hear Daniel and Doc arguing about which tools were the best to bring over and who would be the best at navigating the wheelbarrow up the path.

"Do they always sound like that?" Anna asked, chuckling.

"Always, dear. It's like living with two of the Three Stooges."

"Do you think Daniel is all right with me working at the cottage?"

"Daniel is just worried about you, Anna."

"But I'm doing much better physically."

Marie watched as Anna lowered her eyes.

"I know I haven't made any progress with my memory, but I'm really trying."

"Oh, Anna," Marie said, putting her arm around Anna's

shoulder. "You're doing great! I'm so proud of you! Now we need to show these men just how strong we women are by proving them wrong. They say women are the weaker sex, but there's a reason God chose women to have the babies."

Marie noticed instead of laughing at her joke, Anna was actually creasing her forehead in pain. The moment passed and Anna's strain was replaced by a shy smile and nod of her head.

Chapter Twelve

Anna awoke the next morning excited to start over at the cottage. Finally, she had a way to start paying back some of everyone's kindness. She knew, however, that even though she had a purpose in the present, she couldn't forget the cove and what she needed to accomplish there also. The cove held the answers to her past. Although she had told Marie she would try to live in the present, sometimes the thought of her past left her with swells of such sadness that, at times, she felt too weak to go on.

Those dark times were mostly at night when she had time to think. She had been drowning in guilt, wondering if she had children of her own. If so, what kind of mother must she be if she couldn't even remember them? Was it possible too that she was someone's wife? Or was the longing to be held by someone just another trick of her imagination?

All of these thoughts and more would ricochet through Anna's mind in the lonely hours of the night, until finally the physical exhaustion would blessedly conquer both her mind and body.

In the bright light of day, combined with the beauty of her surroundings, however, Anna regrouped and found the strength to go on.

Anna bent down to put her shoes on before she headed out the kitchen door.

"I'll be gardening out back, dear," Marie said. "So if you need me . . ."

"I'll come back," smiled Anna.

"Doc and I will be working on the fountain in the front." Daniel sounded just as concerned as Marie.

"And I'll shout if I need you two also."

Anna could feel the three sets of eyes following her off the porch and down the path.

"Look at us," grumbled Doc. "We look like we're sending a child off to kindergarten."

Anna had made it to the cottage and was standing in front of the picket fence that encircled the cottage in its own little fairytale world. She knew her first job would be to assess the grounds. Since she was already standing on the outside of the fence, she started with the outer perimeter. She was delighted at the assortment of flowers that grew bold and vibrant against the weathered pickets. Even some of the weeds had a unique beauty of their own.

Still, it would be good to get this all cleaned up and give the gardens a little more formality. Anna decided she was going to ask Marie and Daniel if she could also whitewash the fence. A couple of the pickets needed to be replaced and Anna was pretty sure she could tackle those also.

Anna's tour took her next to the cottage itself. It was European in architecture, made of stone, obviously a long time ago by a patient, loving hand. It looked to be in good shape, but it would be easier to tell when she was able to cut some of the overgrown vines away from the walls and cedar shake roof.

The front part of the cottage faced the cove with Daniel and Marie's house to the right and center. Doc's house was directly across the crystal water and created the other end of the horseshoe formation of the coast.

Continuing around the cottage, Anna was fascinated by the sapphire blue of the sky where it blended into the water. The open sea was not as tame on this side. Anna watched the rolling white caps in the water crash up against the cliffs.

Even though the yellow warmth of the sun did not feel as intense on this side of the cottage, its brightness drew Anna's attention to a slight shimmering that came from somewhere on the roof.

Anna went closer to investigate. The back of the cottage had a slate patio, sporadically covered by weeds and surrounded by a low stone wall. This whole area, including the cottage, was overgrown with, in Anna's opinion, extremely healthy ivy.

Anna saw an octagonal shaped room that seemed more of an attachment than part of the original structure. It had a separate roofline, which had been incorporated into the cottage under the original roof. As the wind blew gently, it separated the ivy leaves and the whole roof began to sparkle like a well-cut diamond.

Curious, Anna stepped up to the wall and started tearing off the foliage. No matter what section she pulled from, she uncovered glass. The room was made entirely of glass.

In no time at all, Anna was searching out the base of the ivy. She didn't want to kill the main plant, just give it a good trim in order to expose this magnificent structure.

After she had cleared a very small portion of the plant, Anna realized her work would be slowed even further because of the care she needed to take in clipping and unwinding the ivy out of the delicate copper filigree that enhanced the support structures of this room. Anna was working so hard and was so fascinated by every inch she uncovered, that she hadn't heard when Daniel approached.

"I see you found the glass conservatory."

"I thought that's what it was. I was trying to clear enough

off so I could see inside, but I guess I haven't gotten very far. It's still too dark to see anything when I look in."

"Take a break and I'll tell you what you've been uncovering." Daniel handed Anna a bottle of water he had brought with him.

Anna settled herself on the stone wall and Daniel sat down next to her.

"Once upon a time . . ."

Anna smiled, raising a teasing eyebrow toward Daniel.

"I'm just kidding," Daniel smiled. "But there is a nice story that goes with it."

Anna listened intently as Daniel began.

"Marie's ancestral grandparents immigrated here from England. The grandmother was from nobility, but the grandfather was a simple merchant. They weren't even supposed to converse with each other, but Marie's grandmother defied her parents and the society that dictated the separation of classes, and ran away with her one true love. They secretly got married and immediately left for the Americas so no one would ever be able to separate them again.

"Her grandfather became a successful merchant in his own right and eventually he was able to build this cottage for his beloved wife. He was worried he had taken her from her family and her homeland, so he created their home to be something she could feel familiar with—an English cottage by the sea. The conservatory was added later, after the birth of their child.

"She never really missed England, but it saddened her that her husband was gone for such long periods of time. He added the glass structure so she could share the same wonders of the universe with him—the same stars at night and the sunrise in the morning. They were indeed separated, but in many ways as close as a single glance.

"When you get more of the ivy off, Anna, you will find the

French doors. Marie's grandmother would run out of those doors with a smile in her eyes, never missing even one of her husband's returns."

"Whatever happened to them?" Anna asked, intrigued.

"Eventually their son took over the business and they spent the remainder of their days holding hands on the beach, under the stars."

"Thank you for sharing that with me, Daniel."

Anna stood and started to clip the ivy again, but this time on the side where Daniel had pointed out the French doors.

Daniel came up beside Anna and quietly began clipping and pulling.

"Anybody here?" Doc shouted, rounding the corner.

"Back here," called Anna, watching Doc stop abruptly.

"This is like finding a needle in a haystack, isn't it Anna?" Doc asked.

"Actually," said Daniel, "I've always thought of it more like a pearl in an oyster."

"True," agreed Doc. "It will be good to once again see this proud structure uncovered from the yards and yards of this cold, green ivy, strangling its beauty."

Anna watched as Doc also started untangling and pulling the greenery from the walls.

Erik walked into his cottage after being at the police station with Dennis. He had been helping at the station in the mornings. He and Dennis had worked it out with Marie, Daniel, and Doc, that as long as Anna was with one of them, he'd be only a phone call away. But she was never to be left entirely alone. So, when he was home, Erik was frequently checking out of the window with his binoculars.

For the last few days, Anna's routine had been rather easy

to follow: a morning walk with Daniel and Doc and working in the gardens with Marie in the afternoon. The problem was that this afternoon, Erik could only make out Marie's form in the garden.

He set his binoculars down and was headed out the door when he caught a movement and splash of color over at the overgrown cottage next to his. Curious, he left his cottage.

Erik knew Doc and Daniel had seen him coming, but Anna seemed to be too intent on her work to notice him. He was glad when Daniel had given her at least some heads up, by calling out a greeting.

"Hi Erik, how do you like your new place?"

"Place is great," laughed Erik. "It's the landlord who's hard to put up with."

"Just remember," said Doc, smugly, "you have a golf game with that very same person in a couple of days. We'll see who's laughing then."

"Anna," Erik nodded in greeting.

He noticed Anna's head and shoulders starting to slump the minute she realized an outsider had entered into her world. He didn't want this chance to interact with her to go by, but how was he going to force his intrusion on her when it clearly upset her?

"Erik, there's a ladder in the shed over there." Doc pointed to a small building a few yards away. "Quit standing around and go get it. You can work on the roof."

Erik walked to the shed, stunned at how Doc was forever barking out orders and, what was worse, Erik was always following them.

The only person with more emotional turmoil going on inside besides him was Anna. Erik could tell she was not happy with this turn of events, but she was too polite to say anything. They had backed her into a corner, but hopefully she would come out fighting and not run away this time.

Erik came back with the ladder and began clearing the roof. A couple of times he pulled so hard that the ivy's tentacles released quickly from the structure and his ladder tipped backward, leaving him flailing in mid air, desperately trying to regain his balance.

"You know, Erik," Doc commented, "you have to be careful pulling this stuff off. The copper work is very delicate."

"You're more worried about the copper than me risking my neck on this ladder," Erik answered angrily.

"I'm a doctor, Erik, not a builder. You I can fix, this building I can't."

Unfortunately, Erik had not had the luxury of knowing Doc as long as the others, so the incredulous look Erik bestowed upon Doc must have struck Anna as funny, for a spontaneous chuckle slipped from her lips.

"I'm glad you're all having a good time at my expense," Erik snapped, returning to the tug of war he was having with the ivy.

"I'm sorry," Anna said sincerely.

"I'm not looking for an apology from you. It's that—"

"So I see the party has moved over here now," Marie appeared from around the corner of the cottage carrying a basket of goodies. "I knew this would be the first thing you would find, Anna."

"Why didn't you tell me about it?"

"I thought it would make for a nice surprise."

"It was," agreed Anna.

"Erik, dear," Marie shaded her eyes as she looked up the ladder, "did Doc bring over the cookies I baked for you?"

"As a matter of fact," Erik replied, looking smugly at Doc, "the only thing he's given to me today has been orders."

"Then it's a good thing I brought more cookies, so we can all take a break," Marie said, opening up the basket.

"I would love some," said Erik, climbing down the ladder

before Daniel and Doc could veto his break.

"I brought one more thing over." Marie reached into her pocket. "I brought this over for you, Anna."

With one of Marie's cookies melting in his mouth, Erik watched as Anna put her hand out and took the thin, metal object Marie had offered her. It was an old-fashioned key that surprisingly had been kept in good shape.

"It's the key to the French doors," explained Marie, smiling. "You can't be over here working without being able to get a drink of water or wash your hands when you need to."

"You mean I can use the cottage for that?" asked Anna. "I don't know what to say. Thank you."

"Shall we try the key?" Marie asked and took Anna's arm in hers.

Erik watched as Marie and Anna entered the cottage. After a short tour, both women emerged back out into the sunlight with tears glistening in their eyes and a smile lying gracefully on their lips. Erik could tell they shared a silent agreement, even as he watched Anna cup her hands against the glass to look back into the room she had just departed from.

"I think we should call it a day," Marie suggested. "The sun is almost down and we all need a good supper. Besides, Anna wants to get an early start tomorrow. She's decided to fix up the inside of the cottage as well."

Erik stood stunned looking first at Marie and then Anna. Glancing at Daniel's and Doc's wide eyes and open mouths, Erik realized he wasn't the only one surprised at this announcement. Was it possible for Anna to have that much energy? In his opinion, this place needed more work than any one person could handle. He knew it would certainly try his patience.

"Erik, would you like to join us for supper?" Marie asked.

Erik tried focusing his attention away from the cottage and back to Marie.

"I'll have to take you up on that another time. I've already promised Dennis and Susan I'd bring pizza over and baby-sit Brandon and Katie tonight."

"That's nice of you, dear." Marie patted Erik on the arm. "We will see you tomorrow then."

"Absolutely," grinned Erik.

At least he had somewhat regained his wits about him. Daniel and Doc were still standing with their mouths wide open, doing a great impression of baby birds.

"I wouldn't miss tomorrow for the world," laughed Erik.

Chapter Thirteen

The next few days flew by in a blur for Anna. Since it was already August, she decided she should concentrate on the gardens and the fixing up of the outside of the cottage. Hopefully, she would be able to get that much done before fall and the cold weather set in. Still, at times when she was in the cottage getting a drink or washing her hands, she would have to force herself to show some restraint and head back to the work outside. That didn't stop her, though, from forming ideas and imagining color schemes as she worked, bent over, pulling weeds and planting flowers.

At the moment, however, Anna was pushing a wheelbarrow down the path to the main house. This was her third trip today to the house and its garden shed, which held many delightful treasures for her to use over at the cottage.

"Hi," said Anna, approaching her three friends.

"Hi, yourself," answered Doc, smiling.

"I came to get a bird bath, if that's okay?"

"Of course it's okay," said Marie. "But don't you think you should slow down a bit? You make me exhausted just watching you."

"I'm trying to beat the snow," Anna replied, laughing.

"I'd say you've got a good start on it," uttered Daniel.

"Actually, all this physical work feels good. My muscles were a little sore the first few days, but now it seems to give me more energy. Besides, in another week or so, I should be mending the fence and that will seem like a piece of cake compared to pulling weeds."

"Speaking of painting," Daniel said, "all of the paint is in the garage over here. I was thinking that Doc and I could go over to the cottage and clean out the small shed over there. That way, when you pick out the paint that you want, we can bring it over and store it. It would be all ready then when you need it."

"I don't want you to go to all that trouble."

"It's no trouble. I need to see what's left over in that shed anyway and Doc doesn't mind helping, do you?"

"Of course I'll help," said Doc, glaring at Daniel. "But just don't go getting bossy on me. I don't want to end up the worker and you the foreman."

Anna knew if she wanted to get a word in edgewise, she would have to be quick.

"I would really appreciate that. I guess I'll be getting that birdbath now though."

"I'll come help you load it into the wheelbarrow," Daniel said as he followed Anna to the shed.

"I know you think she's working too hard, Marie," Doc began. "But look how healthy and content she looks. It's really rather interesting to watch, but as the outward appearance of the cottage improves daily, so does Anna's physical and emotional state. She's become stronger and more confident. It's as if one can't do without the other. The cottage regains its respectability and so does Anna. You can see it in the way she stands just a little taller or holds eye contact just a little longer. You were absolutely right to encourage this project for her, Marie. Never doubt that."

"I just worry about what she's been through. What if she

wakes up one day and finds she just can't cope any longer?"

"This morning during our walk," started Doc, "Anna made it four more steps down the incline. She was pretty shaken up when she made it back to Daniel and me, but the point is, she's not giving up. That's the biggest gain—she's not a quitter."

"I hope you're right." Marie was wringing her hands. "It's just that—"

"It's just that Anna has become more like a daughter to all of us," Doc interrupted. "And like any parent, it's hard for us not to want to jump in and try to fix all the hurts. You and I both know though, that's not how a person learns. Life is all about lessons and coping and the best lesson by far is experience. As painful as it is to watch sometimes, we're going to have to let Anna experience the bad as well as the good."

Anna could sense as she approached Marie and Doc that she had been the subject of their conversation. She wished they didn't worry so much about her. At their age, it couldn't be healthy.

"Doc, I thought you and I might go over now with Anna so we can start on that shed," announced Daniel.

"I'll make lunch and bring it over," offered Marie. "That way you can all take a quick break and then get back to work."

"That would be perfect," agreed Daniel.

"Oh, I have ulterior motives," Marie said with a smile. "I'm hoping Anna will give me a tour of the new gardens she's planted."

"I would love to," replied Anna shyly.

A little while later, Anna was standing up, shaking dirt off of her hands. She couldn't believe how fast the time flew. There was Marie, standing on the back patio, setting lunch on the wicker table and chairs that Anna herself had brought over from the shed.

"Lunch is ready!" Marie shouted loud enough for everyone to hear.

Anna watched as Daniel and Doc came around the corner grumbling at each other, cobwebs clinging to their bodies.

"You two can just brush off and then head straight inside to wash off," Anna heard Marie say as she advanced closer to her friends. She looked at her own hands caked with mud and by the looks in everyone's eyes, her face must have shared a generous amount of that same earthiness.

"Come quick," Anna heard Daniel whisper, as if he were the leader of some covert operation. "This way before Marie sees you and none of us gets any lunch."

"Do you think it's possible to get that cleaned up in such a small amount of time?" laughed Anna.

"I think the smell of fried chicken is incentive enough to try," Daniel said with a wink.

Within a few minutes, they were all back outside, waiting to see if they had passed Marie's inspection. They ate lunch with a kind of gusto that comes from working out in the fresh air and sunshine. After lunch, Anna helped Marie clear the dishes and take them inside to be rinsed off before being put back into the wicker basket.

"Isn't there any warm water?" Marie asked, rinsing a dish.

"No," Anna replied. "It's really not necessary for washing my hands and getting drinks."

"There's no reason why it shouldn't be on. When the weather turns colder, you'll end up with chapped hands. I'll have Daniel look into it along with the furnace. You'll be needing heat soon also."

Anna was grateful for the thoughtfulness, but the twinge of guilt seemed to always lie just below the surface. How was she ever going to repay her friends?

"Anna," Marie's voice interrupted Anna's thoughts, "how about giving me the grand tour of your gardens?"

Anna felt like a child waiting for her parents' approval as she watched Marie carefully inspecting the gardens. They were standing in Anna's favorite spot now, a circular garden bed, splashed with an array of multicolored flowers, adorned in the middle by a spherical sundial. Anna had envisioned the sun nourishing the flowers, while seeking out the arms of the sundial to share its knowledge of time.

"You've done a wonderful job here. You should be proud of yourself."

Anna looked into Marie's eyes, misty from unshed tears. "Thank you."

"No Anna, thank you. You'll never know what this has meant to me, to see the cottage on its way back to what it was, what it was intended to be."

Anna smiled in acknowledgement.

"Daniel and I are planning to attend church on Sunday. We didn't want to go until you felt better."

"I'm sorry," Anna said, feeling guilty. "You shouldn't have stayed home because of me."

"Don't be silly, dear. We were right where we were supposed to be at the time. Anyway, I was just telling you because we would like very much if you would go with us. Doc goes too and afterward we all go over to Millie's café to have breakfast."

"I don't know," Anna said, hesitantly, while laying her hand to her cheek.

"Anna, surely you're not concerned with your looks anymore. Have you looked lately? You're beautiful and now with your tan, you look like the poster woman for good health."

"Do people know about me?"

Anna was being forced into thinking about one of the hundreds of things she didn't want to think about, much less talk about.

"Of course they do," Marie stated frankly. "It's a small town and something like this has never happened around here before."

Anna lowered her eyes and felt huge weights pushing her shoulders down as her posture began to wilt. Instantly, Anna felt her chin being gently, but determinedly lifted, until her gaze met Marie's.

"This is the level you must keep your head at, Anna. Never lower your gaze to anyone. Breathe in the world. God gave you that gift and no matter how hard someone may try, no one can take that from you unless you let them. Don't let them, Anna. Use your strength.

"I can't think of a better place to find strength than in church. You know what they say, there's power in numbers. One becomes many and the chain of life becomes strong. You have to start facing people again, Anna. What a wonderful place to take that first step."

Anna knew Marie was right. Although she was afraid of the gossip and what people thought of her, staying secluded from the world couldn't make her happy indefinitely. Anna was already beginning to feel that she wanted more, needed more, she just hadn't known where to start.

"I would love to join you on Sunday."

"Good, dear," smiled Marie. "Now how about showing me the rest of your creation on this little bit of earth?"

They finished touring the gardens then went to check on Daniel's and Doc's progress.

"Anybody in here?" Anna asked, sticking her head inside the shed.

"I am," came Daniel's voice. "But I'm having trouble keeping Doc concentrated on this job."

"What are you complaining about?" grumbled Doc. "You just sent me out there with all those old windows and besides, I don't see you lugging them around. If you didn't keep everything under the sun, you wouldn't have such a mess."

"I thought I would need them someday," said Daniel defensively.

"That's what you say about all this junk," snapped Doc.

"Well, I'm getting rid of it now, aren't I?" barked Daniel.

Anna had been watching the whole encounter. In fact, she found the old storm windows with the cross-section panes quaint and maybe useful.

"Really, if you are just going to throw them away, would it be all right if I take them?"

Anna knew they were all looking at her as if she'd sprouted another head. She saw the look of defeat that crossed Doc's face, while the look of triumph graced Daniel's.

"See, you old coot," boasted Daniel. "I was saving them for Anna."

Even Doc, who was fit to be tied, burst into laughter. The rest of the afternoon was devoted to cleaning out the shed. When it was completely swept spotless, Anna carefully put the old storm windows back in, against the wall. With that done, they called it a day.

Chapter Fourteen

Church on Sunday went far better than Anna had anticipated. Her fears from the drive there began to dissipate as she soon realized that Daniel, Marie, and Doc seemed to be well liked by everyone in this small community. Not a person went by them without a friendly greeting. Anna understood they all probably knew about her circumstances, but they were all too polite to be nosy.

It didn't take Anna long to relax and begin focusing on her surroundings. Marie had told Anna that the old stone church, in which they were in, was one of the original structures of the town. It certainly reflected that in its architecture, boasting a pristine white bell tower that stretched gracefully upward toward the heavens. Its many majestic stained glass windows were splashing color on the inside floors and walls, as the sun brilliantly flowed through them. The church was notably cared for by loving hands, from its freshly painted walls to its glossy polished wooden pews. Anna felt herself glad that she had come and let some of her burden be lifted.

As they walked out of the church, Anna was amazed at what she had actually missed going in, when her mind had been so focused on meeting new people. Directly across the street was the town square, complete with an abundance of trees and flowers. Memorials depicting the different wars were placed honorably throughout the park. From each outer corner of the square, a brick walkway cut diagonally across the park, intersecting in the center, where a large fountain cheerfully tumbled water from one level to the next. An immense gazebo with its polished copper roof took up a good part of one of the four sections, while another section with its swings and slides, enticed the little ones to come and have some fun. This was definitely the hub of the town, for all of the quaint shops sat across the street, bordering the park on all four sides.

They crossed the brick street to go to Millie's café. Breakfast was friendly and informal, as everyone in the town knew each other, making it seem more like having family home for the holidays. No one pressed Anna to join in their conversations, but they did, however, make a point of never excluding her either. On their way out, Millie had made Anna promise to come back for one of her famous brownie sundaes and Anna had happily agreed.

They all got back into Daniel's car and the ride home had seemed much shorter to Anna than she had remembered from earlier this morning. She could easily walk the distance if for some reason she should ever need to go into town. She had said as much to Daniel and caught a glimpse of his smile before he turned to walk into the house.

The rest of the day, Marie and Anna spent leafing through magazines to get ideas for Anna to use over at the cottage.

Anna had gone to bed early and now here she was, gazing up into the morning sunshine, ready to tackle her next project. Earlier she had noticed some of the cedar shakes on the roof had come loose and in some places fallen completely off. She wanted to get a better look so she could figure out what she needed to fix them. The lowest part of the roof that also looked to be the best part to supply her with a good footing seemed to be by the front door. Anna took the tallest ladder out of her shed and, after leaning it against the house, started the climb up. The inspection was going well as she waved across the lawns to Marie, until Anna started over the peak of the roof and on to the other side. She began to slide on the moss that had grown on these shaded shingles. Between the moss and the steep pitch of the roof, once she began to fall, there was little help for anything to stop her, except the ground.

"Are you hurt?" Erik was demanding, appearing out of nowhere.

Startled, Anna wiped the tears in her eyes and looked up. "I'm fine."

"You're not fine," countered Erik. "You just fell off a roof!"

"I didn't fall all the way off," Anna replied stubbornly.

"Yeah, I forgot, the ground broke your fall."

"Very funny. I meant I caught the edge of the roof before I fell. It slowed me down some."

Anna was not only in pain, but also feeling humiliated. She was hoping to keep what little pride she had left in tact.

"Let's get you up and see how you're doing." Erik's arm slipped around Anna, lifting her up gently.

"What were you thinking sending her up on that roof like that?" Doc yelled, as he, Daniel, and Marie came racing around the corner of the cottage.

"Me? You're the ones who told her she could fix this dump up!" shouted Erik.

"Well, why weren't you up there?" continued Doc, angrily.

"I wasn't even over here," answered Erik. "Do you think I'd be working on a roof dressed like this?"

All eyes were turned to Erik now and for the first time, everyone realized the state of dress, or rather undress, he was in.

"I had just gotten out of the shower and was putting on my

jeans when I saw Anna starting to slide on the roof," Erik explained. "I didn't have time to finish dressing."

"What were you doing on the roof by yourself?" scolded Doc, turning toward Anna.

"Obviously the roof needed repair," Marie said matter-of-factly.

Still mortified by the chain of events this morning had evolved into, Anna was glad for Marie's support.

"I'm taking Anna back to the house to find a pair of tennis shoes," continued Marie. "She's going to need something with a little more traction to stay up there."

"She's not going back up there," stated Daniel.

"What do you think, Anna?" Marie questioned.

"I want to go back up and finish what I started." Anna gave Marie a grateful smile.

"Daniel and Doc, you're too old to get up there like you used to. So you two can direct Anna and Erik on how to do it."

"Who said I'm going up there?" replied a stunned Erik.

"You'll be fine," continued Marie. "Daniel and Doc will show you how to put the roof braces on, so even if you start to fall, you'll stop at the brace."

"I'm not worried about that," grumbled Erik. "It's having those two as crew bosses."

"Erik doesn't have to help," Anna said, wishing they would all quit forcing this job upon him. "I'm fine doing it myself, really."

"No offense, but I witnessed first hand your carpentry skills," Erik teased. "I'm not sure mine are much better, but you know that old saying, two hands are better than one."

"Good then, it's settled." Marie turned toward Anna. "Let's go and get those shoes now, while the men gather all the things you will need."

"Thank you," whispered Anna, linking her arm in the older woman's.

"How bad is it?" Marie whispered back.

"Not too bad, nothing's broke."

"Go get some clothes on," Doc instructed Erik, while turning him toward his cottage.

"I am. Don't get pushy."

"I'm not. But I am going over with you."

"Are you playing landlord again?" asked Erik.

"No, I'm playing doctor and I want to get a good look at those cuts on your feet."

"My feet are fine," Erik was saying, but Anna watched him begin to gingerly walk up the path. She felt guilty that because of her, Erik was now suffering from many cuts and probably some embedded stones in his feet.

"I'm not asking you," continued Doc, "I'm telling you. I'm going to look at those feet and clean up those cuts, if I have to get Daniel to help me tie you down."

"You better watch it, Doc," Anna heard Erik say. "You know what happened to the Grinch's heart on Christmas day?"

"Come on, Cindy Lou Who," chuckled Doc. "The sleigh's this way."

That was two days earlier and now through hard work and much arguing amongst Daniel, Doc, and Erik, the final shingle was nailed down just as the first raindrop began to fall. Anna and Erik had worked hard with no more accidents or incidents, even though Doc and Daniel had sworn their lives had been scared out of them at least a dozen times. Now, as Erik and Anna removed the last of the roof braces, they shared a moment of content at their accomplishment.

"I can honestly say that was the first time I've ever fixed a roof," sighed Erik. "What do you say we go into business together, Anna?"

"Sure," laughed Anna. "But right now with this lightning, I think it would be wiser to go into the house."

Chapter Fifteen

Anna was sitting in the library, listening to the rain and mentally adding up the little odds and ends of work that needed to be finished yet on the outside of the cottage. A loud crashing of a door snapped Anna's attention back to the present and she headed in the direction in which she thought it had come. As she entered the kitchen, two small forms in yellow ponchos were standing in puddles that were forming around their tiny, booted feet. A woman had just entered the French doors, while closing an oversized umbrella.

"Hurry in out of the rain," Marie was hustling them all farther into the kitchen.

The bigger of the two ponchos was doing a good job of unfastening the hooks and buttons, while the little one was getting assistance from Daniel. When both children finally shed their wet cloaks, Anna could see that the oldest was a boy and the little one a girl. As Anna was observing, the boy began to head toward her.

"Hello," he said, putting out his hand, as he must have seen his father do on some such occasion. "My name is Brandon."

"Hi," replied Anna, smiling and accepting his small, warm hand. "I'm Anna."

Not to be overlooked, the little girl came barreling into Anna's knees with her arms stretched upward.

"I'm Katie," she said, standing as if waiting to be picked up.

"It's nice to meet you, Katie," said Anna, instinctively, bending over to pick the child up.

"I'm sorry about Katie," apologized the woman. "Being shy will never be on her resume."

"Anna," Daniel was saying, "this is Susan, Dennis's wife. You've met Brandon—"

"And I'm Katie," the little girl interrupted.

"Yes you are, squirt," Daniel said as he reached over to take Katie from Anna. "Now you and your brother get to stay in here and make cookies and play crazy eights, while your mommy gets a little grown-up time with Anna. I imagine after two days of this rain, your mommy's ready to climb walls."

"My mommy can't climb walls," Katie said innocently.

"Oh, Katie, dear," uttered Daniel, patting the little girl's head. "Give it time."

"Anna, can you stimulate Susan's brain for us, with some adult conversation, while we try to tire these two munchkins out?" asked Daniel, while shooing both Susan and Anna back into the library.

"That would be great," Susan agreed. "It's been nothing but Barbie dolls and Hot Wheels. My brain is turning into mush."

Anna was nervous as she followed Susan.

"Marie mentioned to me that you were fixing up the cottage," started Susan. "That's such a great place. Dennis always told me I was crazy, but I always thought that place had such great potential."

With the conversation on the cottage, Anna's nerves began to relax.

"I've got the outside almost finished. I was lucky to get the roof done before all of this rain set in."

"I understand you had a little help with that."

Anna was curious how Susan had known about her drafted help.

"Erik is a good friend of ours. My husband and he were partners in the city before we moved here," explained Susan.

Anna shook her head in acknowledgement. Erik had mentioned that previously.

"How did you ever get Erik to do anything so domestic? I didn't even realize he knew which end of a hammer to pick up," laughed Susan.

"Actually, I don't think he really wanted to. Daniel and Doc kind of enlisted him after I fell off the roof."

"You fell off the roof!"

"Really, it was more like I slid off when I was inspecting it. I ended up with a sore ankle and a lecture from Erik, who had apparently seen the whole thing from his cottage. He ran over immediately, with Daniel and Doc not too far behind. Anyway, it turned into a three-ring circus and somewhere within all that yelling, Erik had been drafted to go up with me to finish the job."

"I would have given anything to see his face," smiled Susan. "Erik's afraid of heights."

"Oh, I don't think he was too happy at first, but when we were done, he was pretty proud of it."

"I'm sure he was, but I'll still have to tease him about it when I go over to pick up his laundry."

"Why are you washing Erik's clothes?" Anna asked, blushing, as she realized it was really none of her business.

"I feel the need to take care of him now that Elaine is gone."

"Who is Elaine?"

"She was Erik's wife and my best friend," continued Susan sadly. "When she and Mandy—his daughter—were killed by a drunk driver, I felt I had lost a sister. I wanted to take care of Erik for her, to help ease his pain. Up until now, however, he has made that almost impossible. We finally have him here and now I can finally keep my promise."

Anna was feeling guilty. She hadn't even tried to look beyond Erik's stubborn, brash personality. Once again, her own life was put into perspective by someone else's. Perhaps our lives are lived like chapters in a book. Chapters that need to address one issue before we can continue and turn the page.

"Dennis has told me a little bit about your circumstances," admitted Susan. "I just wanted to be open with you on that. I want you to know how sorry I am that this has happened to you and if you ever need anything or just want to talk . . . well, I just wanted you to know, I'm here and I'd like you to consider me a friend."

Anna was touched by Susan's offer and maybe at some point she might feel more comfortable.

"Well," said Susan lowering her gaze and picking up a magazine, "Marie tells me you've been getting ideas for different rooms over at the cottage."

When Marie brought tea in, Anna couldn't believe an hour had already gone by while she and Susan had been engrossed in different designing magazines.

"Marie," chuckled Susan, "Anna doesn't believe me when I tell her I have no concept of decorating."

"Did you ever get any curtains up in your dining room yet?" Marie winked at Susan.

"Nope," replied Susan. "And I rest my case."

"Maybe when Anna finishes her own project, she'll consider helping you with yours." Marie set the tray down on the coffee table.

"I would love to, but maybe you should wait and see how much damage I do first," responded Anna.

"Mommy! Mommy!" Katie shouted, entering the room as Brandon followed with a plateful of cookies. "Look what we made."

"Would you like one?" asked Brandon, offering the treats to Anna.

"They smell delicious." Anna was enchanted with the two little faces smudged with flour.

"Anna," Marie was saying, "would you mind if I took Susan for a minute? I want to show her some material I have that might work for her curtains."

"Oh, Marie!" cried Susan. "That's not fair to leave Anna with these two bundles of energy."

"It's more than fair," smiled Anna. "Maybe they'll give me the secret recipe to these yummy cookies."

Anna watched Marie and Susan leave the room, as Katie began telling her of gooey eggs and sticky butter.

"Could you read to me?" begged Katie.

"Katie, you're not supposed to bother her," corrected Brandon.

"It's quite all right," Anna reassured the children. "What would you like to read?"

Brandon found his favorite book of fairytales and, before long, Anna found herself with Katie on her lap and Brandon snuggled up against her side. The two children were very attentive listeners, but the busy day and the lull of Anna's voice had eventually won out and the two fell asleep within the circle of Anna's arms.

Anna was afraid to move a muscle and take the chance of disturbing either child, so she relaxed and leaned back into the sofa. She absentmindedly stroked both children's hair, while her senses took in the essence of them—the way their long lashes lay on their chubby cheeks and the way they smelled of baby shampoo and sunshine. Slow tears were working their way down Anna's cheeks when Marie and Susan came back into the room.

"Anna," whispered Susan, "are they hurting you?"

"No, not at all," Anna whispered back sadly. "It's just that I know this feeling, I'm sure of it. I feel it here." Anna pointed to her heart. "I have children and this feels very real to me."

Brandon turned and curled up on the other end of the couch and Anna gently laid Katie across from him and stood up.

"I'm sorry, Susan," Anna said, touching her forehead. "My head is hurting terribly. I think I'll go lay down for a little while."

Anna withdrew quickly from the room, before her despair began to show.

"I'm sorry, Marie," Susan apologized. "I forgot what a handful these two can be."

"Susan, Anna's worked five times harder than this over at the cottage. Yes, this was draining, but emotionally draining. It had to happen. We've all noticed, including Anna, how she seems to get terrible headaches when something seems familiar to her regarding her past. Sometimes it's a smell or something she sees. Other times it's a word or a sound."

"Is this bad for her?"

"Doc is confident that her health is progressing nicely. She did have a severe blow to her head and that could certainly have caused her memory loss, but the headaches seem to appear only when something triggers them. Some of her worst episodes come when she is trying to face the incline going down to the beach, but then the headache always go away, after she's turned and walked away."

"Why does she do that then?"

"She and Doc both feel that if she can conquer that fear and face the reality of what happened to her, the rest of her life will start coming back also. It's the only common ground she has. It's her one foot in the past and her other in the present."

"How is she doing?"

"For what she's gone through, I think she's made remarkable

progress. She's made it about a quarter of the way down. Unfortunately, Anna doesn't feel as satisfied with her accomplishment. She feels she's a failure. That's why the project of the cottage is so important. She needs to know she can have control over herself and her accomplishments."

"From what I can see, it's working."

"Yes, it really is and I know it meant a lot to her when you told her that earlier. I think sometimes she thinks we'll tell her anything just to make her happy. She's probably right," chuckled Marie. "It's good for her to have a friend closer to her own age."

"I like her a lot." Susan's voice was sincere. "I hope the pain of seeing children doesn't keep us all from having a friendship."

"You would be surprised how strong she really is. These bits of remembering take her by surprise. But lately, after reflecting on them for a while, she seems to come out on the other side even stronger. This was a big step for Anna today. Now she has to work out remembering the specifics. That's when she begins to doubt herself and starts to waiver and that is when she needs all of us even more. Don't stay away because you think you're doing her a kindness, Susan. She needs to see you and the children so she can start to embrace her reality."

"If I've learned anything from my husband, it's how to be stubborn and persistent."

"Haven't we all learned that from the male population," laughed Marie.

Brandon and Katie started waking up from their impromptu naps.

"Where's Anna?" Katie demanded.

"She was tired and had to lie down for a nap too," explained Susan.

"Will we see her before we go?" Brandon asked.

"Probably not," Marie answered. "But I'll tell you what you can do, you can go in the kitchen and get the crayons and paper out and make Anna a card."

The two children jumped up excitedly, ready to sprint down the hallway.

"You have to be very quiet and walk," said Susan.

"Susan," began Marie, "you don't have to walk on eggshells around Anna. We need to just be ourselves. Noise and laughter are good for her. It's the quiet that reminds her of the voids and offers her only emptiness."

"Marie's right you know," said Daniel entering the room. "Anna needs us to go about our every day lives, or even with all of our good intentions, we take the risk of secluding her. She needs a friend right now."

"I can do that," stated Susan.

"I know you can," smiled Daniel. "Now, however, we have to get in the kitchen and rescue Doc from two little Picasos with paintbrushes."

"Paintbrushes!" cried Susan

Later that day, after Susan and the children had gone home and all traces of watercolors had been removed from the kitchen, Anna emerged from her bedroom. She was feeling exhausted, but thoughtful.

"How's your headache?" Doc asked, concerned.

"Better. I feel so foolish when I get them. I'm sorry if I seemed rude to Susan."

"Don't worry about it, dear," said Marie. "You can't help them. I hope you don't mind, but I did explain to Susan what we think causes them. She was worried it was their fault."

"That's okay," Anna replied. "I'd rather she knew the truth than think I was trying to avoid her."

"She understands," Marie said as she handed Anna the cards Brandon and Katie had made for her earlier.

A smile was on Anna's lips, but fresh tears were forming in her eyes.

"What of my children?" was all Anna could choke out.

"If God is here for you, Anna," Marie said gently, "surely you must know He is also there for those you love. It may not be everything you want to hear right now, but it is the most important thing you must remember."

Anna looked out the window. The rain had stopped and outside she could see the start of one of the most beautiful sunsets. The colors were refreshing and bright as they reflected off each tiny crystal droplet left behind by the storm. It was a fresh start, as old as time. The old and the new were working harmoniously to bring about perfection and it was working extraordinarily well.

"Could I please use your phone to call Susan?" asked Anna, thinking it was nice to have someone to call. "I thought maybe I could give her and the children a tour of the cottage tomorrow."

Marie smiled and at that moment, Anna felt as fresh and sure as the cleansed air drifting in from the open window.

Chapter Sixteen

Anna put the final brush strokes on the pale green walls of the living room. She was still finding it hard to believe two more months had passed. The days were still sunny and warm, but the nights were starting to get crisp, leaving the slightest hint of frost behind by morning. The spectacular colors that overwhelmed Anna's vision were definite testimony that fall had majestically arrived. Anna had agreed to spend the rest of this day carving pumpkins and making candied apples.

Yes, Anna thought, today would be a fun break, but tonight she would have to work twice as hard to catch up. A few weeks ago, Anna had retrieved the old storm windows from the shed and given them a fresh coat of paint. When she was cleaning off the glass, ideas began jumping out at her. Anna began painting the glass, as if it were a canvas, creating a scene that reminded her of the person or persons she intended to present the window to. Marie and Daniel's window had been abounding with splashes of many flowers and, of course, Marie's beloved cottage. Doc's hinted of sailboats and sailing, while Dennis and Susan's, gave a glimpse of two children, playing on the beach. On Erik's window, Anna had worked hard on capturing one of the sunsets she had noticed him admiring daily. Her friends gave her rave reviews about her work and even convinced Anna to take one of the windows to the local art gallery. To Anna's amazement, this proved to be a huge success. Anna instantly had over a dozen orders and people weren't even blinking at the hefty price tag that Karen, the owner, had assigned to each piece.

Karen also wanted Anna to consider letting her bring a couple of the windows to her sister's gallery in the city. Karen was convinced Anna's work would sell for double the amount there. Karen had been right and now with the work Anna was trying to get done at the cottage and her new means of supporting herself, she found herself wishing for more time in each day.

She would never complain though, because this gave her the ability at least to begin to pay Marie, Daniel, and Doc back financially. Anna reached into the refrigerator to grab a quick glass of apple juice before she washed up to join the others.

That's when it struck her—all the necessities that made a house a home were here. Anna had cleaned and refinished floors, furniture, walls, and appliances until her arms ached, but looking around, she felt her efforts had been well worth it. The cottage was completely furnished, but more importantly, it looked and felt comfortable. Even Erik, who thought she had been crazy for agreeing to take on this task, seemed to spend an awful lot of time here with his feet up.

Anna always felt lonely when she had to close the door on the cottage and walk away from it at the end of each day. She loved Daniel and Marie and would be forever grateful to them, but she needed to start depending on herself not only financially, but emotionally as well. She needed to have a life that was on her own terms, her own time schedule.

"Hey, Anna!" She heard Erik shouting and knocking loudly on her door.

"Erik," she replied, rushing to open it, "come in."

Anna began to laugh before the door was even swung fully open. There stood a man with an angry scowl on his face, half hidden by a larger-than-life potted plant.

"What were you doing? I was yelling and knocking out there for a good five minutes."

"Sorry, I guess I was daydreaming."

"Just don't do it again."

"Yes, sir," smiled Anna, giving Erik a mock salute. "It won't happen again, sir."

"Good. I brought you a flower for the conservatory."

"That's not a flower, that's a man-eating plant. I think I saw a play like that once."

"Where do you want this oxygen treatment?"

"I guess next to the other three plants you brought over. You know, Erik, this has to be the very last plant you bring over, or pretty soon I'll have to move the furniture out."

"I know," agreed Erik, looking through the glass toward the ocean. "I just feel so connected with this room."

"If I remember right, you hated working on this room."

"No, I hated being told and not asked to work—there's a difference."

"I'm sorry," Anna said sincerely. "That's just Doc. He means well, he just likes to fix things up and make them right."

"Yeah, and I'm his biggest challenge," winked Erik. "I love the power that gives me."

"You are two of a kind," laughed Anna.

"Now you're insulting Doc, because whether anyone believes it or not, I think he's a great guy. I have a lot of respect for him."

"Don't sell yourself short; you're in that same category."

Before Anna could go any further, she heard Doc shouting from the front of the cottage.

"We're in here!" Anna called out.

"I knew we shouldn't have sent a boy over to do a man's job," grumbled Doc, as he and Daniel entered the conservatory. "See, now we had to come over to retrieve both of them."

Erik turned to Anna, laughing. "If you repeat any of our prior conversation, I swear, I'll deny it."

"Your secret's safe with me," winked Anna.

"Will you two quit talking gibberish," Doc said impatiently.

"Let me just change my clothes." Anna headed off toward the bedroom.

"I've been called off the case," Erik whispered as the sound of Anna's door closing echoed in the cottage.

"What?!" shouted Doc.

"A little louder, I don't think the squirrels in the front of the yard could hear you," replied Erik.

"Sorry." Doc blushed.

"They feel that since Anna's life hasn't been threatened again in this length of time, she won't be needing around-the-clock protection," continued Erik. "I disagree—time is her assailant's biggest weapon. The waiting and planning are part of the thrill for this scum. I've talked to Dennis; I have about three months vacation time built up, so I intend to take that all right now.

"Hopefully, this will all be sorted out in that amount of time. I just wanted you both to know, because technically, I have no authority over this case any longer. I'm good at my work though, so I know this is far from over. This isn't just a hunch; this is just how cases like this work. If he's realized she's alive yet, he's probably also realized she's well protected. As long as she can't point a finger at him, he's willing to give it time. Then when she starts to feel safe again, he'll hunt her down."

"Thank you for staying," said Doc humbly.

"Don't go making it more than it is," Erik said, noticeably

uncomfortable with the intended praise. "He's the kind of guy I've been trying to get off the streets my whole life. I want him locked up so he can't hurt Anna or anyone else ever again."

"No matter how you put it," said Doc, "it's a noble thing you are doing."

"What's a noble thing?" Anna asked, joining the men.

"Erik's agreed to clean the 'goop' out of the pumpkins," smiled Doc.

"I told you guys, absolutely not," muttered Erik.

"Come on, Anna." Daniel took her arm and lead her out the door. "We have pumpkins to carve and candy apples to eat. These two can stay and bicker all they want, that just means all the more apples for us."

"Not on your life," Doc said, passing the pair.

Anna noticed how quiet Erik was on the walk over to Daniel and Marie's. It wasn't until Brandon ran and jumped into Erik's outstretched arms that Erik seemed to come out of his thoughts.

"Hey, Uncle Erik," greeted Brandon, giving Erik a huge hug. "Look, I've got my face already drawn on my pumpkin."

"Yes, you do," agreed Erik. "And it's a scary one."

"Look at all of these pumpkins," Katie said, twirling and clapping her hands together.

Anna looked at the two dozen or so pumpkins scattered around the deck. She was caught up in the children's excitement and the smell of fall in the air. However, the nagging reminder she had to work late tonight prompted her to gather her courage and share her newest idea.

"I was thinking," Anna began, speaking directly to Daniel and Marie, "maybe, if it would be alright with the two of you, I could move into the cottage and start paying rent."

It was so quiet, Anna could hear the autumn leaves rustling as they floated off the trees in the warm breeze. Even Brandon and Katie seemed to be holding their breath waiting for Daniel's and Marie's answer.

"You must be getting tired of me always being underfoot," Anna continued, before she lost her nerve. "This way, I could work late without bothering anyone."

"Don't you like it here?" Katie asked, breaking the silence.

"Yes . . . I do," Anna stammered.

"She just needs some quiet time and some space of her own," Marie said with an understanding smile. "It's just like when you like to go to your room and play with your dolls, Katie. Anna needs her own room too."

"But she has a room here," stated Brandon.

"Yeah," agreed Erik, sounding to Anna like one of the children. "She has a room."

"Well," Marie continued, while bending down to Brandon and Katie, "you know how you're in charge of taking care of your room and keeping it clean?"

Anna watched as Brandon and Katie began nodding their heads in unison.

"Adults need rooms to take care of too. But because we're bigger, we need more room."

"I wouldn't want anymore room to keep clean," Brandon said seriously.

"Precisely," smiled Marie. "But look what a good job Anna's done cleaning and taking care of the cottage. I think she'll be just fine over there."

"It's not a good idea," persisted Erik.

"Why?" Anna asked, feeling hurt, but her emotion quickly turned to anger as she started to walk inside. "I'm beginning to think you don't want me for a neighbor, Erik. I promise to keep the parties down to a minimum."

Susan, Marie, Brandon, and Katie followed Anna inside.

"Now you've done it!" Doc whispered angrily.

"I've done it? I thought you two—three," Erik continued,

pointing at Dennis, "agreed to help me keep Anna safe."

"Keep your voice down," reprimanded Dennis. "We'll just have to come up with a plan."

"I thought we had a plan," Erik replied, through clenched teeth. "I thought the plan was never to leave Anna completely alone. It seems to me that the plan was working quite well."

"It was," said Daniel thoughtfully. "But we can't keep Anna locked in a tower forever. She's already starting to feel the walls closing in."

"All right," agreed Erik. "But we do things my way. No exceptions, got that?"

"What are we agreeing to?" Doc asked.

"You're not agreeing to anything," answered Erik, calmly. "This is just the way it is going to be. Since someone will not be able to be with Anna one hundred percent of the time, I'll have to put a one-way communicator in the cottage."

"A bug?" Daniel asked, looking stunned.

"In layman's terms, yes," replied Erik.

"That seems to be a drastic step; an invasion of her privacy," stated Doc.

"I don't think when her attacker comes back to finish the job he'll be worrying about her invasion of privacy," Erik quipped.

"He's right," added Dennis.

"So here's the thing," Erik continued, "we either alert her to the real danger she might be in, in which case, she would probably never leave this house, much less her room again. Or, as in your very own words, we try to make her life as normal as possible. I'll only have the device on when no one else is in the cottage with her, especially at night.

"The length of time we have to fit this puzzle together depends on Anna or her attacker and I can guarantee you, the minute he knows she's alive, the game has begun for him."

"We'll support you," sighed Doc.

"Now, I just need a good block of time to put the transmitter in and check the locks on all of the doors and windows." Erik turned toward Dennis. "Do you think Susan could get Anna out of the cottage tomorrow for a few hours?"

"Sure, I'll talk to her tonight."

"I know this is going to be hard," said Erik. "But I think it's best if Susan and Marie don't know about this either. It will be hard enough for all of us to act natural about it."

"How am I suppose to get Susan out of the house without giving her any explanation?"

"I don't know," laughed Erik. "She didn't seem to need too much coaxing last time we watched the kids. She told me over and over again how much fun she, Anna, and Marie had at the flea market."

"Can we carve pumpkins now?" asked Brandon, running out of the door with Katie on his heels.

Anna looked at Erik skeptically as she, Susan, and Marie followed the children outside.

"Anna," said Erik, "I'm sorry about what I said earlier. I didn't mean for it to sound . . . I meant . . ."

"He meant that although you've done a wonderful job over at the cottage, it's not safe," Daniel interjected. "The old electrical wiring needs to be checked. Tomorrow, why don't you ladies take another 'ladies day out' or whatever you call it and give us some time to give the wiring the old once over."

"Well," Anna sounded a little concerned.

"I promise we'll be careful and not make a mess," Daniel offered.

"It's not that . . . I have all of those window orders to work on, I was hoping to use a good part of the day tomorrow to work on them."

"It will probably only take a few hours," coaxed Dennis. "Why not leave in the morning, run some errands, and stop for lunch? By the time you get back, it will all be done."

"I do need to get some more paint and brushes." Anna started to warm to the idea. "Do you mind, Susan?"

"Are you kidding? You're the best thing for me since Sesame Street. Marie, you pick the restaurant and tomorrow we're out of here."

"Okay," laughed Anna. "But only for half a day."

By the time the pumpkins were carved, the sun was slipping away to a distant land. Marie had given Dennis and Erik candles to put in each of the pumpkins. As the silly and scary jack-o-lanterns glowed around them on the deck, the group of friends sat bundled up.

The famous candy apples they had made this afternoon were now dessert and as Anna sat back, wishing it could stay this way forever, reality hit her like a bucket of cold water. What was she thinking? She already had a life somewhere. She had her own children, she could feel it, just as she knew she had carved pumpkins and dipped apples before.

This day had been bittersweet for Anna and suddenly she just wanted to be alone. She wanted to try to transport herself back into her other life, as she had tried so many times since she had awakened here months ago. She heard Erik's voice now interrupting her thoughts.

"Thanks for supper," Erik was saying, laying his napkin down on the table. "It was all great and way more than I should have eaten. If I don't get up now and walk home, I'm afraid I'll still be sitting here when the sun rises tomorrow."

"That's okay," smiled Marie. "I would throw a blanket on you, dear."

"Thanks, Marie, but I have a little reading to do on electricity. I can never remember if it's the red wire that's the positive or the black one."

"Please tell me you're not on the bomb squad," uttered Doc, shaking his head.

"Well . . ." Erik began.

"Never mind," Doc interrupted. "I don't want to know."

"Then before I take any more abuse, I'm leaving," laughed Erik. "Anna, why don't you walk with me, if you're still determined to work for a while yet tonight."

"Sure, just let me help clean up first."

"Nonsense." Marie waved her hand in the air.

"I'll help," said Susan, standing up. "Besides, I get the whole morning off. If I'm not careful, I might become lazy."

"I doubt that," Anna said and bent down to give the two sleeping children a kiss. "This will be my first night in the cottage."

"Tonight?" Everyone said in unison.

"I have to start sometime," Anna said, turning toward Daniel and Marie. "I really need to work late and I don't want to keep you two up waiting for me."

A small twinge of guilt settled in Anna's stomach as she and Erik walked off into the night. She hated to upset Marie, but this was for the best for all of them.

"So what were you thinking about earlier?" Erik asked as they continued to walk.

"I don't know what you mean," sighed Anna, not wanting to put words to thoughts that were so painfully locked away in her own mind.

"I think you were remembering," pressed Erik. "Remembering something similar to the events of today."

In the darkness, the reflection of the moon made the silent tear Anna wiped from her face sparkle on her hand like a diamond. She could see Erik's compassion as she looked into his eyes.

"Every day," Anna began, softly, "I do things, see things, feel things that seem so real, so familiar. Yet, I can't find anything solid to prove that they ever really existed. I know I have children—why can't I find a way back to them? I should have been with them today, yesterday, and what about tomorrow?"

Anna let Erik take her shoulders and turn her toward him.

"Listen to me. I know you're feeling guilty. Guilt for not being there when they need you. Guilt for not sharing their accomplishments and disappointments and guilt for not spending a beautiful, fall day with them."

Anna watched Erik's face, noticing how her pain became his pain.

"The night I lost my wife and daughter was the very same day I had made a promise to change. That morning, Mandy had asked me to go to one of her swim meets that night. I had easily promised her I would. When Mandy had gone off to school, like so many mornings before, Elaine had begged me to keep my promise. Then we had one of our many fights about how Elaine thought my working was more important than my own family and how I never seemed to have any time for them. I was determined to prove Elaine wrong. I told her that I would come back to the apartment and pick them up and we would all drive over to the meet together.

"Unfortunately, Elaine was right. I didn't keep my promise and I keep telling myself it was because of my job, but that will never bring back Elaine and Mandy. I should have been there in that car with them, to either save them or die with them, but once again, they were without me. Now I have to live without them the rest of my life. It's a just punishment, don't you agree?"

Anna took Erik's hand. "Marie says there are lessons, challenges in life. And the only way to go on is to have learned from them."

"Oh, I've learned. I've learned what I missed and what I am missing, but what good is that to me now? Today I did something I very rarely did with my own family; I took the time to have fun. Was I wrong in doing that?"

"Erik, you can't change that now, but you can change. You can grow."

"That's easy for you to say, Anna," said Erik bitterly. "There's no miracle that can bring my wife and daughter back to me, but you, you have a chance."

Erik's words, hit Anna like a blow to the face. She sadly turned and looked across the water.

"I'm sorry," Erik said regretfully. "You and I are nothing alike. You're kind and caring. You were hurt, you have to heal, and I know you will because you're determined. I threw it away, Anna. I threw it away, all on my own."

Anna understood Erik was hurting. "You're a good man, Erik, and if you won't have any faith in yourself, I'll have it for you."

Not another word was spoken as they finished the walk to the cottage.

"Goodnight," Erik said when they reached the door. "I'm sorry that . . ."

"Erik, there's no need. Friends?" Anna asked, while putting her outstretched hand toward Erik.

"Friends."

Anna entered the cottage, closing the door to the cool night air.

"It's gonna be a chilly night." Daniel's voice came from just behind Erik.

"Yes, it is," replied Erik, sitting down on a bench.

"I knew you'd stay out here." Daniel sat down next to Erik and handed him two blankets.

"Without the tapping device in place, there's no way I can leave her here alone tonight."

"You're a good man, Erik. Don't you ever think otherwise."

The phone rang inside the cottage, bringing both men to their feet and to the window.

"Thank you, Marie," Anna said into the phone. "I don't think I could have gone to sleep without it."

Anna hung up the phone smiling.

"What was that all about?" asked Erik.

"My guess is, Marie was checking up on Anna. From the bits of Anna's conversation, Marie must have given Anna her nightly blessing. Anna says she feels safer and can sleep better with it.

"Try not to get too cold tonight. I better get back, before Marie catches me gone. I told her I had something out in the garage I had to turn off. Now I understand why she was glad to get rid of me. Oh well, I guess she got her phone call in and you got your blankets. It worked out pretty well I think. Goodnight, Erik."

"Goodnight, Daniel, and thanks," said Erik, holding up a blanket.

"You're welcome."

"Daniel, do you believe in second chances?"

"I do." Daniel started down the path. "And thirds and fourths. Frankly, in however many a body needs. See you in the morning, Erik."

Chapter Seventeen

Walking up to Anna's cottage, Erik could hear the comforting structure of classical music Anna listened to while working on her paintings. Since Anna's work had begun showing in the city, her workload had tripled and with Christmas just a little over a month away, it seemed a paintbrush was never far from her reach.

Erik knew that with each holiday or event that passed, Anna became more depressed and demanding of herself to regain the memory of her former life. Most of the time, it only gained her severe headaches and great disappointments. Doc told her perhaps she was trying too hard and Erik agreed. He thought she should try to relax and let the memories flow out of her, just as her ideas for the windows she painted.

Erik took hold of the doorknob and was surprised when it turned easily in his hand. Opening the door, he stepped into the cottage and began to call out.

"Hey, Ann?"

Anna appeared with paint smudged on her clothes and a guilty look on her face.

"I thought we agreed you would keep the doors locked when you were inside," said Erik frustrated.

"I know, but Marie was just here and . . ."

"Marie was here over two hours ago."

"How do you know?" Anna asked, surprised.

"I uh, I saw her leave." Erik sounded guilty even to his own ears. "Anyway, that's beside the point."

"But I like having you guys being able to walk in. It's just more comfortable that way. Besides, what could happen on such a gloriously sunny day?"

Outwardly, Anna always tried to project to the world she had no fears, but Erik knew all too well of Anna's terrors. He heard every scream and every sob that exploded from her body, as she relived the attack, over and over again in her nightmares.

The dreams had started about two nights after Anna had moved into the cottage. It was also the first time she had made it halfway down the incline in the cove. Erik would never forget the sickening fear he felt when he had heard her thrashing and screaming on the other end of the transmitter. He had jumped up, grabbed his gun, and was running to her cottage, formulating a plan that would keep Anna safe, while he took care of her attacker.

When he had reached her cottage and looked into the windows, however, he was confused at what he saw. Anna was crying and restlessly rolling around on her bed. Erik had scanned the room, but neither saw nor heard anyone else in there. Yet, Anna still had been begging over and over again for her life. Then Erik had realized Anna's eyes were closed and the heart wrenching pleas were only a dream, but as real to her now as they had been that frightful night in July.

Anna was regressing, but to a place where reality could be all too real—a place that controlled time and showed no mercy. Anna was stuck in her nightmares. Erik had watched as Anna awoke, sitting straight up in her bed, sweat drenching her body. She seemed to look around frightened and confused. Then, almost hesitantly, she walked toward the mirror slowly lifting her hands to her face as her trembling body seemed to force her to stand there and look back at the reflection. Then a new set of sobs had brought Anna to her knees and Erik had the feeling these tears stemmed more from relief rather than fear.

After a couple of weeks of these nightmares, Erik began to notice the purple smudges under Anna's eyes. He was getting ready to share his insight of the situation with Doc when Anna herself came over to see Erik on this matter. He wasn't surprised that Anna had chosen him to confide in, after all, what had started out for Erik as just another job of protection, had easily turned into a trusting friendship.

Erik was still trying to pinpoint when that change had occurred; yet, weren't they continuously being thrust together by Daniel, Marie, and Doc's insisting that Anna live a normal life? When Marie had given Anna her old bicycle so Anna would be able to ride into town, Doc had smugly given Erik his. When Marie had insisted Anna share her beautiful voice with the church choir, Erik had been appointed her chauffeur. Every Wednesday night, Erik found himself right next to Anna, but in his case, trying to find at least one note to hold on to.

Amusing as all of this probably was to Daniel and Doc, Erik found he actually didn't mind doing the everyday things that most people do. The more time he spent with Anna, the more he realized they both shared a great sense of loss and wanting to be able to fit in somewhere. It seemed to be a continuous struggle for both of them, but together it gave them an unspoken strength that just felt comfortable.

As Anna had stood there with the trust of friendship in her eyes and the sound of tears in her voice, Erik had known he had been listening as a friend, her friend. Anna had spoken to Erik of her nightmares and how though she could never clearly put a face to anyone in her dreams, everything else about the dreams were vividly real. She could smell the salt water and sand on the beach, feel the moist breeze as it swept over her body, hear the lulling tide, and know the dread, as her mind relived the terror.

Erik had held Anna while she had worried she was loosing her mind. He tried to ease her thoughts by telling her how normal her reactions were. He also went on to explain to her how she needed to gain the control back from these dreams so she could move on.

Erik had promised to help her and an exhausted Anna had listened. She was to phone him immediately after she had awakened from one of her nightmares and together they would talk past the fear, until her mind was ready to fight again.

After the first night and the first phone call, Erik thought Anna seemed to be a bit more relaxed. She was still having the reoccurring dream, but it seemed to come much later in her sleep cycle, allowing Anna's body the much needed sleep it had been craving. It also was becoming easier for Erik to settle her down after one of the nightmares. Maybe just the fact that Anna knew someone was there who knew what she was going through gave her at least some peace of mind.

Whatever it was, it seemed to be helping, and as Erik lowered himself into one of the chairs in Anna's cottage, he wondered how to once again give Anna the lecture on locking her doors, even during the day. He was afraid everyone, including himself, was beginning to treat a beautiful sunny day with a false sense of security. Erik still felt uncomfortable when he knew Anna was over here alone and he found himself once again walking that fine line between scaring her and instilling common sense.

Watching Anna paint, he noticed the deep furrow forming on her forehead. "I wish I had a penny for your thoughts."

"What makes you think I have any thoughts?" Anna asked, pointing to the half-done painting.

"Exactly, I've never seen you at a loss of what to paint."

"Maybe I'm running out of ideas."

"Whoa! I think you need to analyze this."

"Analyze what, Dr. Freud?" chuckled Anna.

"Seriously," Erik continued, while looking into Anna's eyes. "You seem distracted, worried. What's the matter?"

"I guess I'm more worried than I thought about tomorrow."

"You're worried about Thanksgiving?" Erik asked confused.

"No, not Thanksgiving," Anna began slowly. "I'm worried about meeting Michael and his family."

"Why are you worried about meeting Daniel and Marie's son?"

"I can't imagine what they must think of me. Wouldn't you be a little leery of a stranger your mom and dad took in, a little concerned about the situation?"

"Maybe," Erik replied honestly. "But I've also learned a thing or two since I've been here. For instance, I've learned to trust in people and friendships. I've learned patience and . . ."

Erik heard the faint sound of laughter as he looked up to see Anna hiding a grin with the back of her hand.

"Okay," Erik said smiling. "I'm still working on patience, but I've made a great deal of progress since I've come here. I'd have probably accomplished that virtue by now if it weren't for Doc and Daniel."

Erik was getting annoyed as he watched Anna's grin turn into a full-fledge smile.

"Anyway, my point is, if Michael was raised by these people, he has to have a lot of their good qualities too. I wouldn't write him off prematurely. Give him a chance."

"I guess you're right," conceded Anna, picking up her paintbrush.

"Besides, we'll go over to Daniel and Marie's together tomorrow; there's safety in numbers."

"What are you afraid of?" Anna sounded astonished.

"Doc—I'm in charge of bringing the wine and he's convinced I'm no wine connoisseur."

"Are you?"

"Not in the least," Erik admitted miserably.

"Well then," said Anna putting a brush stroke on her painting, "I'll help you blow Doc's socks off."

"You'd do that for me?"

"Oui Monsieur." Anna winked. "Your secret's safe with me. Just let me clean these brushes up and we'll go shopping. I need to get some ingredients for the pumpkin pies I'm bringing."

The next day, Erik and Anna gathered the wine and the pies and headed over to Daniel's and Marie's.

"I think we should use the front door and knock," declared Anna.

Erik agreed; now that Marie and Daniel's son and his family were here, knocking was the best plan. When Erik raised his hand to knock, he noticed Anna shaking lightly from her head to her toes. He reached over and put his arm around her shoulders for support.

"Remember what we talked about, Anna. Give yourself a chance. You can control this situation. You can make people pity you or you can be the open and generous person I know you to be."

"You're right. I'm the one putting expectations on others, not the other way around."

Before Erik could reply, the door suddenly opened and a younger version of Daniel stood within the frame.

"You must be Erik," he said extending his hand. "I'm Michael."

"This is Anna," Erik said, finishing the introductions.

"It is so good to finally meet you." Michael firmly took Anna's hand into his own.

"For heaven's sake, you two," Marie said, coming down the hallway. "What are you doing out there?"

"We have been waiting and watching for you in the kitchen," announced Daniel, standing next to Marie now.

"We thought we'd use the front door and knock for a change," explained Erik.

"Daniel, you didn't tell me this was to be a formal occasion," joked Doc. "I would have worn my tux."

"It's not," murmured Daniel, turning back toward Erik and Anna. "You two get in here out of the cold and next time walk in the back door like everyone else. No more knocking. I'm too deaf to hear it anymore, got it?"

"I don't know. Could you repeat that last part?" Erik asked mischievously.

"You're good," smiled Michael. "It took me years to give as good as I got. I think if we work together we might actually get somewhere."

"Marie, shut and lock the door and if those two smart alecs are on the other side," Doc called out as he stared at Erik and Michael, "I know my heart won't break."

"Come on in, Anna." Daniel took one of Anna's pumpkin pies and headed for the kitchen. "I promise the rest of the family has more manners."

Erik liked the sound of Michael's laughter as he and Anna stepped into the kitchen. He was also glad to see Susan and Dennis had already arrived. It was a little like having reinforcements.

A movement out of the corner of Erik's eye caught his attention, but before his mind had time to react, a woman wrapped her arms around him first and then Anna.

"Hi, it is so good to finally meet both of you," the woman was saying. Erik watched her turn her attention entirely to

Anna. "When I woke up this morning and looked over at the cottage, I was so amazed. What an extraordinary transformation."

"Anna, Erik," started Michael laughing, "this is my wife Cheryl. She hugs a lot and speaks her mind, always. That's one of the reasons I married her."

"And that's precisely what makes you my favorite daughter-in-law," added Daniel.

"I'm your only daughter-in-law."

"You'd still be my favorite," Daniel said with a wink.

"It's nice to finally meet all of you too," said Anna.

Suddenly the back door burst open and the sound of happy children filled the room. Brandon and Katie were uncontrollably giggling as they were being bounced up and down on the backs of two teenagers.

"This is Garth and Megan," Cheryl introduced, walking over and putting an arm around each of the older children. "The very reason my and Michael's lives are never without a dull moment."

"Mom, you know you wouldn't have it any other way," said Garth.

"True, honey," laughed Cheryl. "But I could have done without your ten stitches from skiing and Megan's broken wrist from volleyball."

Erik felt Anna stiffen next to him. Some things and some people seemed to jar her memories like cables used to jump start a car. Erik had become good at recognizing this when it happened.

"You okay?" Erik whispered into Anna's ear.

"I'll be fine," whispered Anna, crossing the room to meet the older kids.

The rest of the day was full of good food and laughter. After Erik and Anna were bundled up for the walk back to their cottages, Erik watched Daniel approach Anna.

"I have a favor to ask of you, Anna. Marie has delegated Doc and me to go up into the attic tomorrow morning and get the Christmas decorations down. I was hoping you wouldn't mind taking the morning walk with Michael."

"Hey, you'd be doing me a big favor," begged Michael. "I'd get out of working with those two. I always end up the worker. One worker and two foremen just doesn't seem fair."

"I know what you mean," concurred Erik.

"Sure," said Anna hesitantly.

"Good," said Michael. "I understand you like to go pretty early, I'll come over around six thirty, if that's good."

"That's fine," Anna replied weakly.

After talking and walking Anna home, Erik was not surprised when her nightmares that night lasted longer than usual. New things and new people were always hard for Anna. Erik knew Anna was uneasy about being alone with Michael, not because she was afraid of him, but because she was afraid of herself and the embarrassment she harbored within.

Erik wasn't the least bit surprised when he heard the transmitter pick up the knocking at her door the next morning and what seemed to be Anna scrambling to wake up and get dressed. He figured she must have overslept from the exhaustion her mind and body had put her through last night.

"Hi," Erik heard Anna say, along with the click of the door opening.

"Good morning," came Michael's voice over the transmitter. "I hope you're wearing more than just a sweatshirt and jeans, it's freezing out here."

"I'm sorry, please come in. I sort of overslept and I guess my mind is still a little groggy. I hope you haven't been out here long."

"Not at all."

Erik could hear their steps now on the wooden floors.

"Wow!" Came Michael's voice. "You've really done a great

job with this place. It's been so long since I've actually been in it. It's even better than I remember."

"Why don't you go into the conservatory and I'll make us some tea."

Erik knew when Michael had stepped from the kitchen into the conservatory, even though the two rooms were open to each other. The conservatory, made entirely of glass, gave everyone's voice a distinct acoustical quality.

"I'd forgotten," came Michael's voice. "I'd completely pushed out of my mind the beauty and awe I'd always felt here. All I remembered was the loss and loneliness. How could I have forgotten the good?"

"Well, you've come to the right person," Erik heard Anna say, pain lacing her voice. "I'm an expert at forgetting."

"Anna," Michael was saying, as Erik heard him walking across the room. "I wanted you to know Cheryl and I know about everything. Doc called me right from the start to get my medical opinion on a couple of things and mom and dad have kept us informed about your recovery. It seems you are making great progress in healing."

"Your parents have been so generous and have taken such good care of me. Were you upset when they had told you they had taken me in?"

Erik held his breath, but he could appreciate the slight pause Michael gave, before answering Anna's question.

"I was never worried about you—my parents and Doc are a good judge of character. But I will admit that for a while I was worried about what your circumstances would bring to their doorstep."

"I worry about that too," agreed Anna.

"Let me finish. It wasn't long, however, before it hit me that those are three of the most orneriest people I have ever met. Nobody in their right mind would dare mess with them."

Erik had to chuckle in agreement on his end of the receiver.

"What I do know for certain," Michael continued, "is how good you have been for my parents and Doc. You may think they're doing all of the healing, but you have miraculously opened up their old hurts and wounds and let the festering out.

"You saved them when they didn't even know they needed saving. I could hear it in their voices when I spoke to them on the phone and I can see it in their eyes when you walk into a room. I know they've talked to you about Julie and I have to agree, there are some similarities between the two of you. I've missed my sister terribly, Anna, and I'm not saying you are her, but I've dreamed for so long to catch mere glimpses of my past you now offer. You've been good for all of us, so I don't want to hear any more about paybacks and one-sided healing. We all have different needs, Anna. Let's work on them together, agreed?"

"Agreed," Anna answered.

"I've decided to take a lesson in courage from you. It seems you've made it farther down the cove than I have since the morning I lost my sister. Do you care if I take a few small steps with you this morning?"

"No," answered Anna softly. "I would be happy for the company."

"Then get your coat. You and I will need all the warmth we can get."

Chapter Eighteen

Anna heard a knock at her door and instantly fear seeped through her body, along with a paralyzing numbness that caused her to loose her grip on the paintbrush that she held in her hand. When Michael and his family were here, people were coming and going all of the time, but they left days ago and wouldn't be returning until Christmas Eve. Once again, a spasm of fear knotted her stomach.

"Anna, it's me!" Erik shouted. "Open up, it's freezing out here!"

"What's wrong?" asked Anna, hurrying to open her door.

"Nothing's wrong," smiled Erik, as he entered the cottage. "Dress warm, it's payback time."

"For what?"

"Doc's Christmas tree," grinned Erik. "If I have to have one, so does he."

Anna was thinking fondly of the day after Thanksgiving when they had all gone to the tree farm to cut down trees. Erik had been angry that a tree had been forced upon him and even angrier when Doc didn't have to have one. Doc claimed he didn't need one because he was always at Marie and Daniel's anyway, which meant he could just "borrow tree time" from them. Erik had been grumbling so much all week about how there was no such thing as borrowing tree time that Anna had suspected he must be up to something.

"Do you realize that's been over a week ago?"

"Yeah," said Erik, rubbing his hands together. "I figured it would throw Doc off. Besides, it took me that long to string the popcorn and cranberries. Do you know how hard it is to not burn popcorn?"

"And do you realize it's nine o'clock at night, pitch black, and freezing outside with two feet of snow on the ground?"

"Then I guess you'd better dress really, really warm."

"Why is it men can be worse than little kids at times?" Anna asked, bundling up in her warmest clothes.

"Pride's a funny thing, Anna. It can be used for good or it can bring a man down."

"Which is this?"

"In this case it's just used for inspiration." Erik winked and headed out the door.

When Anna stepped outside, she saw the Christmas tree tied on an old Radio Flyer. Erik had fastened a rope to the sled, making it easier to drag.

"What's my part in this conspiracy?" Anna asked reluctantly.

"If you could carry the bag of lights and strung popcorn, I think we could get over there faster."

"And just where do you intend to put this monstrosity?"

"I figured right on Doc's back deck. That way, he'll have to see it every time he looks out. That'll get his dander up."

"Honestly, I can't believe I'm helping you with this scheme," Anna said, knowing deep down, Erik was doing this for all the right reasons; he would just never admit it.

By the time they reached Doc's house, Anna's fingers were numb, despite the thick woolen gloves she wore.

"Okay," instructed Erik, untying the tree, "we have to work quickly and quietly."

"Why is it I feel as if I'm in training for the navy seals?"

"Get serious now, Anna. That old coot doesn't miss a thing. You don't want to get caught, do you?"

"You honestly don't think he'll know who did this?" Anna asked in amazement.

"Of course he will, but I want to see the look on his face when it's all up, not when he could still make us take it down."

Anna helped Erik quietly carry the tree onto the deck. When Erik ran back down to get the tree stand and bag of lights, she prayed he wouldn't bail on her if Doc suddenly decided to look out of his back windows. In a matter of seconds, however, Erik was back up, taking the tree from Anna and lifting it into the stand.

"It looks straight to me," whispered Anna, stepping back for a better look.

"Good," said Erik, getting the ropes he had used to keep the tree tied to the sled. "Now you take a rope and I'll take one. We need to tie it taut to the deck railings, so the wind won't knock it over."

That done, Anna watched Erik reach inside the bag and retrieve a huge, three-dimensional star, which he gently placed on the very top of the tree.

"Does that light up?" Anna asked, stunned by the simple beauty.

"Let's finish up and we'll find out."

No more words were spoken as they continued working, stringing the lights and garlands of popcorn.

"All right," Erik whispered, bending down for the extension cord. "Do you mind gathering up the boxes from the lights while I run this cord to the nearest outlet?"

"No problem."

"When you're done, go down by the shed around the corner," directed Erik. "We'll watch from there."

Anna finished and hurriedly walked down the steps. She

stood watching as Erik plugged in the lights, banged loudly on the glass door, and dove down the steps, landing right next to her.

Anna crouched in wonderment at the sight she and Erik had just created. The nine-foot tree, with its glowing star and thousands of smaller lights accentuating its shape, was a mystical vision against the majesty of the starry night sky. Crashing the serenity of the moment, Doc shoved the door open and stepped out into the frigid winter night, wearing only his pajamas and robe.

"What in blue blazes—" Doc was shouting, as his hands rested on his hips. "I told that boy, I don't do trees! That stubborn young whelp!"

Anna watched as Doc continued to stand there, staring at the tree and shaking his head. Then ever so slowly he moved toward it, arm outstretched, and very gently touched one of the brightly lit branches. Now that Doc had moved closer to the tree, his face was illuminated by all of the tiny, bright lights adorning it. Anna could see the tiny teardrop, as it slowly made its way down Doc's weathered cheek.

He stood there a few more minutes, oblivious it seemed to the bitter cold around him. Then he turned and simply walked back inside. Anna took Erik's hand and silently they walked away. Glancing back, Anna could make out Doc's silhouette sitting very still by his window, gazing out at the tree. When they had walked a little ways, Erik finally spoke.

"I'm glad he liked it."

"I think he loved it," replied Anna, squeezing Erik's hand as they continued to walk past Daniel and Marie's house. Suddenly the front door flew open and Anna knew they had been discovered.

"God gave you a brain to use," grumbled Daniel. "Do you two know what the temperature is outside tonight?"

"Stop lecturing, and get these two in out of the cold,"

Marie scolded, coming up from behind Daniel.

Anna was silent and noticed Erik was also, as they moved into the house. Marie scooted them into the kitchen and sat each of them in front of a steaming mug of hot chocolate. Instantly, Anna wrapped her frozen fingers around the mug. Twinges of thawing pain registered in her brain as she noticed Erik mimicking her movements.

"You couldn't have done that during the day?" demanded Daniel.

"No," Erik replied stubbornly.

There was a minute of silence before Daniel finally spoke again.

"I would have loved to have seen Doc's face," smirked Daniel.

Anna looked at Erik; Doc's secret would be kept safe with them.

"You know," continued Daniel, "he'll be complaining for weeks, probably even years to come."

"We're ready for him," Erik said, winking at Anna.

"You're just lucky we noticed you two outside," said Daniel. "You would never have made it back to your cottages without some part of your bodies frost bitten."

"You didn't just notice them," laughed Marie. "You were spying on them."

"And you weren't?" Daniel raised an eyebrow.

"I glanced now and then," admitted Marie. "And by the way, it is simply beautiful. It should be an inspiration to us all for the upcoming Holiday season."

"That's what Erik called it earlier," grinned Anna, directing her gaze at Erik. "An inspiration."

Anna knew her play on words was not lost on Erik, but even he had to admit, the feeling of doing something good for someone was much more satisfying than settling an old score.

During the next week, Doc complained continuously about the Christmas tree. He told Anna, however, that as long as it was there, at least the birds should get some use out of it. So he bought suet and birdseed in the shape of ornaments and hung them along with the popcorn on the mysterious tree. Not a single night went by when Doc's tree wasn't shining like a beacon in the night and not a single person visited his house without getting a personal viewing of the mysterious tree that had just appeared one night.

Chapter Nineteen

Anna began furiously working to fulfill her window orders. On the bright side, she had most of her Christmas presents bought and wrapped, with the exception of putting the finishing touches on the window she was making for Michael and Cheryl. She had thought about what to paint on their window all last night. Now, knowing she wouldn't be able to fall back to sleep anymore, she got up and began transferring her thoughts onto the window.

Anna could hear the wind whistling around the cottage and see the sparkle of frost patterns etched onto the cottage's windows. Looking outside as she warmed some tea, Anna noted the grayness of the early morning sky against the angry white caps of the sea. This could only mean snow would be starting to fall again soon.

Anna found she loved the sound the cold blowing wind made, forcing the cottage into groaning and moaning at times. She loved to watch the swirling snow as the large drifts formed dunes in the yard. She especially liked being cocooned inside, with a fire in the fireplace and Christmas music drifting throughout the cottage. It seemed to Anna that this was her own personal winter wonderland. The extraordinary beauty of it seemed to put her small life into a greater perspective.

Anna was startled from her thoughts by the ringing of her telephone. She picked it up, hearing Susan's frantic voice from the other end.

"Anna, I can't find Katie. I went to take a shower and she was playing . . ."

Susan was speaking so quickly and with her sobs in between; it was difficult for Anna to get a good understanding of what was going on.

"Take a breath, Susan," Anna said, as fear began to creep into her stomach. "Slow down and start again."

"Katie must have heard Dennis get up and leave earlier this morning," Susan started again. "After I saw Dennis out the door, I heard a noise in Katie's room. I peeked in and she was up, playing with her Barbie dolls. Brandon was still asleep, so I told Katie if she promised to be quiet while I took a shower, I would make her favorite breakfast when I got out."

Susan started crying again and Anna was afraid Susan wouldn't gain any of her control back if Anna didn't force her to continue.

"Then what happened?" Anna tried to remain calm.

"When I got out of the shower, I couldn't find her. I thought she was playing a game, but after a few minutes, I became frantic. My yelling woke Brandon up and he helped me look for her. I never locked the front door when Dennis left this morning."

"Susan, that doesn't mean anything."

"At first I thought someone did come in and take her, but then I noticed her coat and boots were gone, so I ran outside to look for her. When I couldn't find her, I called Dennis."

"What did Dennis say?"

"I could only get a hold of Ginny." Susan started to cry again. "Dennis and Erik were out of the office together. A power line had gone down somewhere. Ginny was going to track them down."

"I'm sure they're on their way."

"But I can't wait that long, Anna. I'm going out again to look for her."

"No, you need to stay close to the phone," Anna said, quickly trying to devise a logical plan. "Katie might come back looking for you. I'll go over to Daniel and Marie's, we'll get Doc, and between all of us we'll find her, Susan. I promise."

Anna knew she was trying to comfort herself as well as Susan, but this was Katie—sweet, bold, little Katie. Anna ran to get her coat, boots, and gloves. When she opened the door to what moments ago seemed like her own wonderland, she now saw it for what it really was: a harsh winter storm and Katie was somewhere out in it.

Anna put her head down and started running as fast as she could to Daniel and Marie's. The blowing snow and icy road was hampering her pace, but what proved to be her biggest obstacles were the images forming in her mind. Images of Katie being scooped out of her home transformed into Anna, herself, fighting off an intruder.

Anna's thoughts became all twisted up, making it hard for her to distinguish reality from illusion. She forced herself to move on. For a moment, she thought she was weeping out loud, but then the fog in her mind lifted and she realized the crying was actually coming from somewhere below where she stood.

Anna looked around to get her bearings. She had passed Marie's house. Instantly the fear that gripped her every morning during her walks washed over her like the angry waves spewing from the sea. She was standing at the top of the cliff, looking down at what she came to think of as her own personal hell, the cove. The waves were menacingly crashing against the beach and the snow was making it difficult to determine the safest route down. Anna could barely make out a splash of color, down near the beach, but her ears confirmed her suspicion as the sound of a whimpering child began again.

"God, please," Anna begged, starting down the slippery descent. "Please, let her be okay."

The whimpering stopped and so did Anna's heart.

"Katie!" she screamed. "Katie, I'm coming to get you."

"Anna!" cried Katie. "It hurts."

"I know, honey," Anna shouted, not even noticing when she had passed the spot that had always brought her to a stand still before. The farther down she climbed, the icier it became. The spraying water from the waves had frozen to the surrounding rocks and sand, making it nearly impossible for Anna. Suddenly, Anna's feet went completely out from under her, and with great force, she found herself sliding right at Katie. Anna stuck her foot out just in time, bouncing off the rocks instead of slamming into the little girl.

"I'm scared!" cried Katie.

"I know, sweetie," Anna said, taking off her own coat and putting it on the trembling little girl. Immediately the cold started numbing Anna's exposed body.

"Where does it hurt?" Anna asked gently.

"My arm," sniffled Katie.

While approaching Katie, Anna had in fact noticed her arm was positioned at an awkward angle.

"Does it hurt anywhere else?"

"Not really. I'm cold."

"Well then," Anna said, putting on her most confident smile, "let's get you out of here."

Anna tried to stand, but there was nothing for her to gain a footing on. Katie wailed as Anna landed once again on the ground.

"That's what happened when I fell down the hill."

"Katie, how far did you fall?" Anna asked, worried that

Katie had fallen the entire way and was perhaps hurt more than Anna had originally assessed.

"I thought I heard a kitty," Katie was saying, pointing to a spot halfway up the incline. "I came down . . . he wasn't there. I tried to go back up . . . I fell down here. My arm hurts."

"It's okay, Katie. I will get you out of here."

Just then, Anna could hear the sirens of a squad car and Daniel and Doc were beginning to yell down the incline.

"Don't come down," Anna yelled up to them. "It's too slippery. You'll have to get some ropes."

"Dennis and Erik are here and tying ropes off right now," Daniel yelled back. "They'll be down in a second."

"Daddy! Daddy!" screamed Katie.

"Katie!" Dennis shouted back, his voice filled with anguish. "I'll be right down, baby."

Anna held Katie as she watched Dennis and Erik make their way down the incline, holding tightly to the ropes. Daniel and Doc were lowering a rescue gurney that was attached to a third rope. Dennis was the first to reach them and the fear and worry Anna saw in his eyes sent shivers of sympathy to her very soul.

"I think her arm is broken," Anna said through chattering teeth. She was starting to realize just how cold she really was, now that some of the responsibility of Katie's rescue was lifted off her shoulders. Anna felt the weight of a coat being placed on her shoulders and realized Erik had given her his.

"I'm sorry," Katie began between sobs. "Are you mad?"

"I was scared," Dennis admitted, brushing back hair from Katie's eyes.

"Is mommy mad?"

"Mommy's worried too, Katie."

"I'm sorry I snuck out of the house," admitted Katie, displaying a stubborn look on her face. "Nobody would take me to Anna's. We were supposed to help her decorate gingerbread men."

"We'll talk about that later," replied Dennis, gently lifting Katie onto the gurney.

"It's nice to see she's inherited some of your genes," chuckled Erik.

"No way. She gets that stubborn streak from her mother," replied Dennis, tugging on Katie's rope so Daniel and Doc could start pulling it back up the incline. "I'm going up with Katie, then Doc's driving with us over to the hospital. Anna, I can't thank you enough."

Anna could only nod, as Dennis turned and made his way back up the incline. Anna slowly exhaled the fear she had felt for Katie only to have a new fear rush in right behind it, consuming the void. She glanced around at the beach. The terror she felt made her begin to shake. She couldn't breathe. Suddenly, she was screaming, fighting, pleading. She felt searing pain all over her body. She was so cold; she must be drowning. The pain was so great and she was so tired, she decided to let it wash right over her. From somewhere far away, she heard a strong, familiar voice. It called to her, but she was just too tired to go in search of it.

Erik had watched as Anna went completely white. Just as he had suspected, her mind grasped the reality of what she had done. The nightmares Anna had been having in her dreams ruthlessly followed her now into this waking moment. Erik helplessly watched as Anna's body began to tremble. He tried to hold on to her and reassure her she was all right, along with transferring some of his body heat to hers, but then the screaming began.

Eyes wide with fear, Anna began fighting Erik with such

force that the surprise caught him off guard. As he fell backward, he saw Anna frantically trying to make it up the slippery incline. He was yelling her name, but Anna had retreated into a world where she was fighting her demons alone.

Erik could hear Daniel's voice shouting from above, but Erik's reply hung on his lips, as he watched Anna begin to fall back down the icy slope, her body grotesquely pinballing off the rocks on its way down to the beach.

He rushed to her side, only to see the haunting gaze of intense fear and to hear her tormenting pleas that could only have been her last words spoken on that warm summer's night in July. Erik watched as Anna's body gave in and she quietly slipped into a state of unconsciousness.

Erik knew he had just witnessed first hand the horror and inhumanity this woman he had come to think of as a friend had lived through that night and every night since. Never before in his career had a crime scene been so real, so vivid.

Erik could sense the evil, feel it, and taste it. It made him unsure of his existence, unstable in his beliefs. He knew that this glimpse of Anna's attack was the stuff nightmares were made of and Anna's haunting gaze would forever be burned into his memory.

There was no doubt in Erik's mind now that he would hunt down and find Anna's assailant. Erik wanted this man, this thing, to experience the same kind of fear Erik had seen in Anna's eyes. He wanted this evil to feel fear coming closer, to feel hunted like the animal he was.

Erik's anger was so strong by the time he reached Daniel at the top; he couldn't even remember how he had gotten himself and Anna up the icy incline.

"What happened?" Daniel asked breathlessly.

"What did you expect?" Erik sneered. "She made it to the bottom. I hope it was worth it."

"Erik," Marie's voice was calm. "We need to get her inside."

Daniel gently wrapped a blanket around Anna as Erik held her. Both men headed toward the house.

"I think we should take her in the car over to the cottage," Marie suggested, coming up behind them.

Erik looked incredulously at Marie.

"Yes, she's scared," continued Marie. "But she's made such a selfless step, going down there to get Katie. I don't think we should belittle that by making her start all over again. She won half the battle by just going down there. Now she needs to stand up to the rest. Even her past life depends on her moving forward."

Erik went to Daniel's car, keeping Anna cradled in his arms as he carefully got in the backseat. Daniel and Marie got in the front and they silently drove the short distance to the cottage. When they arrived at the cottage and laid Anna in bed, Erik could already see the bruises forming from where she had hit the rocks on the way down. Anger once again caused his body to become stiff and rigid.

"You are going to have to change your attitude around her when she wakes up," insisted Marie.

"How can I, Marie? I saw it all today down in that cove and when I get my hands on—"

"You'll what? Become him? That's not you, Erik, and it's definitely not Anna. That day we found Anna we saw the same things you saw and more. My anger and grief for her were so strong, I felt like I was suffocating. I wept for her when I was alone, but I knew pity and anger would not help to heal her. Anna's soul needed our love and friendship and by giving her that, we've watched her live and take interest in life again.

"Don't you dare show her anger, Erik! That's not who she is and that's not what she deserves. Anna trusts you to be strong, don't take that away from her."

Erik sat holding Anna's hand until Doc arrived several hours later. Doc checked Anna's various cuts and bruises and reassured everyone that Anna's state of unconsciousness was due to nothing more than exhaustion and being out in the cold. Erik continued to sit by Anna's bed, barely noticing when Marie would occasionally peek in or bring him food and coffee. That night after Daniel and Marie went home, Doc stayed and slept on the couch, while Erik kept his silent vigil next to Anna's bed.

Close to dawn, Erik was awakened by Anna's whimpering. He knew what she was dreaming about, but noted that her soft moaning never crescendoed into the heart-stopping screaming that had pierced through every one of Erik's nights since he had installed the transmitter in Anna's cottage. Doc came quickly into the room.

"How's she doing?" Doc whispered, joining Erik by Anna's bedside.

"Bad dream," Erik replied. "I've heard them much worse though."

"Maybe that's a good sign."

"Maybe."

Anna's eyes fluttered open and Erik could read first pain, then confusion pass through her gaze.

"Good morning, sleepyhead," Erik greeted Anna, releasing her hand.

"Do you remember being the heroine yesterday?" Doc asked gently.

"Oh my God, Katie! Where is she?" Anna asked, sitting up.

"Whoa," Doc said. "Katie's fine, she broke her arm and was a little dehydrated, but I'm sure she's back to being mischievous Katie again."

"I talked to Dennis last night," added Erik. "And from what I understand, she's grounded for the rest of her life."

"It's not entirely her fault," explained Anna. "I did promise her she could help me decorate cookies and somehow we hadn't gotten around to that yet."

"Well then," said Doc, "perhaps this was a hard lesson on patience for her. One that would do her good to remember for next time."

Anna leaned back in the bed.

"I'm going to go tell Daniel and Marie you're awake and doing better," Doc continued. "I'll try to keep everyone away as long as I can, but Susan especially wants to come and see you."

When Doc left, an awkward silence filled the room.

"How about if I make us some breakfast?" Erik asked.

"Can you cook?"

"I think I can manage not to burn your house down."

As Anna was trying to get out of bed, Erik saw her startled expression as her eyes saw the bruises that had formed on her legs. She looked at him like a wounded doe.

"Anna, do you remember everything that happened yesterday?"

"I remember getting to Katie, then you and Dennis were putting her on a gurney."

"That's right," Erik said reassuringly. "But once Dennis got to the top, it was like something snapped in you and you started fighting and screaming. You broke away from me and tried to run up the incline and that's when you fell. I'm so sorry, Anna, I should have held you tighter."

"I remember." Anna's gaze dropped to the floor.

"Anna, don't. I'm your friend."

"Thank you for helping me," said Anna, quietly. "I'm going to take a shower now."

"Sure." Erik understood Anna's need to be alone. "I'll go and start breakfast."

It was only seconds before Erik heard a loud bang and then glass shattering. He ran to the closed bathroom door, unsure of what to do next. He could hear Anna crying softly on the other side.

"Are you okay?" he asked, straining to hear what was going on behind the closed door.

"Fine," came Anna's feeble voice. "My glass of water slipped out of my hand."

He thought that perhaps the slight bruising the rocks had caused to Anna's face might have startled her. The bruising caused no significant distortion, but even so, the injuries could only have added to Anna's long list of chilling memories.

"I made it down the cove," came Anna's soft voice, through the bathroom door.

"Yes, you did, Anna," praised Erik, relief rushing over him, as he rested his head on the door. "And now it's time to climb back up and out."

Late that afternoon, a tearful Susan, carrying Katie, flowers, and balloons, came rushing in to hug Anna. Erik was so proud of Anna as she rose to the occasion, decorating cookies with the children and managing to stay awake through supper that included everyone who cared about her. By seven o'clock, everyone was bundling up to head to their own homes. Erik said goodnight, closing the door behind Daniel, Marie, and Doc. He looked at Anna whose weary face openly exposed the exhaustion she had desperately been trying to hide all day.

"Come on," Erik said, crossing the room and sweeping Anna off the couch. "Bedtime."

Erik tried not to notice Anna's shocked expression, as he continued to carry her down the hallway into her bedroom. "Just yell if you need anything."

"What do you mean? Where are you going to be?"

"Right out there on the couch," Erik said matter-of-factly, laying Anna on her bed.

"On the couch! You can't stay here."

"Why?"

"Because."

"Look, Anna, last night I slept in here, tonight I'm moving to the couch. I'd say our relationship is regressing, wouldn't you?"

"Ooo . . ." squeaked Anna, rolling her eyes. "You're impossible!"

"So I've been told," Erik laughed, walking toward the door. "Need anything before I bunk down?"

"Just for you to leave."

"See you in the morning, sunshine," Erik said, sarcastically, just before turning off the light.

Erik heard when Anna's breathing went from regular to relaxed. He knew she was in a state of some much needed sleep. He pulled out some reports Dennis had wanted him to review, but within a few minutes, it became hard to concentrate and his head began to nod.

Hours later, Erik jumped off the couch, papers flying off of his lap. He was confused as to where he was. He had been having a horrible nightmare in which a woman was softly crying, but he couldn't get to her. He heard a clock chime four, and then the sobbing that he thought had been part of his dream shook his mind into reality. It was Anna.

He ran to her bedroom, only to find her bed empty. He checked the room she used for her painting, but it too was empty. He headed for the kitchen. Even though all of the lights were out, the glow from the moon reflecting off the water shown brightly through the conservatory windows, illuminating the entire room. There silhouetted in the middle of the conservatory, stood Anna, hands to her face, softly crying.

"I was so sure if I could only make it down the cove, I would remember everything," Anna said as if in a trance. "I'm sorry I woke you. I don't sleep well most nights."

Erik knew better than anyone the truth in that admission, but now was certainly not the time to reveal his knowledge.

"No, I'm glad you did," Erik said, carefully choosing the right words to continue this conversation. "I needed to talk to you on what you remember. I was just waiting until you were feeling better."

"You mean, you were afraid of sending me even further over the edge."

"No, that's not it at all," said Erik, crossing the room and taking Anna by her shoulders. "You can't even begin to know how much I admire your strength."

"What strength would that be, Erik? The strength that couldn't keep me from being raped or the strength that keeps me from knowing who I am? Better yet, how about the strength that keeps me from finding my family, my children? Which of those strengths should I be most proud of?"

Erik had never heard Anna angry before, even though she had every right to be. He knew her anger at this moment was really hurt in disguise. As much as he hated to hurt her more, he needed to continue this conversation, while the anger was giving her strength to push back.

"What did you see in the cove yesterday?" Erik asked, firmly.

"I told you nothing made sense to me."

"Anna, I was there with you. I saw the fear in your eyes and the pain in your screams. What was it?"

Erik saw Anna's shoulders begin to slump and her anger turn to despair. He had to concentrate hard on listening, as Anna's voice changed into a hushed whisper.

"Every night, I relive what happened to me. I feel being dragged, each cut, each hit, each humiliation."

Erik watched Anna's face contorting in pain as her mind relived the attack.

"When I wake up, I race to the mirror to see if I am living

it or reliving it." A sarcastic smiled played on Anna's lips. "Reality is a shaky commodity for me these days. Sometimes I feel just being here is a dream within a dream and soon I'll wake up."

"You are waking up, Anna," Erik said gently. "What else was in the cove with you?"

Silent tears once again were glistening in Anna's eyes as she stood shaking her head. Maybe it was too soon, Erik thought. Maybe he had pushed her too hard. Erik stood perfectly still and for the first time in his law enforcement career, he didn't know how to proceed. He had gotten too close, too personal with Anna. That's what had been blinding his ability to do his job, but now that he had enlightened himself of his own weaknesses, he was confident he would find a way to put this whole situation into a better perspective. He was Anna's friend and that friendship gave him more of a responsibility to be Anna's protector. Once again, Anna began to speak and Erik focused in on her words.

"When I was on the beach, I didn't really hear or see anything differently than I do in my dreams, but I felt fear. A fear that I couldn't get a way from, and even if I could, I knew I would never get far."

"I don't understand."

"I knew that whoever did this to me," explained Anna, staring blankly ahead, "I had known him well, personally."

The coldness gripped Erik's stomach. Perhaps that was why no one was looking for Anna. Erik could sense that Anna had been thinking the same thing. She had said before she felt she was married. Was it possible?

Chapter Twenty

Two days later, Michael and his family were back to join everyone for Christmas. Garth had made it over early Christmas Eve morning to Anna's cottage. While she was letting Garth in, she noticed Erik was adding another setting to the breakfast table.

"Are you excited about tonight?" asked Garth.

"Nervous," replied Anna.

"My grandparents say you have the voice of an angel."

"I don't know about that," said Anna, choking on her hot chocolate. "Somehow I don't think angels worry much about making mistakes."

"Don't let her fool you," said Erik. "I've been with her at practices for weeks now and not once have I heard her make a mistake. Me on the other hand . . . Well, let's just say if the choir director could find a way for me to sing from the outside of the church, he would."

"That's not true," laughed Anna. "They were ecstatic to have another male voice."

"If anything," winked Erik, "I make a good page turner for the organist."

"I don't believe it," smirked Garth.

"You'll get your chance tonight," Erik said as he grabbed his coat. "Dennis and I have got a little business to take care of today. I'll meet you guys over at Daniel and Marie's later this afternoon. I understand we're having dinner, then opening presents before we go to church tonight."

"It's kind of a tradition," explained Garth. "When Megan and I were little, we'd try like crazy to hurry the adults through the food part of the evening. Now I'm counting on Brandon and Katie to pick up the slack."

"This sounds like it could take all night," sighed Erik.

"Usually right up until midnight service. After we go to church, we come home, warm up with some eggnog, hang our stockings by the fireplace, and go to sleep with visions of sugar plums dancing through our heads," Garth laughed.

"Whatever happened to counting sheep?" grumbled Erik.

"They don't fit in the stockings very well," chuckled Anna.

"Anyway, the next day we wake up early to see what Santa left."

"I bet Doc's got the market cornered on coal," grinned Erik.

"Perhaps this year he'll have some real competition." Anna winked at Garth.

"Okay, that's it. I'm outta here," said Erik, turning toward Garth. "Do you think you can get Miss stocking full of apples and oranges over to the festivities this afternoon?"

"Yes sir," replied Garth.

"Sir? Now I'm an old man as well as one deserving of coal. I believe that Christmas story has already been written. I'll see you two conspirators later."

Moments later, with the warmth of a hot mug in their hands, Anna and Garth sat in the conservatory watching the elements of nature form a symphony all around them. Anna looked at Garth, who was watching the snow dancing and swirling on the glass roof. This gave Anna the perfect opportunity to study the young man's face and try to read his emotions.

"How's school going?" Anna asked, breaking the silence.
"Good."
"Any girlfriends?"
"No."

These one-syllable responses were making for a very one-sided conversation. Anna knew Garth wasn't trying to be rude; he just had something weighing heavily on his mind. Anna would wait patiently until he was ready to talk. As it turned out, she didn't have to wait long.

"My dad's decided to take over Doc's practice here. The new doctor isn't working out and Doc feels since everyone knows my dad around here, it would be a perfect fit."

"How do you feel about that?"

"Mom and Dad feel it would be good for Meg and me to get away from all the materialistic influence of urban society and spend some quality time doing . . . I don't know, quality things."

"Wow." Anna smiled gently. "That's a mouthful."

"Yeah, I can't say that I agree with all that, but Mom's right about one thing, Dad needs to slow his pace down. Even I can see the toll double shifts and no days off are taking on him. Besides, maybe he and I can spend more time together my last couple of years before I go off to college. When I used to stay here over the summers, Doc would let me tag along with him on house calls. Maybe my dad will let me go too. Did I tell you I want to go to school to become a doctor?"

"No." Anna was not the least bit surprised. Garth's decision must have been greatly influenced by growing up around two doctors; still, it also took someone special with a lot of compassion. Even at this young age, Anna could tell Garth possessed that quality. "I bet your mother and father are proud."

"I don't know, sometimes I get the feeling they're trying to steer me away from it. Dad always kids me about getting a real job, with real hours."

"Maybe that will change, even for your dad. When will you be moving here?"

"Not until after the school year," said Garth solemnly. "Man, I'm really going to miss my friends and soccer and baseball . . ."

"Believe it or not," Anna interrupted, "they have all of that here."

"I don't know. I mean, what if I don't fit in? What if no one likes me here? I'm not as outgoing as Megan. I wish . . ."

"What do you wish, Garth?"

"I guess I wish half of my life could stay the same and half of it could be different. I wish my life could be perfect."

Anna understood what Garth was trying to say. She herself had one foot in one world and another foot somewhere else. Unfortunately, she didn't know where that somewhere else was for her.

"I hear perfection isn't all it's cracked up to be," smiled Anna. "I hear it can get pretty dull."

"Who says I don't like dull?"

"You're sixteen, Garth," laughed Anna. "I have yet to meet a teenager who likes dull."

Anna watched Garth as he worked at absorbing this bit of information.

"Hey," Anna said, changing the mood. "Want to help me pack up presents and drag them over to your grandparents' house?"

"I have my license now," said Garth excitedly. "Want me to get my grandpa's truck and we can haul them over that way?"

"Sure, if it's okay with your grandfather. It really would save us from making half a dozen trips back and forth."

———⁂———

Dennis was fidgeting in his office at the police station.

Today was the day Erik had to make his big decision. Erik's personal vacation time would be running out at the end of this week. Dennis always felt he could read Erik like a book because they were so much alike, but try as he might, Dennis had no idea where his friend stood on this matter.

For Erik to stay would mean that he'd have to give up his job in the city. A job that he was the best at, a career that he had been at for a long time, while accumulating retirement benefits that were sitting back, waiting to work for him some day.

On the other hand, money wasn't everything—not to Dennis and certainly not to Erik any longer. What did mean a lot to both of them, however, is what they thought of themselves at the end of the day. When Dennis had been Erik's partner in the city, on some days they wondered if they even made a difference. Those were the days they had to remind each other they gave it their all. They had done the best they could.

Because of this very motto, Dennis felt Erik would choose the city over a sleepy little town. There were plenty of bad guys still left in the city. On the other hand, wouldn't there always be? Dennis was concentrating so hard; he hadn't even heard the object of his thoughts enter the room.

"Man is it cold out there." Erik was rubbing his hands briskly together.

"You're getting old," teased Dennis. "This weather never used to bother you."

"This weather always bothered me, you just never heard it over your own complaining."

"Did you get all of your Christmas shopping done?"

"Yeah, but I'm not sure if I'm ready for the marathon gift giving festivities."

"I felt that way, too, the first time we were invited, but since neither I nor Susan have any family left, we appreciate even more how they've all adopted us. They are the closest things my kids will ever have to grandparents."

"They really are some amazing people, which is why I feel bad having to give them my decision."

"So when do you leave?" Dennis tried to hide his disappointment.

"Who said anything about leaving? I'm genuinely sorry for the inconvenience, but Doc's just going to have to put up with me for good."

"Are you kidding?" Dennis asked, slapping Erik on the back. "He's only scratched the surface on his lists of insults for you."

"Then I hope he can take as good as he gives."

"Seriously, I'm really glad to have you as a partner again," smiled Dennis, while shaking Erik's hand.

"I hope you're glad enough to give me a few days off in January."

"You're incorrigible," Dennis said, shaking his head.

"It's business. The gallery in the city Anna has her paintings at wants to do a showing of her work. There are many people who would like to meet the artist behind the cottage windows."

"Do you think it's a good idea to let her go so public?"

"I think she can't hide forever. She also has a right to accept acknowledgement for her work. Besides, I would put money on it that the person who did this to her isn't drawn into artists' circles.

"I gotta believe he's been checking up on her by now, however, and unfortunately the ball's in his court since he holds all of the puzzle pieces. He'll mess up though, he obviously can't figure out a way to get the puzzle back together, or he would have tried by now. I think he's scared and that usually translates into sloppy, impulsive behavior.

"All we have to do is stay on our toes and let him come to us. He'll try to get her alone again, so there won't be any witnesses, but as long as we keep that in mind, we'll stay one step ahead of him."

"Do you think Anna will recognize him? What if she's already run into him and never even knew it?"

"It's hard to know. We'll just have to continue to take it one day at a time."

"Come on," Dennis said, grabbing his coat. "It's Christmas Eve."

Dennis knew the many words and feelings compacted into that little phrase must make it larger than life itself for Erik. Although Erik was starting a new life for himself now, this time of year could only be bringing him loss and sorrow over his wife and daughter. The way Dennis saw it, Christmas was a time to reflect on the past, but also a time to live for the present, and hope for the future.

"Wait until you see what I got Brandon and Katie," said Erik, walking from the office.

"Does it come with a safety lecture from Susan?"

"What do you think?" Erik grinned.

By the time everyone was gathered in Daniel and Marie's kitchen, Brandon and Katie were more than ready to start opening presents. Anna watched Megan laughing as she lifted an overly excited Katie into her arms.

"Did I used to get this wound up?" Megan asked innocently.

"Worse," Michael was saying, patting his daughter on the head.

When everyone had their fill of food, Brandon was put in charge of passing out the presents. Garth had been right, although time seemed to fly by for Anna, the last present was opened around eleven o'clock.

Katie and Brandon had both fallen asleep and were wrapped in blankets when they were carried out to the cars. Once inside the church, however, the fascination of the brightly lit candles woke the two children up.

Halfway through the service, Anna sang her solo. Anna had been afraid about facing Christmas when so much had been lost to her, but now the music flowed from her, comforting her, even as she sang.

She tried even harder to focus on the things she was grateful for. Then a quiet serenity overcame her, holding a promise that the rest of her life would work itself out. Anna looked out over the congregation, especially her precious friends. They had all faced losses that had changed the direction of their lives, yet everyone chose to go on and become strong with the precious silken thread of friendship. Anna knew she was catching a glimpse of what made for a successful, fulfilling life and she would be forever grateful to have learned this secret.

When the service had ended and everyone was bundled up to leave, the confusion of who was riding in which car began. Anna had been with Dennis and Susan coming to church, but now they were going straight home to put an exhausted Brandon and Katie to bed. Everyone was talking and laughing at the same time as they rushed out into the cold night air.

"I'll ride back with Zach and Callie!" Anna called out, heading for Daniel's old truck. Instantly Anna froze to her spot in the middle of the parking lot. The snow was starting to come down harder now, but still Anna didn't move.

"What's the matter?" Michael asked, coming up to Anna's side.

"I'm not sure," replied Erik, coming up on Anna's other side "I think she might have just remembered something in those names."

"We need to get her out of the cold," ordered Michael, as he and Erik each took one of Anna's arms, forcing her forward toward the truck.

"Garth," said Erik, tossing out his car keys, "take your parents back in my car and I'll drive Anna back in the truck."

"Dad?" asked Garth.

"She's all right," said Michael, closing Anna's truck door. "We just need to get her home."

Anna was silent on the ride back to Daniel and Marie's. In reality, she knew where she was and wasn't upset beyond functioning, but back there in the parking lot, her mind had brought up images that were, for a change, perfectly clear. For a moment, Anna had remembered another parking lot where she was laughing and running toward a car.

When the memory had crashed into her, she had been afraid to move or breathe, for fear the vision would vanish into thin air. Even now, sitting here with Erik, Anna was forcing herself to focus on her precious moment, but parts of it were already beginning to fade.

Erik and Anna were the last to arrive. When they pulled up to Daniel and Marie's house, Michael came rushing out to help Anna inside. She had no idea what all the fuss was about. She felt fine, she thought to herself, rushing inside.

"Thank you for helping me remember," said Anna, first hugging a stunned Garth and then Megan.

Anna followed as Marie ushered everyone into the living room, where everyone was silently waiting for Anna to explain.

"My son's name is Zach," started Anna, excited. "He drives like you do, Garth. I also have a daughter; her name is Callie."

"There's something about Christmas and miracles," sighed Marie, reaching over for Anna's hand.

"Wait," said Anna, smiling through tear-filled eyes. "I have one more miracle, another son. His name is Ken and he's my youngest."

Anna's ecstasy was short-lived, as that was all she could remember. To have her children so clearly in her mind, but yet to still have them out of her grasp was pure torture.

"You will be with your children again," Marie assured her. "I think they are trying just as hard to find you. Maybe your prayers and their prayers will find each other tonight. You have to keep praying, Anna. Keep believing."

"That's such a beautiful thought," whispered Anna. "Maybe we did meet tonight—for a moment I hadn't felt lost. I felt whole and everything seemed so perfect."

It was close to one o'clock in the morning when Anna and Erik made it back to her cottage. Anna disappeared into the room she used for her painting, only to emerge several minutes later, with three red Christmas stockings she had painted her children's names on.

"I miss them. I'm missing their lives." She took one of the metal cup hooks she held in her hand and began twisting it into the underside of the mantel, feeling the catch of wood, as it began to accept the intrusion.

"I miss my daughter, too," started Erik. "Every day, with every breath. If I had any reason, any hope of seeing her again, I would hang a stocking as well."

Anna knew this omission was painful for Erik, but it was his way of telling her that she was having a perfectly natural reaction.

"Maybe Marie is right," Erik continued. "Maybe if we pray hard enough, our prayers will meet the ones we love, wherever they are."

"I know they will, Erik, I'm sure of it." Anna reached for Erik's hand.

Chapter Twenty-one

"Are you all right?" asked Erik.

They had been sitting in Erik's car, in front of the gallery for the last ten minutes now. Why had she ever agreed to do this show anyhow?

"Cheryl's right, you know," continued Erik. "People love your work."

Anna had been glad she and Erik were able to squeeze in an overnight visit to Michael and Cheryl's on their way up here. Even though they had just seen them a little less than a month ago at Christmas, it had proved to be a good distraction to Anna's overly wrought nerves.

"What if I'm not what people expect?" Anna asked, once again thankful Erik had loose ends to tie up in the city, making it easier for her to accept his generous offer of escorting her to her art debut.

"You're not what anybody expects," said Erik tenderly, rubbing his thumb across Anna's cheek. "You're much more."

Before Anna could analyze the warmth that was spreading throughout her body, Peg, the owner of the gallery, was opening Anna's car door.

"How are you doing?" Peg asked, looking from Anna to Erik.

"Nervous," Anna replied. "Peg, I want you to meet a friend of mine."

"Actually, we met on the phone, when I gave Erik the directions on how to get here and other details that needed working out," smiled Peg, shaking Erik's hand. "But it's nice to meet you in person."

Anna had a feeling she was missing something in Peg's and Erik's exchange. She guessed it to be something having to do with her safety, but before she could analyze it further, Peg was whisking them through the massive oak doors of the gallery and past paintings and sculptures in various stages of being displayed.

"We are introducing three new artists, including you, Friday night," explained Peg, looking around frantically. "Believe it or not, this chaos will all come together by then."

Anna stood in awe in the middle of all the commotion buzzing around her. Each artist's display had a theme that expressed the feel of the artist's work. The pulse of the theme was the artwork itself, giving the viewer a sense of looking into a painting within a painting.

"I've never had so much fun designing a show," confessed Peg, clasping her hands. "Come see yours, Anna."

Anna and Erik followed Peg toward the back of the gallery. Halfway across, the ceiling opened up and, looking back, Anna saw the open loft that made up the second floor of the gallery. This back section was filled with glorious light as the room's ceiling stretched up to the second story, boasting a circular stained glass skylight that offered an array of color, as it filtered down through the gallery.

"I had hoped to be further along than this when you arrived," Peg said apologetically. "We had a little trouble getting the sod and bedding plants shipped into this frigid climate. The first group got frostbite and turned a disgusting shade of gray, but we've been working around the clock with this second batch and I'm confident we'll be ready by Friday."

"I'm sure it will be lovely," affirmed Anna.

"I must warn you," continued Peg, "I wanted to get a real feel for what you feel when you are painting, so I called Marie and asked her to send me some pictures of the cottage. It was supposed to be a surprise, but as I said, it hasn't worked out exactly as I had planned."

Anna watched as Peg bent over to unroll a large drawing.

"Would you like to see the plans?"

"No, I trust you completely," smiled Anna. "Besides, rumor has it, it's a surprise."

When Erik and Anna left the gallery, they headed to the bureau offices so Erik could put his paperwork in order and clean out his desk. After Erik had apologized to Anna for the third time for having to leave her sitting in the lobby, Anna became intrigued by the steady stream of activity unfolding right in front of her. With Erik gone, she had time to observe the hushed tones and professional manner that seemed to lend its credentials to the occupants who worked here. Anna's thoughts were interrupted when she noticed two men walking toward her.

"Hi," one of the men greeted.

"I'm waiting for someone," Anna replied nervously, afraid these men were mistaking her for someone who needed assistance.

"We know," commented the other man. "I'm detective Larson and this is detective Williams. We were the first ones put on your case last July."

"You probably don't remember us," added Williams. "We only met you a couple of times before Erik was assigned to protect you."

"No," uttered Anna, beginning to feel a chill from Williams's admission. "I mean, I do remember you, it just took me by surprise."

"Imagine the surprise we felt when we found out Erik was quitting the department," said Larson. "It didn't surprise me when Erik was taken off your case and he opted to take all of his personal time, but even I would have never guessed he would have taken a case this far, giving up his job and all."

"I understand you really haven't made much progress," stated Williams, matter-of-factly.

"No," said Anna, barely audible. The shame and embarrassment was resurfacing from the dark places inside of her, where she had been storing it since the day she had awakened in Daniel and Marie's house. Now, not only was her life changed, but because of her, Erik was giving up his life also.

"I see you two are reacquainting yourselves with Anna," Erik said snidely, walking up from behind Larson and Williams.

Anna knew Erik must have heard at least some of the prior conversation.

"It was nice to see you again." Anna never once took her eyes from the floor, as she walked out of the building.

"You know what? You two need to work on your people skills, learn some manners. You'd be surprised what a couple of months away from this job could do for you," Erik said, turning and following Anna through the exit.

While in the city, they would be staying at Erik's apartment so the movers could come and pack things up. On the ride over there, the silence was deafening, as Anna tried to process all the information Larson and Williams had just revealed to her.

Her angry self-centered thoughts took a complete one-eighty, however, as she watched Erik tentatively begin unlocking his apartment door. She could see the rush of emotions attacking his senses as he stood battling with himself to step inside.

Anna felt awkward, as if she had entered a type of shrine. She too felt uneasy crossing the threshold into Erik's former life. She watched as Erik crossed the room and stood before a table filled with what Anna could only assume were photographs of his loving family. Her mind screamed at the world's unfairness that had caused both of them to lose those they loved.

"They're beautiful," commented Anna, coming over to stand next to Erik. When she looked at the array of photos, each with Erik's wife and daughter smiling back to the world, it was hard for her to grasp the reality that these seemingly vibrant lives were no longer there to be a part of humanity.

"Yes they were," agreed Erik, cradling one of the photographs. "I thought I could stay here while we were in town, but if you don't mind, I'd rather get a couple of rooms up by the gallery."

"I think that would be a good idea," Anna agreed, turning toward the door.

After Erik had checked them into adjoining rooms, Anna began putting her clothes away and settling in. She knew when she heard the knock on the connecting door that it could only be Erik.

"Everything okay in here?" Erik asked, entering the room.

"It's great," replied Anna. After everything that had happened this morning, Anna was finding herself at a loss—a loss of what to think, what to say, and even at what to feel.

"I need to go back to the apartment and pack up a few things. The movers are coming the day after tomorrow to put most of it in storage, but there are a few personal things I want to take back with me."

Anna knew this was going to be hard for Erik, but she understood his need to do this alone. He needed time to say good-bye, time to close this chapter of his life, so he could turn the page, and continue his story.

"Are you hungry?" asked Erik. "I'd forgotten we haven't eaten a thing since this morning."

"No, not really. Besides, I can always get something later."

"Anna," Erik started, "I know you're angry with me from what Larson and Williams said earlier down at the bureau, but you have to trust me, I'm—"

"I don't think trusting you is the problem," interrupted Anna, angrily. "I'm embarrassed to think how I must have acted or am still acting, if everyone sees the need not to trust my stability. I always knew I might still be in danger. I was never unrealistic about that."

"It wasn't like that. We thought we were protecting you and trying to make things as normal as possible."

"My life now isn't normal," Anna said, fighting back the tears. "What happened to me isn't normal, but the reality is. I need the reality, Erik. I can't have everybody making everything perfect for me; that's not normal. I have to feel the pain, along with the fear, so I can stay alert, remember what to look for. I lost my memories, not my abilities. You need to try to get your job back here, Erik. I don't want to be responsible for your life changing because mine has. As much as I love it where I am, it's not where I belong and neither do you."

"Wait a minute, I didn't take that job with Dennis because of you. As a matter of fact, my job here in the city was possibly sending me over the edge. So, if I want to live in the same peaceful little town that harbors an ornery cuss like Doc, then that's my decision."

Anna stood looking at Erik, trying to decide if he was telling her the truth. As her fears of ruining his life began to ebb away, a sad smile replaced her frown.

"Then you are very fortunate to live where you want to and know that you belong."

"Truce, then?"

"Truce," repeated Anna.

"How about if while I'm gone, you get ready to go out and have the best lobster dinner you've ever had?"

"And you know where that is?" Anna asked, skeptically.

"Believe it or not, I can be a most impressive tour guide, so all day tomorrow you have my undivided attention. Tonight, however, we celebrate."

"Celebrate?" Anna asked confused.

"Have you forgotten why we're here?"

"My nerves remind me around the clock," groaned Anna. "I'll be glad when Friday night is over and done with."

True to his word, the next day Erik had shown Anna around what seemed to be the entire city. She had been thankful for the full day of sight seeing and shopping, as it had forced her to keep her mind off the gallery. Now Friday night had come and Anna stood once again before the massive doors of the gallery. Butterflies began to resume their dance in the pit of her stomach.

"Good, you're early!" Peg greeted them with a smile. "I wanted you to see your work before anyone else arrived."

Peg led Anna and Erik to the section she had shown them the other day. Anna stood in awe, feeling as though once again it was a warm summer's day, instead of the cold, blustery January night.

Peg had used Marie's photograph to recreate a section of the cottage's gardens. A white picket fence with an entrance arbor formed the front boundary of the display. A sign outside the fence read, "Please feel free to step on the grass."

The lushness of the grass and the allure of the brightly colored flowers beyond the fence was all Anna needed to kick off the elegant, black heels she had purchased to go along with the designer dress that Marie had insisted Anna have for this special occasion. Through her nylons, Anna could feel the soft coolness of the freshly laid sod.

Her gaze never left her windows as they hung from the entire length of the two-story vaulted ceiling, suspended magically by invisible wire, giving them the illusion of floating. Anna circled her work, pleased that Peg had picked up on the beauty of the simplicity of nature Anna tried to incorporate into each window.

The windows hanging at different lengths and at different angles portrayed each one's uniqueness in a world of common bonds. The three wind chimes hanging from a rotating mechanism created one more layer of richness that tingled Anna's already heightened senses.

She felt almost naked standing there, exposed through her artwork.

"It's a little overwhelming to see yourself for the first time as others do, isn't it, Anna?"

Anna blinked twice and was even more tempted to pinch herself before she turned to the voice she had sworn belonged to Marie.

"We wouldn't have missed this for the world," Marie continued, coming over to hold Anna.

"But how?"

"We've had it planned for quite some time now," answered Marie with a wink. "We wanted it to be a surprise."

By now everyone had entered barefoot into the recreated cottage garden.

"We are all so proud of you," smiled Doc. "You've come a long way, my dear. A very long way."

Peg brought glasses of champagne into the close-knit circle of friends and Erik made a toast to Anna's success. Anna drew strength from her friends and her earlier worries of meeting new people began to fade, as those eager to meet the new artists began filling up the gallery.

Throughout the night, Anna met many people who found her work gave them a sense of peace and tranquility. It was still hard for Anna to believe her windows were considered art, but she did find contentment in the sincerity of those she met. By midnight, she was pretty sure she had met everyone who had attended the opening.

"Well," said Susan, coming up to stand next to Anna, "I guess Dennis and I should go relieve our friends of Katie and Brandon."

"I can't believe you had everything lined up for tonight and I never knew," Anna said, still amazed.

"Believe it," smiled Susan. "It was Erik's idea."

"Erik!"

"I guess he really can have a sense of humor," chuckled Susan.

Anna and Susan were still laughing when Erik and Dennis joined them.

"What's so funny?" asked Erik.

"Not a thing," replied Susan, sharing a look with Anna.

"Michael went to get the car," Marie said, joining them with Cheryl, Doc, and Daniel. "It was a lovely opening dear, but now our old bones are looking for a place to rest."

"Speak for yourself," Doc muttered. "I'm good for another half an hour or so."

"You turn into a pumpkin at midnight," teased Daniel. "Don't kid yourself."

"I think we'll be leaving too," added Anna, helping Marie on with her coat. "It seems to be clearing out."

"You two wait inside," ordered Erik. "Dennis and I will go get the cars."

"Let Erik come in and escort you two back to the curb when we pull around," added Dennis.

"I can't tell you how much I appreciate all of this," Anna said turning toward Peg.

"You don't have to say anything," replied Peg. "I already know. Talent is a funny thing. It doesn't always get recognized, but that doesn't make it less of a talent. I was glad to showcase yours, Anna. It was a secret too hard to keep quiet."

Erik stepped back through the gallery's doors, letting in a quick reminder of the frigid night. "Everybody ready?" he asked, taking Susan on his right arm and Anna on his left.

A crowd of people from what appeared to have been a wedding reception entered the sidewalk from the restaurant next door. There was laughing and rice throwing as the bride and groom worked their way toward a limo parked in front of Erik's car. Soon Erik, Susan, and Anna were caught up in the crowd. Erik felt the tug on his left arm as he and Anna became separated. At first, Erik assumed the push of the crowd had forced Anna from his arm, but as he turned around, he noticed that someone else had replaced his hold and was dragging Anna away.

Erik saw the panic in Anna's eyes. The man, who held Anna's arm, was a good six inches taller than she was and dressed in dirty rags. Nothing this man wore fit right or matched. He had the hood to his shabby coat pulled up so tight, Erik could hardly see any of his face.

When the man realized Erik had spotted him, as fast as the man had grabbed Anna, he now released her and was trying to disappear into the crowd, but not before Erik caught a glimpse of the man's shoes.

Erik was torn between chasing the man and getting a shaken Anna into the car. He quickly released his first thought, as it would probably prove futile with this crowd of people surrounding him, so he reached for Anna and began steering her back toward the curb and Dennis and Susan.

"Is she okay?" inquired Susan.

"I think she'll be fine, once we get her out of here." Erik noted Anna's ashen face as he began forcing her body to bend into the car.

"I didn't even see where that bum came from," confessed Dennis. "I guess I was too distracted by the bride and groom."

"Yeah, me too," agreed Erik, shutting Anna's door. "But not so distracted that I hadn't noticed that bum had on a brand new pair of two-hundred-dollar tennis shoes."

"Let's get her out of here," Dennis said, looking around.

"My thoughts exactly," agreed Erik, knowing that his observation was not lost on Dennis.

While Erik was pulling the car away from the curb, he noticed a woman running toward them and shouting something. Erik couldn't make out what the woman was saying, but it didn't matter anyway, looking at Anna frozen with fear, he had only one thought on his mind: get Anna away from here and quickly.

Chapter Twenty-two

February gave no relief to the bitter cold and blowing snow of January. For Anna, being stuck inside didn't produce the same cabin fever that had become so infectious to everyone else.

After the night of her showing, orders for the windows had greatly increased and she was finding it hard to keep up with the demand. She refused to taint her work by being rushed. After all, mass-producing was not what the customers were paying for and that was definitely not what her windows were about. She had talked with Peg on the phone and they had agreed on a reasonable time frame for each work, allowing Anna a life beyond just painting.

After Anna had returned from the city, she had also thought a lot about the man who had grabbed her in front of the gallery. True, she had been terribly shaken at first, but once away from the situation, Anna began to see it for what she felt it really was, someone in need of a hand out.

While in the city, she had witnessed hundreds of men, women, and children asking anyone who would listen for just a little help. She wasn't so naïve not to realize a good percentage of these people were using their handouts for drugs and alcohol, and Anna thought perhaps that was exactly the reason the man who grabbed her had seemed overly aggressive.

Though many thoughts had raced through Anna's mind at the time, now all she could feel was sadness. Sadness that, for whatever reason, people lived like that. She was sure this way of life could never have been their life's dream, but could only have become their cold, lonely reality.

Anna never forgot that this wasn't her complete life. She would never fully regain all of the things taken from her, but as sad as that made her, she was grateful for the support she had helping her to move forward. Who would help these people climb back out of the gutters of the city? Anna knew she was in a position financially now to help, even if it seemed a small drop in a very large bucket. Maybe though, she could convince others to help her fill that bucket.

These thoughts were never far from Anna's mind, even as February turned to March and the promise of spring slowly began to push its way through the earth's sodden ground, ready to reclaim its glory.

"I should have known I'd find you out here on your knees on the first day of spring," Susan said as she joined Anna outside of her cottage.

"Where are the kids?"

"They're with Marie. She's showing them how to plant seeds in pots. I think this is going to eventually be a Mother's Day present, so they are in step one of an ongoing project."

"That will be fun for them to watch the flowers grow."

"Looks like someone else is having fun," teased Susan, pointing to the rake in Anna's hand.

"I guess I am kind of excited to see if all of my hard work last fall will pay off."

"So what else is on your mind?" asked Susan, taking the other rake that was leaning against the wall.

"What do you mean?"

"When I was walking over here, you seemed deep in thought."

"I was," admitted Anna. "I was thinking about going into the city this weekend."

"Why?"

"I've been thinking a lot about what happened the last time I was there," continued Anna, "and maybe instead of being afraid of the man who grabbed me, maybe I should try to help him. What if he just needed a little food or something? I would like to do something to help others like him."

"And how do you propose to do that?" asked Susan cautiously. "You forget I have lived there and unfortunately, that's part of the way of life in a city."

"But does it have to be?"

"Anna, no matter how hard you try, you can't help everyone and make those conditions just disappear."

"I know that, but I have to try to do at least what I can and maybe I can convince others to as well. I know it will never clear up the problem, but even if I helped just one person, that's one more than yesterday. Sometimes I become afraid thinking that it could very easily have been me in that predicament. It was just the luck of the draw that I ended up here, where there are good people to care for me."

Anna watched as Susan shook her head, then slowly began to smile.

"How can I help?"

"By listening to my idea and telling me it's not crazy," smiled Anna. "That would be a great start."

"A great start to what?" asked Erik, coming from around the corner.

"Anna is going to the city this weekend and she was just filling me in on her plans."

"The city!" exclaimed Erik. "When did this come about?"

"Actually, I just thought it through," Anna responded, wondering why this was so upsetting to Erik. "I thought I'd take the bus."

"What part of this exactly did you think through? Taking the bus in is certainly not thinking it through."

"People take the bus all the time," Anna stated, defending herself.

"You're not people!" shouted Erik.

"Then what am I?" Anna shouted back.

"You're . . . you're . . . just let me know when you want to go and I'll drive you myself," grumbled Erik before turning and walking away.

"He is so stubborn," Anna said, stomping her foot into the freshly raked ground.

Anna and Erik left early Saturday morning. Anna was still angry with him for telling her instead of discussing it with her on how she was getting into the city. He never even asked her reasons for needing to go, so she childishly kept them to herself. This all made for a very long trip and by the time they pulled up in front of the gallery, they both jumped from the car as if it were on fire.

"Would you wait up?" shouted Erik, coming around the car.

"Erik," said Anna, pivoting on her heels and knocking right into his chest. "We've had this conversation before. I know you don't think so, but I can take care of myself. Trust me, there isn't a naïve bone left in my body."

"Is Peg expecting you?" Erik sighed, as he turned and headed for the gallery doors.

"Yes, she is."

Before they had even reached the top step, the doors opened and a smiling Peg greeted both of them.

"All of this secrecy has me intrigued," smiled Peg.

"There is no secrecy," laughed Anna. "It's something I wanted to discuss with you in person."

"So what can I do for you then?" asked Peg, escorting them into her office.

"Actually, it's something I would like to do. I'd like to give a percentage of my income from the paintings to helping out others. While I'm here, I intend to check out the different organizations that help those who need food, medical care, or even just a place to rest their heads at night."

"That's why we came all the way here?" Erik asked, sounding astonished. "Couldn't you have done that over the phone?"

Even though Erik had asked the question, Anna turned back toward Peg.

"I'd like to have another contract drawn up, allowing the money to be automatically deposited into the account of the organization I choose."

"That can be arranged," said Peg.

"I have also drawn up a letter asking the other artists here if they would consider doing the same," continued Anna, handing the letter to Peg. "But only if it's all right with you. I would understand if that's not possible. I wouldn't want anyone to feel pressured."

Anna watched Peg as she read the letter that basically explained Anna's desire for wanting to help out a charitable organization, while asking each artist if he or she would consider joining her efforts, therefore representing the gallery as a whole unit.

"I'll tell you what," Peg said as she looked up from the letter, "let's do one better. We'll make it a challenge to all of the galleries in the city. Who knows, by this time next year, maybe even nationwide."

"That would be perfect," sighed Anna.

It was silent for a moment before Peg stood up.

"Let me show you the display we've set for your windows."

The gallery looked different from the last time Anna had

been there. Instead of the large displays of just a few artists, there were smaller, but just as tasteful displays of many.

"I miss the grass to walk on," Peg admitted. "But it's still my favorite place to come and take a break."

Anna saw that two of her windows still hung suspended from the ceiling. Below the windows sat a sprinkling can with what appeared to be a never-ending supply of water pouring from its spout. The sparkling water gave Anna the feeling that someone from above was nurturing the many potted plants that were set on various pedestals throughout the display.

From the corner of her eye, Anna saw Erik walking around the easel that held a portrait of her, along with a brief description of where her works were born. The information was vague at best, only describing the cottage, without giving a location. Erik hadn't wanted a picture of Anna hung up at all, but Peg had convinced him the public needed to feel connected to the artist. This was Anna's life now and it was what was paying her bills, so Erik had eventually relented and the poster was made with his approval.

"I didn't bother calling you yesterday, since I knew you were coming today," started Peg. "But yesterday, a woman came into the gallery. She went right to your picture, Anna, and called out a name, but I didn't catch it. When I approached her, she said it was uncanny how much you looked like someone she knew.

"She continued to tell me how she had seen this same woman a couple of months ago, right here in front of the gallery. She said it had been dark that night and she had been at a wedding reception. She claims she tried to call out a name, but before she had been able to get the woman's attention, the car she was in drove away."

"Did you get her name?" urged Erik.

"No," replied Peg. "The gallery was fairly busy and I got called away. I had told her I would only be a second, but by the time I got back to her, she had already left. I'm so sorry, Anna, I really am."

Anna had been holding her breath the entire time Peg had been speaking. She had felt her heart racing at the thought that someone might be able to identify her, but the racing excitement slammed into her chest as she realized her hopes had walked out the door with the mysterious lady.

"It was probably nothing," mumbled Erik.

Anna could see her look of disappointment reflected on Peg's face. Peg was too good of a friend to have to bare this guilt over something that might or might not have been significant.

"I've been told, everyone has a twin," smiled Anna, taking Peg's hand. "This woman just mistook me for someone else, just like she thought. She probably took a closer look at the picture, realized it wasn't who she thought, and walked away before she embarrassed herself further."

"I hope so. But if she comes back, I promise she won't be walking out again until I know her name."

"If she does, call me immediately," instructed Erik, handing Peg one of his business cards.

After they had said their good-byes, Erik maneuvered the car back onto the busy city streets.

"Do you think that's more of a case of mistaken identity?" Anna asked eagerly.

"Are you hungry?" countered Erik.

Anna knew Erik was worried about giving her false hopes, but she didn't appreciate this blatant display of closing a subject.

"You promised to let me in on all of the decisions in my life," reminded Anna, more hurt than angry. "No more secrets, remember?"

"I . . ."

"You what, Erik? You only want to protect me. I've got news

for you, your protection is killing me inside, over and over again."

Anna watched Erik process her outburst.

"This woman could be just a coincidence," started Erik. "But I do have a strange feeling about this and my instincts are usually right."

"Thank you," Anna said, feeling the unshed tears in her eyes, as her lips found a smile of their own. "I just wanted to know your opinion."

"What do you think about her?" asked Erik.

Anna knew Erik was making a conscious effort on her behalf. He must have finally realized what she had been feeling like, being the outsider of her own life.

"The night of the showing and then afterward when we got separated," Anna started, trying to recall specific details. "I really didn't remember you putting me in the car, but . . ."

"What?" prodded Erik.

"I really wasn't sure if this had happened or not, but when Peg mentioned a woman had thought she had seen her friend that night," Anna hesitated while looking at Erik. "This sounds crazy, but that night when I heard her calling a name, somewhere in the back of my mind, I recognized it."

"You're not crazy," confirmed Erik. "Peg jarred my memory too. I also noticed a woman rushing toward the car. I couldn't make out what she was saying and at the time I didn't care, I just wanted you out of there."

"So it did happen," sighed Anna relieved. "I've tried a thousand times to relive that moment so I could hear her say that name again, but her lips stop just before they form a word. We've lost her for good now, haven't we?"

"Not necessarily. It's my experience that curiosity gets even the best of us and the fact that she even came back to the gallery is a good sign. I would put money on it, she'll turn up again. I'll talk to the manager of the restaurant also. Maybe they have a guest list from the night of the wedding."

"I hope you're right," Anna said, losing herself in thought. Anna had considered the fact that this woman was not perhaps a friend as she had claimed to be, but whether this woman could help Anna or hurt her was irrelevant anymore. Anna just wanted her life back and even welcomed the risk if need be.

The rest of that day and the next, Anna and Erik kept busy visiting shelters and organizations Anna was considering for the distribution of funds. The rest of the trip and the drive home were uneventful. By the time they had reached Anna's cottage, it was nearly midnight. Erik helped Anna get her bags in the cottage, and then walked back to his car. Erik hadn't been sleeping on Anna's couch as much anymore and she supposed it was to give her more independence, but at times when the nightmares were at their worst, she found she missed him.

"I'll see you in the morning." Erik bent down to give Anna a kiss on her cheek.

"Not too early," Anna yawned.

"Speak for yourself, I have to work."

"No rest for the weary," laughed Anna, as she closed and locked her door.

Chapter Twenty-three

"Hey stranger, how are you?"

Bolting straight up from her crouched position over her garden, Anna came face to face with Dennis.

"Whoa, why so jumpy?"

"Sorry," replied Anna. "We got in late last night and I guess that's why I've let my imagination run wild."

"How so?"

"I woke up to a sound last night and then one of my bedroom windows broke. I talked myself into believing the worst and now I have a stiff neck and sore legs from sitting on the floor keeping an all-night vigil."

"Why didn't you call Erik or me?"

"Dennis, look around you. With all of these branches and the debris blowing around in the yard, I'm sure the wind was strong enough last night to whip a branch from that tree by my window close enough to do some damage. Even I got a good laugh when the sun came up."

"I still want you to call next time. I'll be by a little later to fix it."

"No need to," smiled Anna. "As long as I was up, I tackled it myself early this morning. There was an extra window in the shed. I was just waiting for it to warm up a bit more so I could paint it."

"I would still feel better if I checked the locks on it," replied Dennis.

"It looks to me like you'd feel better if you had a couple hours more sleep," observed Anna. "Long weekend?"

"You could say that. Brandon and Katie came down with the chicken pox."

"Oh no!"

"They were feeling pretty sick the first couple of days," admitted Dennis. "But now it's the itching and boredom."

"I'll go see if I can help."

"I'm sure Susan would appreciate that. I think she's ready to go out of her mind. I know I was glad to be going to work this morning."

"Maybe she'll let me relieve her for a while so she can get out of the house."

"Speaking of work," continued Dennis, "Erik was supposed to meet me a half an hour ago at the station. I suppose he's being lazy and still sleeping in."

"I don't know. Weren't you just over there?" Anna asked, pointing to Dennis's squad car parked in Erik's driveway.

"I knocked loud enough to wake the dead, but there was no answer. I just assumed he was here with you."

"No, he dropped me off last night and was going straight home. I haven't seen him since."

Dennis and Anna looked at each other and then turned and raced to Erik's cottage. They knocked on both doors and some of the windows.

"He gave me a key." Anna nervously pulled the key from her coat pocket.

Dennis took Anna's key ring and inserted the right key into the lock. When they entered Erik's cottage, only a faint buzzing sound broke the silence.

"Erik?" called out Dennis.

A weak moan came from the direction of Erik's bedroom. Entering the room, they saw Erik, still in his clothes from yesterday, lying on top of his covers, shaking uncontrollably. Red spots were forming on Erik's hands and face. Anna placed her hand on his forehead.

"He's burning up."

Erik turned his head deliriously from side to side, trying to focus on the voices that seemed so far away.

"I'll get him undressed and under the covers," instructed Dennis, already pulling off Erik's shirt. "You call Doc and get some cold water and a washcloth."

Anna turned to leave the room.

"Anna," called Dennis, forcing Anna to turn back, "have you had the chicken pox?"

"I don't know," replied Anna. "It wouldn't matter, I'm staying. I'll go call Doc and be right back."

When Anna left the room, Erik's frail hand clutched the front of Dennis's shirt.

"You have to go turn off the receiver before Anna figures it out."

"That's the least of your problems," replied Dennis, removing Erik's shoe.

"Now!" demanded a weakened Erik.

"I suppose if I don't you'll crawl in there yourself," grumbled Dennis, leaving the room.

A second later, Erik watched Dennis quietly step back in.

"Are you happy now?" stormed Dennis.

That was all Erik needed to hear, so he could let his mind and body slip into a fevered unconsciousness. On the fourth morning, Erik awoke from this state and the world was once again coherent to him. He smiled as he saw the blue sky and bright sunshine hovering patiently outside of his window. He rolled over in bed and beheld an even more welcoming sight—Anna asleep, curled up in a chair next to his bed. Her eyes began to blink, as if she sensed him watching her.

"How are you feeling?" she asked, uncoiling her body.

"Did you get the license of the truck that hit me?"

"Actually," smiled Anna, "it was something much smaller than that, that brought a big man down."

"What?" Erik asked, raising one eyebrow.

"Technically, two things: Katie and Brandon."

"Katie and Brandon?"

"They were just sharing," chuckled Anna. "They gave you the chicken pox."

"Chicken pox!"

"Really, Erik, you've got to stop repeating everything I say, or I'm going to be led to believe the fever has affected your thinking process as well."

"As well as what?" asked Erik as if dreading the answer.

"Let's just say, you should stay away from a mirror for a couple of days."

"That bad?"

"Doc says you'll be fine if you don't scratch, which is why I'm going to prepare you an oatmeal bath."

"Oatmeal," uttered Erik, disgusted. "I'd rather eat the oatmeal than bathe in it."

"That's not possible. You, my friend, are on a strict liquid diet. While you are in the bath, I'll fix some nice broth and Jell-O. If you can keep that down, who knows, tomorrow maybe you can have a couple of crackers."

"How's the patient?" Doc asked, entering the bedroom.

"Grumpy," smiled Anna.

"Good," replied Doc. "Then he's already back to his old self."

Erik shook his head in temporary defeat. He still felt weak as a baby, but when he was feeling better, he would show them . . . he would show them how grateful he was to have friends who cared.

By the sixth day of Erik's illness, even he could see the signs of fatigue and strain showing on Anna's face. He was still weak, but he was definitely getting better, which in his mind was the reason he had the temperament of a caged animal. Before he could suggest to Anna to take a break, he overheard Doc handling that for him.

"Go on, Anna," Doc urged. "I'll take that tray of breakfast in to Erik. You get out of here and take a break today."

"I'm fine."

"As your doctor also, I'm prescribing a morning out in this glorious spring sunshine. You won't do anyone any good if you get run down too. Besides, my reinforcements should be here any minute."

Just as Doc had mentioned that, Erik heard Daniel's voice.

"Where's our patient?"

"I was just getting ready to bring him an antihistamine and some breakfast," Anna was saying.

"We can handle that," Daniel said. "Don't forget, you're in the company of a doctor and I've been known on occasion to make a good nurse."

Erik heard the door close and knew instantly that Anna had been sent firmly out it.

"Shall we go into the lion's den?" Erik could hear their conversation as they were inching closer.

"His roar is much worse than his bite," laughed Doc. "Besides, we come bearing gifts."

As they entered Erik's room, he pretended to be sleeping, but Daniel and Doc refused to play along. Daniel tied back the curtain and threw open the window, letting in the fresh spring air, while Doc flippantly placed the tray of food on the small table that Anna had moved next to Erik's bed.

"Where's Anna?" barked Erik, trying to adjust to the brightness that instantly flooded the room.

"Last I saw her, she was getting some much deserved fresh

air and heading over to talk to Marie," replied Daniel.

Erik watched as Dennis sauntered into his bedroom.

"Your door was open, so I let myself in," grinned Dennis.

"All right, that's it!" shouted Erik, pushing back his covers and getting out of bed. He had on a pair of sweat pants, but he grabbed a shirt as he headed out of the room.

"What's with him?" asked Dennis.

"I think he was feeling a bit underdressed," stated Doc. "And not necessarily in the clothing department. Put yourself in his shoes. It's hard feeling like the weakest link."

"Then maybe it's time to catch him up on what's been going on," said Dennis.

"I think that would be a good idea," agreed Doc. "And not just for his sake."

They found Erik at the kitchen table, eating a muffin and drinking a cup of coffee.

"Mind if we join you?" Dennis asked.

"It's a free country," replied Erik blandly.

Erik knew Dennis chose to ignore his moodiness as he continued.

"The day I found you sick," Dennis began, "I was on my way over to share some information with you."

"What information?"

"When you and Anna were gone, I was checking the doors and windows at her cottage and as I was walking around to the back, I noticed shoe imprints in the mud. I know a lot of us have been in and out of Anna's cottage and, at first, I thought it was just one that had thawed out from the winter. But Susan had been with me and pointed out that it was an area Anna had just been raking, so it had to be a fresh print."

"Why didn't you tell me?" demanded Erik.

"Oh, gee, I don't know, maybe because you were sick and pretty out of it."

Erik heard the sarcasm in Dennis's voice and guilt began to rise in his stomach. Dennis possessed all of the same skills he himself had, so why was Erik being so bull headed?

"Sorry," said Erik, humbled. "Can I see the photograph you took?"

"I can do better than that," Dennis nodded.

Erik knew that nod was a silent acceptance to his request for forgiveness and he listened as Dennis continued.

"I measured the print and sent the photo to the lab to be analyzed." Dennis handed Erik a manila folder. "The lab matched the tread of the shoe to a popular brand name. The pattern is clear, so the lab determined that the owner hadn't been in possession of them very long."

"New brand name tennis shoes," said Erik, voicing his thoughts out loud. "Just like the man who grabbed Anna in the city."

"There's another thing," continued Dennis. "It was a size eleven."

"The same size as the original print in the sand," acknowledged Erik.

"And there's another thing," Dennis was saying gravely.

"I'm beginning to feel like Rip Van Winkle," sighed Erik wearily. "I think I've missed a lifetime in six days."

"This might be nothing, however," interjected Doc.

"Why don't you let me decide," Erik replied tensely.

"I checked on a window Anna had replaced in her bedroom the other day," Dennis continued. "She seemed to think the wind whipped a tree branch through it."

"And you don't?" questioned Erik, noting that all three men in the room had skepticism written all over their faces.

"There is no branch from that tree close enough to have ever brushed the cottage, let alone break a window," stated Dennis.

"Not even with the wind that night?" asked Erik.

"Maybe with hurricane force winds, but that night was far from being a hurricane."

"All right," said Erik calmly. "It's begun."

"The other guys down at the station and I have been taking turns patrolling around here at night," informed Dennis.

"Thanks," nodded Erik. "I guess I haven't been too much help to anyone lately."

"I feel kind of responsible for that. After all, you wouldn't be in this predicament if it weren't for my kids."

"How are they doing?" Erik asked, feeling guilty for not having thought of it before.

"You know kids," grinned Dennis. "They're sick for a day or two, then they're up and running around again. Susan's had a hard time with them itching, so, when I left this morning, they were both wearing their socks on their hands. At the time they both thought it was funny, but by now I'm sure the fun has worn off."

"I certainly don't feel like running a marathon yet," admitted Erik. "But I can relate to the itching."

"I can go and get a pair of your socks," winked Doc.

"I think I can show some restraint," grumbled Erik.

"Good," continued Doc. "Then you'll have no problem when I tell you that you need to stay in bed for a few more days."

"Bed! I'll take it easy, but I'm not going to lie around getting bed sores."

"I hardly think you're in a position to get bed sores," snorted Doc. "But if you promise to take it slowly, I'll allow you to stay on the couch. Maybe if you're really good, we'll bundle you up and take you outside on the deck for a short spell."

"You'll allow me?" bellowed Erik. "I don't believe I've been forbidden to do anything since high school!"

"Well then, I hope you remember how."

Erik could feel the challenge in Doc's stare, but already Erik's body was starting to betray him. "A few more days and that's it. How long will it take for these sores to go away?"

"Now that's another story," replied Doc. "But be thankful not every inch of your body is covered with them like Brandon's and Katie's. For now, let's work on gaining your strength back. Make sure you drink plenty of liquids. Your high fever depleted your body of fluids. You'll be surprised how much better you'll feel just by replenishing those, eating well, and continuing to take it easy."

Erik nodded and drank the glass of orange juice that had mysteriously appeared in front of him. He was determined to be the model patient. This feeling of extreme weakness was just altogether unacceptable to him.

Chapter Twenty-four

Four days later, Erik was feeling so much better; he tiptoed from his bedroom into the kitchen. He wanted to surprise a sleeping Anna with breakfast. He had been feeling guilty this last week that Anna had insisted on sleeping on his couch in order to continue taking care of him. Unfortunately, Erik's couch was not nearly as comfortable as the couch at Anna's cottage, but she never once complained. The dark circles under her eyes were sign enough of her fatigue. Erik had made her promise that this was to be her last night she would subject herself to such cruel and unusual punishment.

Erik stepped out onto the back deck and waved to the officer in the patrol car that was sitting in his driveway. It was the only signal the officer needed before he drove back to the station.

Later today, Erik planned to tell Anna about the shoe print and what he suspected was the real reason behind the broken window. He knew Anna had seen the patrol cars at night and he wanted her to know the patrolling would continue, especially with her going back to her own cottage tonight. When Erik stepped back into the kitchen, he heard a soft moan coming from the couch.

"Is it morning already?" asked Anna, stretching.

"Something like that. You were supposed to stay asleep until I had breakfast done."

"The smell of coffee always wakes me up."

"You don't even drink coffee," laughed Erik, reaching for the mug of hot milk he had warmed up for Anna's hot chocolate.

"That doesn't mean I can't appreciate the smell."

Side by side, they began cooking. Before long, a morning feast weighed down Erik's small kitchen table.

"Were we expecting someone?" laughed Anna.

"You forget," replied Erik, eyeing the mounds of bacon, sausage, potatoes, and eggs crammed onto every square inch of the table, "I haven't really eaten anything in over a week. I'm starved."

"Then by all means, don't let me hold you back."

"I won't," grinned Erik, never once laying down his fork.

Although Erik consumed a lot of food, breakfast went by rather quickly. He watched as Anna insisted on cleaning up and putting things away. Then, she reached for her jacket.

"I'm going to run home and take a shower before the rain starts."

Erik had also noticed the ominous clouds rolling in off the water. "According to the forecast, we're in for some pretty rough weather."

"I'll be back soon, but I also want to start a load of laundry," Anna said, gathering up some of Erik's things.

"You know, you don't have to do my laundry too." But Erik had to admit his cottage had never looked so good. While he had been sick, Anna had cleaned every inch of it and added small touches to make it feel like a real home. She had taken Erik's precious photographs of his wife and daughter out of the box, and displayed them openly on the fireplace mantle.

Amongst the pictures, Anna was careful to keep small vases of colorful spring flowers she had cut from her own garden.

At first, Erik had felt too open, too raw. But he soon realized as the days went by that by facing his loss, he could begin to endure the anger, hurt, and sadness.

The blast of wind that whisked through the room as Anna opened the door brought Erik back to the present. He could hear the thunder rumbling in the distance. Erik watched as Anna started down the path, the wind whipping her hair around her face.

He closed the door, realizing now would be a good time to get cleaned up himself. It always felt good to Erik to wash off all of the lotions and creams Doc insisted he kept plastered on his chicken pox. Anna would force Erik to put them back on when she returned, but at least he would have some time to be free of the smelly ointments.

On his way to the shower, Erik walked over to the transmitter and set the volume level on high. With Anna staying here, there had been no need to be using this lately, but with his health returning and things getting back to usual, Erik wanted to make sure he would be able to hear a pin drop in Anna's cottage if necessary. The storm was really breaking, as Erik stepped into his warm paradise. As the water began to relax his muscles and ease the intense itching, Erik's mind began to drift.

Anna had made it all the way to her cottage when the nagging thought struck her that perhaps she hadn't turned off Erik's oven. A few raindrops were starting to fall, but she decided to run back to Erik's instead of calling him on the phone and risking the chance of dragging him out of his shower. She would just use her key, slip in, turn the oven off, and slip out.

By the time she reached Erik's, the wind and rain had

started coming hard and fast. The thunder was so loud; she could barely hear the shower running in Erik's bathroom. Anna went over to the oven and gave a small chuckle; all that way over and the oven really was off.

She looked at the phone on the wall and decided to give Daniel a quick call to see if there were any storm warnings before she headed back out to her own cottage. Anna picked up the phone, only to hear another voice already on the other end.

"Hello?" answered Anna curiously.

"Anna, I've been trying to reach you."

"Who's this?" inquired Anna, realizing she must have picked up a call before it got the chance to ring.

"Peg, and like I said, I've been trying to get a hold of you for a few hours now."

"I've been taking care of Erik; he came down with the chicken pox. He's doing much better though."

"Listen, Anna, your line is breaking up, so I'll talk quick. I was calling Erik to let him know there was a man in the gallery who bought one of your windows. Unfortunately, one of my newer people was waiting on him and when he asked for a little information on the artist, she looked you up in the file and gave him some."

"What did she give him?" Anna felt her hand grasping tighter to the phone.

"He knows the town you live in, Anna. I'm so sorry, I know this doesn't mean much, but I let that employee go. She was clearly explained the procedures and this was one rule too important for me to overlook."

"He was probably just another coincidence anyway," said Anna nervously.

"Let Erik decide that," added Peg firmly. "Can I talk to him?"

"He's in the shower," answered Anna, as a loud buzzing

sound began to draw her attention from somewhere in the room.

"Do you promise to tell him I called? I'll be expecting his return call sometime today."

Anna heard a muffled knocking on the door, followed by Daniel's greeting.

"Hey, anybody home?"

"Just a second!" shouted Anna. "Peg I gotta go, Daniel's at the door and it's raining cats and dogs outside."

"I understand, tell everyone hello," Peg said, before the phone line went dead.

Anna ran to the door and opened it, ready to scold a soggy Daniel for being out in this weather. To her amazement, however, the other side of the door was barren. Movement caught her eye over at her own cottage. She could clearly make out Daniel standing in her doorway and knocking on her door. She could also see Marie, waiting in her driveway in their car, but Anna's mind was having a difficult time sorting all of this out. Daniel spoke again.

"We're picking Doc up and going over to Susan's. The kids are a little upset with the storm. I was checking to see if you needed anything."

Anna felt like she was in a dream. It was like watching a movie, where the lip movement and the words didn't quite move in sync. She turned to the electronic device on the table that she had been dusting around all of last week and instantly knew what it was that was projecting Daniel's voice so clearly.

"Get in the car, Daniel," Marie was saying. "You'll catch your death in this rain. She's obviously with Erik. She's in good hands and we promised Susan we'd be right over."

Anna watched as Daniel and Marie pulled out of her driveway. Then silently, as if in a trance, Anna walked over to the receiver and turned the knob until the hideous buzzing stopped.

"Anna," groaned Erik, appearing next to her, wrapped only in a towel.

"I thought there were no more secrets," uttered Anna sadly. "Who all knew about this?"

Anna watched as a defeated Erik seemed to be trying to form a sentence. After an extended silence, the sentence Anna had been hoping for was condensed to only a couple of painful words.

"Almost everyone."

Anna ran out the door straight into the grips of the storm. She knew Erik had sense enough not to follow her in just his towel, but she could feel his eyes following her as she fought the wind and rain, back to her cottage.

The sound of thunder shook her cottage, as she entered her own shower. She needed the warmth of the shower because she had been soaked to the bone. But even more so, she needed the healing properties of washing away the pain and humiliation that always seemed to seep in when she least expected.

Dressed now after her cleansing shower, she found herself pacing back and forth in the glass conservatory. The raging storm outside seemed only to feed more into her hurt and anger. Anna had her back to the French doors when she heard the loud knocking that she knew would eventually come. She had been tempted to let him stay out there in the rain and if Erik still hadn't been getting over his illness, she knew she would have done just that.

"Why would you think I would want to talk to you?" Anna shouted angrily as she made her way to the door. "Why would I believe anything you would have to say?"

Anna swung the door open, only to have her heart stop and her mind begin to fog.

"Elizabeth, it is you," said the man angrily, pushing down the hood of his coat. "Didn't you think I would find you eventually?"

"No!" screamed Anna, as she felt herself falling, unable to stop herself from hitting her head on the table on her way down.

Erik walked back into his living room, fully clothed and feeling a little closer to being his old self again. He couldn't get out of his mind the painful expression Anna had minutes earlier before she had run out of his door. He walked over to the window to take a look over at her cottage. It was so dark and the rain was coming down so hard, Erik had to wait for a flash of lightening in order to see better. He thought his mind was playing tricks on him, until the next flash of light confirmed that Anna's French doors were, in fact, standing wide open. The next flash showed Erik a glimpse of an unknown car parked on her lane.

Erik grabbed his gun and handcuffs and quickly headed out his door. He would have liked to have taken his car because his knees still felt like jelly, but he wanted the element of surprise on his side if this was more than just a friendly visitor. The closer Erik got to Anna's cottage, the more the hair on the back of his neck stood up. Erik was close enough now that with the help of the lightening, he could make out a man's form bending down to the ground right inside Anna's doorway.

"Elizabeth!" The man was yelling repeatedly. "Lizzie!"

Erik came up from behind the man and ripped him away from Anna's limp body. As Erik shoved the man against the wall, he noticed the blood that was staining the man's hands.

"She's hurt," the man was saying. "Let me go help her."

"I think you've helped her enough," spat out Erik, dragging the man into the kitchen and handcuffing him to the refrigerator. Next, Erik turned and walked back toward Anna.

"I'm her husband!" the man shouted.

Erik turned back toward the man slowly; he knew his anger and contempt was written all over his face. "Then I guess you've lost the vote for husband of the year."

"What are you talking about? I really am her husband."

Erik knew Anna needed him, so he refused to waste any more time on this man.

"You try to move or make any sound," Erik said, pulling his gun out, "I'll shoot you."

The man stood there angrily shaking his head, as Erik got on his knees next to Anna.

"Anna," Erik said gently, cradling her head in his arms. He noticed the blood grotesquely smeared across her forehead and the bruise that was forming beneath it. The cut appeared to be superficial, but the bruise caused Erik some concern. Gently laying her head down, Erik went to the phone to call Doc. To his dismay, Anna's phone line was dead. Erik picked up an afghan from the chair and went back to wrap it around Anna. He was afraid she was slipping into unconsciousness, but just then, her eyes opened.

"Anna," Erik said tenderly, "how are you feeling?"

Looking into Anna's eyes, Erik could see the confusion that mirrored back. Erik continued to watch Anna's face as she first sat up and then tried to stand up. He caught her around the waist and helped her to the chair. Erik knelt in front of her, holding her hands as he spoke.

"Listen to me," Erik began slowly. "I tried to call Doc, but your phone is out."

"I'm okay," Anna said softly.

"Elizabeth," came the man's voice from the adjoining kitchen.

Erik watched as Anna slowly turned her head toward the voice. When she saw the man handcuffed to the refrigerator, her face turned ashen and her body began to tremble.

"Terry," she whispered, putting her fist to her mouth.

"Do you know him, Anna?" asked Erik.

"He's my husband."

"Are you sure?" Erik asked, thinking Anna was still acting as a spectator in her own life.

"I feel so many things," Anna whispered. "Love, hurt, anger, sadness. I don't know what's real anymore."

Erik could see Anna's shoulders begin to slump, her sanity begin to slip and it reminded him of the wounded lost woman he had met months ago on the cliff.

"Anna," Erik started, gently taking her chin and forcing her to look at him, "I promise you we will get this straightened out. I'm going to take him out of here and try to get some answers. I need you to try to calm down and keep trying to call Doc. Do you understand me?"

To Erik, Anna seemed to be in a deep trance. The man in the kitchen was still calling out to her and Erik held Anna back, as she stood to walk over to him.

"How are my children?" asked Anna sorrowfully.

Erik kept watching helplessly, as Anna tried desperately to hold back the flood of tears.

"How do you think they are without a mother?" answered the man cruelly.

Erik was across the room in three strides. He showed no mercy in uncuffng the man from the refrigerator, only to recuff him again, but with his hands behind his back this time.

"If you need me, I'll be at my place, until I know Doc is here with you," instructed Erik, dragging the man with him through the front door, so as to avoid having to pass Anna.

Once outside, Erik turned and punched the man square in the face. As Erik watched the man lying in the mud, with the rain pelting his body, Erik became frightened at his own violence and the taste of revenge.

"That was for Anna," grumbled Erik, dragging the man to his feet and pushing him toward his cottage.

Chapter Twenty-five

"Who are you?" The man demanded for the fifth time.

"I believe I was the first to ask you that question," said Erik dryly.

"I told you, not that it's any of your business, I'm Elizabeth's husband."

"I think you would be surprised how much of my business this is," replied Erik coldly.

"I gathered as much."

"What's that supposed to mean?" Erik asked, leaning into the man's face.

"I think any fool can see," muttered the man, overly calm. "And I guess I'm that fool."

"Oh, I don't think you really believe yourself to be a fool. In fact, last July, I bet you were hailing yourself at being quite the genius. Funny how things don't always work out though, isn't it?"

The man leapt to his feet and with his hands still handcuffed behind his back, charged at Erik like an angry bull. The movement caught Erik off guard and they both went sprawling to the floor. Erik still had the advantage, however, and within seconds, the man was pushed back into the chair.

"You surprise me," said Erik, with a wicked grin. "I would

have never imagined you would take on someone your own size and strength. Guess what? You've hit the jackpot, I'm also a cop."

"Gee sorry," the man said sneering. "I mistook you for a jealous lover."

"You know I'm having a real hard time stomaching you. It will be a real pleasure to get you down to the station, get some fingerprints, and run your license plate. Do you want me to take a guess on what will show up?"

"Be my guest, you seem to know it all."

"Well," admitted Erik picking up his phone, "I guess I can't blame Anna's lack of telephone service on you—mine's dead too. Here's the deal, I'm cuffing you to this wooden pillar that separates the living room from the kitchen. I'm going to go dry off and change. If you move . . ."

"I know," answered the man furiously. "You'll shoot me."

"Something like that," agreed Erik, walking toward his bathroom. "But if you're really good, I'll bring you back a dry towel."

"Don't do me any favors," the man said blandly.

After they had left, Anna's shaking became uncontrollable. She held on to the blanket Erik had given her as if it were the last life preserver on a sinking ship. She closed her eyes to the headaches, but the bright images kept flashing sporadically on the lids of her eyes. She wasn't sure just how long she had been sitting there.

When she finally fought down the intense pain and forced her eyes open, by some miracle, the sun was out and shining brilliantly.

She stood up and looked out. Other than the puddles that had formed on the ground, she would never have believed the havoc the weather had been creating for the last couple of hours.

Like the storm, she was in the midst of havoc. Would her life ever be normal? Where was her rainbow that pushed away the clouds? The images kept ripping through Anna's mind, but still there was so little connection between them.

Anna decided to try doing what lately gave her a feeling of having a core to her being. She would paint. Hopefully, this would calm her down and the images would flow into perspective and form her life, just as the images flowed from her paintbrush to create her art.

Anna went to the room she kept her work in. Lying on two sawhorses was one of the old windows she had already cleaned up and given a fresh coat of paint to its frame. Her mind wandered back and forth between reality and fantasy. She started painting flowers that she envisioned to be in window boxes directly outside the window.

She held her breath, as her mind snapped before her, giving a clear image of all three of her children. She missed them so much. She thought of her husband and knew she had an overwhelming feeling of love and loss for him also. It just didn't make sense.

Anna looked hard at her painting and realized she had unconsciously painted a family of five in the distance on a beach. The tears began to flow as she remembered how happy her family had been at one time. What had happened?

Anna needed answers. She had given up enough of her life and her children's. She was going over to Erik's to confront her husband. After all, she had a right to these answers. Anna's fallen tears had left smudges on the loving cozy scene she had just created on the window. She reached across her work to get a rag.

When Anna started to lift the rag from the window, something drew her attention—a ghostly image of a man's face. In one painful memory flash, Anna recognized the reflection that was hovering in the depths of the painting and branded in the recess of her mind. Her breathing quickened and her hands began to sweat. Cold chills ran down her spine. He was standing right behind her and his presence engulfed her. She could only pray he hadn't realized she knew he was there. She felt like she was moving in slow motion, but she knew she needed to remain calm. She would rather die first than to let this man touch her again. She started to act like she was putting her brushes away. As Anna saw his hand come up in the reflection of the window, she grabbed the paint thinner and spun around, spewing it in the direction of her attacker.

"You bitch," he growled, as Anna ran past him and out of the room.

She made it to the front door and was desperately trying to force the bar back in the bolt. A searing pain washed over her scalp; she was being pulled by her hair. As she felt strands of it being savagely ripped out, she fell backward onto the couch. It was happening so quickly. Anna never saw the hand that came from behind slap her with such force that her mind fogged and her vision blurred.

"You're still a whore," he sneered, twisting her hair tighter in his hand. "Another man, Lizzie? Really, you'll never learn."

Terry had sat fuming as he watched the man Elizabeth called Erik dry off. Cop or no cop, what was he doing, pushing him around and demanding answers? From what Terry had lived through these last eight months and from what he had just witnessed this morning, they had both better have a pair of good lawyers.

Terry knew Elizabeth had been unhappy, truth be told, they both had felt the pull of growing apart, but how could she have put her own children through the pain and humiliation of being deserted? Perhaps it was possible to never really know a person.

Terry's thoughts were interrupted by a scratchy, static sound coming from the radio on the table next to him. He could faintly hear what seemed to be a man's agitated voice.

"You can imagine my surprise when I found out you weren't dead," came the man's voice over the radio. "How did you manage that?"

Terry looked from the radio back to the room Erik had just gone into. What if this wasn't really a cop? What if they were just trying to intimidate him with this recording? Terry looked around, trying to devise a plan to free himself. As he was calculating his options, he continued to listen to the voice from the machine.

Anna was sitting on the couch, forcing her mind to clear and her vision to come back into focus. She knew he had just asked her a question, but she refused to answer it. Suddenly she felt her body being projected over the couch. He then began dragging her across the floor and into the kitchen. Next, she was being tossed up onto the counter with such force that her head snapped back, slamming into a cabinet. He stood between her legs, pushing her shoulders back into the cabinets in order to keep her head up.

"I asked you a question!" he yelled. "I expect an answer."

Thinking she was going to retch any minute, Anna pushed the pain and sickness into the back of her mind. With the last breath of strength she possessed, Anna pushed herself off the counter. Surprise was on her side and she sent him reeling backward onto the floor. Anna half ran, half crawled to the French doors, but once again, the locks that kept her safe from the outside, managed to ruin her chances of escape.

Terry strained his ears, listening to all of this from the other end. An uneasy feeling crept over him. He had heard the man speaking and the unmistakable sounds of struggling, or . . . Terry's heart was pounding so loudly; he had to take a few long breaths in order to calm himself down. The man's voice was back, angrier than ever.

"I think," came the sinister voice, "since it worked so well the first time, we should go with the same plan. Can you imagine a second lover jilted by a letter? That's something I'll have to hang around to see this time."

"I remember," came Anna's voice. "You'll never get away with this a second time."

"But I have for so long," said the man mockingly. "I'm sorry to say it, but you're just as unstable this time as you were the last time. Look how easily your own husband thought the worst of you."

After hearing Elizabeth's voice, the realization of what this machine possibly was forced terror into Terry's mind. At the mention of a letter, the anger Terry had felt toward Elizabeth for these last several months suddenly became replaced by doubt and guilt that perhaps he impulsively read a situation so wrongly that he had endangered his wife and destroyed his family. He still wasn't sure what Erik had to do with this, but for now, Terry had to assume, Erik was his best option to help.

Hearing more struggling coming from over the receiver, Terry began to desperately yell out for Erik's attention, but Erik was already rushing into the room with the sound of scuffling and glass breaking. Erik looking confused, eyed

Terry warily, but quickly turned his attention toward the receiver. Terry watched as Erik ran to turn it up.

"Thank God Anna hadn't turned it off completely," Erik was saying to no one in particular.

Now with the volume turned up to full, Terry heard the brunt of Anna's attack, as if it were happening right before his very eyes.

"I recognize that man's voice," said Terry horrified.

"No!" screamed Erik, as he ran out the front door.

Terry could hear Elizabeth's cries over the receiver, as he began kicking the wooden pillar with his feet. He had not fought hard enough for her once, and he had no intention of making that same mistake twice. Thankfully, the pillar was of a hollow construction. After four kicks, it gave way, allowing Terry to pull his handcuffs down and through the separation. As awkward as it was to run with his hands cuffed in front of him, Terry still caught up with Erik who was looking pale and exhausted. Outside of the cottage fence, Terry grabbed Erik by his shirt.

"That's my wife in there," informed Terry, releasing Erik and holding his cuffed hands out in front of him.

Terry was amazed that Erik hadn't even questioned him on how he had gotten free of the pillar, but instead silently took out the key to the cuffs and freed Terry's wrists.

"Now you listen to me," Erik was saying, "we can't just go rushing in there. We could do more harm than good. I've got a key to the front door; I'm going in that way. You hang to the side of the house and watch the doors off of the conservatory."

Both men ran low across the fence, until they came to the front of the cottage. Terry separated from Erik and continued along to the back of the cottage. He could see Elizabeth struggling with the door and then suddenly, she was miraculously out and running from the cottage. Terry could see the red welts on Elizabeth and could sense her fear. He ran after her, just as he heard Erik's voice shouting.

"Drop the gun!" Erik was shouting while pointing his gun at Elizabeth's attacker.

The man had his gun aimed at Elizabeth and in the seconds it had taken Erik to yell that warning, time suddenly stood still. Elizabeth looked back frozen with fear. The man fired his weapon at Elizabeth and Erik fired his weapon at the man. The span of that one second held the weight of a lifetime. Then, just as quickly, time seemed to lurch forward and the confusion was compounded as more people entered the yard. Terry, who had been running toward Elizabeth when the guns went off, was able to reach her before her crumpled body hit the ground.

"Elizabeth," said Terry, gently cradling her in his arms. He noticed a bright red blood stain on her right side that was quickly spreading across her shirt.

"Terry," replied Elizabeth, faintly, "the letter . . ."

"Bring her to the cottage," commanded one of the older men that had entered the yard.

"Anna," said the older woman holding Elizabeth's hand, as Terry carried Elizabeth back inside. "It's going to be all right."

"For eight months I've been trying to find myself," whispered Elizabeth, barely audible. "Now it seems as though I have too much life for one person. I don't know who I am at all."

Terry watched as the loss of blood and the physical pain finally took its toll on Elizabeth's body, taking any hope of getting this straightened out now with it.

Chapter Twenty-six

"Dennis," grumbled Doc, while continuing to work on Anna, "get these two idiots out of here. I can't think with all of their fussing and arguing."

"I'm not leaving until I know she's going to be alright," said Terry.

"I'd say your concern is about eight months too late," challenged Erik.

"Anna's going to be fine," Doc said calmly, looking up from where he was stitching up Anna's side. "The bullet just grazed her side and the other wounds will be sore for a while, but they aren't life threatening. Now if the two of you want to continue fighting like children, I'm ordering both of you outside."

"Come on." Dennis reached for Erik's elbow. "You're ready to fall over."

"My name is Daniel," stated Daniel, offering the other man his hand.

"I'm Terry," responded the man. "Elizabeth's husband."

"I gathered as much. What do you say we go try to untangle this mess and leave Doc to his business? I'll make us some coffee."

When Daniel and Terry entered the kitchen, they could

see Dennis and Erik outside. The glass walls gave them an all-too-clear view of the two men taking photos of the fatally wounded man who had attacked Anna.

"On second thought," Daniel said, looking around the disheveled cottage, "I don't suppose we should touch anything until this area has been fully investigated. Let's go have a sit on a bench outside."

Terry began speaking after they had silently reached the bench and sat down.

"There were times when I would sit alone, wondering where she was, or what she was doing. Then I would look at the kids and see how distraught they were and the anger and bitterness would come crashing back. You can't imagine how hard it has been on us."

"Maybe," conceded Daniel. "But you can't seem to imagine how hard it's been on Anna."

"For one thing, I don't care what she is calling herself now, her name is Elizabeth. You're wrong if you think this could have possibly been any worse for her," denied Terry, reaching into his pocket, and then showing Daniel what appeared to be a letter. "I admit the last couple of years hadn't been the happiest for us and when her mother died last spring, it was as if she became a different person. I knew she wanted things to change, but I couldn't believe this was her answer. Pretty selfish, wouldn't you say?"

"Come on," instructed Daniel, finishing the letter and then standing up. "I believe you missed a great deal by not reading between the lines."

"What's that supposed to mean?" asked Terry, following Daniel back toward the cottage.

"I'll tell you what," Daniel said as they were approaching Erik and Dennis, "let me give you something to read now and then you can ask me that question again."

"I want some answers," demanded Terry.

"Me too!" shouted Erik, standing next to Terry now.

"Dennis," began Daniel, "do you happen to have Anna's file in your squad car?"

"Yeah, but . . ." stammered Dennis.

"I believe it's time Anna's husband got a good look at it," said Daniel, shaking his head. "I think a picture will speak a thousand words for him."

"Over here." Dennis headed for his car as Terry followed.

"What was that all about?" inquired Erik.

"A letter," replied Daniel, handing Erik Terry's piece of paper.

"This letter doesn't make any sense."

"Exactly," replied Daniel. "That's what makes it so obvious. Anna wanted nothing more than to get back to her family, not to run farther away. She would never have written or acted in the way this letter implies."

"We still need answers only Anna can give us. When he's done reading that file," sneered Erik, pointing at Terry, "he can start filling in at least some of the blanks. Within the hour, this place will be swarming with detectives, so we better at least have some of the answers by then."

"I'd say we have a match to the shoe print," said Dennis walking back to the crime scene.

"I guess that takes the husband off the hook for that one," grunted Erik, covering up the dead man.

"You don't honestly believe he had anything to do with this?" asked Dennis.

"Maybe not criminally," replied Erik. "But indirectly, now that's a whole different ballgame."

"Marie called," shouted Susan, running breathlessly up the driveway. "How's Anna?"

"Elizabeth," corrected Dennis, "is going to be all right."

"Is this him?" asked Susan, backing away from the covered form.

"Apparently he knows," said Dennis, pointing toward Terry. "But Daniel has forced a time out between him and Erik, until tempers cool."

"Erik," said Susan gently, "maybe you should go back to your place and rest for a little while. I can't imagine what's keeping you standing at all."

"I'm not taking my eyes off of him for a minute." Erik stared intensely.

"You will when you have a relapse," commented Susan, shaking her head. "I'm going to go in and check on Anna."

"Elizabeth," reminded Dennis.

"That's going to take some getting used to," admitted Susan.

"Maybe now we can get a glimpse of what Elizabeth has been going through," said Daniel, coming up from behind them. "She'll need your friendship now more than ever, Susan. Go on in."

"Whoa!" exclaimed Susan, as the man who claimed to be Anna's husband ran into her.

"Sorry," said the man, scattered. "I didn't see you."

"I'm Susan, I'm a friend of Anna's."

"I didn't know," confessed Terry, clutching the manila folder to his chest. "I didn't know."

"She's been trying to get back to you," Susan said sadly. "She's been trying so very hard, you would be proud of her.'"

"Then why did she leave?" a dazed Terry asked.

"I don't know," replied Susan honestly.

"I need to go talk to the police," Terry said after an awkward pause.

"I'm going to check in on Anna."

"Elizabeth," Terry reminded softly. "Her name is Elizabeth."

"Sorry," Susan apologized awkwardly. "I'll check in on Elizabeth and let you know how she is doing."

"Thank you, no one else seems to want to give me the time

of day. The doctor's banned me from her room and everyone else thinks I'm some criminal."

"I think perhaps there's more than one victim here," said Susan, touching Terry's arm. "I've watched Elizabeth become strong once and overcome her circumstances. I have complete faith in her, that she can do so again. She needs us all now, including you, to help her straighten out her life. Don't back down now. Please help her."

Terry nodded and walked away.

"Oh my God!" exclaimed Susan, entering the cottage.

"God's had nothing to do with this," sighed Marie entering the room.

"All of her hard work, changed in a heartbeat," cried Susan. "How much can one person take?"

"It will be all right," said Marie, putting her arm around Susan. "That's why God gives us friends, He may not be able to stop all of the pain in this world, but he can help to ease it. Come on, Doc's just finished stitching her up and I think she's starting to come around."

"What should I say?"

"You're her friend, Susan," said Marie firmly. "Treat her like that and that will be enough."

"Hi," Susan greeted, entering the bedroom. "And I thought I was having a bad day," she continued, gently pushing a piece of hair from her friend's swollen face.

"My husband . . ." Elizabeth tried to sit up.

"Is just outside." Susan gently pushed Elizabeth back against the pillows.

"But I need to talk to him. I know now what happened."

"He's talking to Dennis and Erik. It might be a little while. I noticed more police arriving as I was coming in."

"He doesn't understand," uttered Anna, desperately. "He must think the worst of me. I know why no one ever came looking for me."

"I promise, Anna," said Susan. "This will all get straightened out."

"My name is Elizabeth and it won't work out or make sense until someone comes and talks with me."

Elizabeth watched Doc and Marie nod their heads and come closer to the bed.

"We're listening, Elizabeth," said Marie, unshed tears shining in her eyes. "Tell us."

With Susan holding one of Elizabeth's hands and now Marie the other, Elizabeth began.

"I'm sorry I'm not an Anna," apologized Elizabeth, feeling guilty for having traded names. Actually, for as glad as she was to know her true name, it saddened her to give up the one she had grown to live with. It once again felt to Elizabeth that a part of her life was being ripped away from her. She had thought this feeling would disappear when she remembered her own life, but the intensity of trying to shed this new life was leaving her just as confused and empty.

"Elizabeth," Marie patted her hand, "I told you before, a name doesn't make up a person. What's inside does and I've always liked what I saw inside of you."

"Go ahead, Elizabeth," encouraged Doc, "tell us what you remember."

Elizabeth took in a deep breath and let it out slowly. She wondered what her friends were going to think of her. Even now after living through it, it seemed almost impossible to her. Elizabeth scooted up straighter in bed, using the headboard for support. She winced as she felt the pull of the stitches and pain in her side. Her hands felt clammy as she continued to hold Marie's and Susan's hands.

"Terry is my husband," Elizabeth began, unsteadily. "But the other man has been a part of my life even longer."

Silence filled the room.

"What happened to him?" Elizabeth asked out of fear.

"He was shot and killed," Doc answered simply.

"Are you sure?"

"Erik ordered him to drop his gun," continued Doc. "But when he shot at you, Erik shot at him. He died instantly."

Elizabeth let go of the breath she hadn't realized she'd been holding.

"Why was he after you?" Susan asked.

"It all seems so very long ago now," replied Elizabeth, shaking her head sadly. "I had agreed to marry him. We became engaged, but the wedding never happened. I was very young at the time, my parents were going through an ugly divorce, and I was stuck in the middle. A few years later, when someone actually seemed to take an interest in me, I think I mistook love for a way to break away from my parents' games. I thought I had found someone who wanted to be with me, just for me, not because I was a stepping stone for others' feelings."

Marie squeezed Elizabeth's hand, giving her the acceptance of her past and the reassurance she needed to continue.

"Anyway, it wasn't long after we were engaged, when my fiancé started seeing other women, or maybe he had been all along, but at that point he no longer cared if I found out about it or not. At the same time, he wiped clean all of my savings and I found out he was buying drugs with the money."

Elizabeth's breathing began to quicken and although she tried to control it, her body began to shake.

"It's okay, Elizabeth," Doc was saying. "Take a few deep breaths and rest a minute."

"No," answered Elizabeth quickly. "Please, I want to go on."

"Then remember you're not alone," said Doc warmly. "We're all right here with you. Now take those deep breaths, then you can continue."

Elizabeth did what she was told and after she settled down some, she continued.

"When I confronted him with all of this and tried to break off the engagement, he became angry, shouting and throwing things. He threw me against the wall and as I felt my body sliding downward, he began to tell me of the horrific things he had done to others who wouldn't do what he had wanted. Then he just left.

"The next morning he was back as if nothing had happened, but once the dam was open, his actions and anger increased with any given incident. Sometimes he didn't even need to have a reason to be mad. Other times, he would be gone for a couple of weeks at a time, without even a phone call, only to return extremely intoxicated. That's when the beatings were at their worst.

"At first, I was so embarrassed that I had gotten myself into this situation, I never told a soul what was really going on. I became an artist at hiding bruises and a good liar at making up excuses. Then during one of his drunken beatings, I realized he was gaining more power each time one of these incidents took place.

"He beat me up pretty severely one time, but the next day, I went for help. I got a lawyer and a restraining order. That was twenty years ago. I've had over a dozen restraining orders since then, to protect myself and my family from his constant intrusions into my life.

"He pushed the boundaries of those legal documents to the limits and at times beyond. He always managed to find the loophole and was good at being sneaky. He has been able to harass me and keep me in fear for the last twenty years of my life. I always knew he wasn't finished because it was never about love. His power was his ownership. It was hard for other people to imagine this and understand and at times even I found his constant interruptions hard to believe. I guess last July even he felt he'd played his game long enough."

Elizabeth could feel her face was wet and wondered when

she had begun to cry. She had been tired from living in the shadow of fear for all of these years, with the very laws that were meant to protect her, ending up always protecting the rights of the guilty one.

"Elizabeth," Marie asked gently, "what happened last July?"

Elizabeth wiped her tears with the back of her hand and wrapped her mind around the sickening fear she felt from within.

"My mother had just died from a long bout with cancer. I spent her last year taking care of her. We buried her at the end of June and I was trying desperately to pull out of the depths of such a great loss. I knew I needed to get back to being the wife and mother I had been before, but it seemed to be such a huge struggle.

"I can't pinpoint why exactly, but prior to my mother's illness, my marriage was in a fragile state and now, part of my struggle was having to face the reality of that situation once again. Whatever it was, I was searching for the energy you feel when your life is in balance.

"I was focusing on accomplishing this when the constant uproar in my life resurfaced. All of these months, I couldn't remember anything and now, everything is so clear, it feels like it was just yesterday. It was the second of July, a sunny warm day. My husband had gone to work. My daughter had spent the night at a friend's house, and my sons had gone off for an early morning round of golf. I was going to the store to pick up a few groceries. We were all going to meet back home around noon to go on a much-needed holiday weekend up north."

Elizabeth paused, trying to sum up the courage to continue. "I never made it to the store that morning."

"Breathe, Elizabeth," Doc urged. "Don't forget we're here now."

Elizabeth nodded her head in acknowledgement and continued.

"As I was heading out the back door, my body was being forcefully pulled back inside. It was the oddest sensation. I suddenly had a great fear of my own home, where I had always felt the safest.

"In that short moment in time, a hundred thoughts raced through my mind. Then he spoke my name and the fear instantly seized me. He finished dragging me in and locked the door.

"As the shock began to wear off, I tried to twist away. I kicked backward and connected with his leg. Immediately I felt the cool metal smoothness of a gun being pushed up against my temple.

"I began praying not for myself, but that my children wouldn't make the mistake of coming home early. He had been rambling on about a note and how he would love to see my husband's face when he found it, but the majority of my attention was focused on trying to figure out a way to get out of this.

"He was pushing a piece of paper and pen at me, yelling for me to write something convincing. I was so confused; he wasn't making any sense. Then he started telling me what to write. He wanted me to tell Terry that I was leaving him to sort things out and that he shouldn't try to find me.

"When I didn't start writing, he pushed the gun even harder against my head, until I gave up and began to write. When he was satisfied with the letter, he turned to get my purse that I had dropped when he had grabbed me. While he was busy looking inside of it, I quickly wrote a message of my own, in small print on the bottom left-hand corner of the paper. I told my family I would love them forever.

"I guess I wasn't quick enough, because he noticed. He became angrier and started pummeling me with his fists. He ripped the pen from my hand and started crossing out my message, but a sound from the front of the house stopped him before he had finished. He wound my hair around his hand and, grabbing my purse, pushed me out of the house. He told me to get in my car and drive while he got into the passenger side. If I didn't, he would shoot me and whoever made that sound in the house.

"I was so worried that it was my daughter coming home early from her friend's house, that I sped backward out of the driveway, not once looking back. Next, he ordered me to drive to my bank's drive-up window and withdraw a large amount of money from my account.

"After that, it seemed like he just picked a direction and had me drive until the gas tank was almost empty. Then he had me pull off in a secluded area, where he tied my hands together behind me. Next, he bound my feet together and when he found duct tape in the trunk, he covered my mouth by completely winding the tape around my head. If I tried to move my head even a half an inch, my hair would pull so hard, it literally ripped from my scalp. His next big find in my trunk was a blanket, which he covered my entire body with, after he had shoved me face first onto the floor of the back seat.

"After driving all day in these conditions, the ropes cut into my wrists and ankles, leaving no feeling to any of my limbs. I was incredibly thirsty and my determination to find a way out of this horror was increasing with every mile I felt as the road moved beneath me.

"At the second stop for gas, I used my feet, kicking on the door and making as much noise as possible. I knew as he sped away from the station, that I had made a futile attempt . . . one that would probably cost me my life.

"On another deserted road, he pulled me by my shoulders out of the back seat. I hit the ground with such force that I could feel the rocks cutting my body, through my clothing. He started yelling and kicking at me and when his shoe hit my head, I was thankful to feel myself reeling into a blackness that was even darker than the night sky.

"The sun was setting again when I came to with water being forced down my throat. I had no idea how much more time had gone by, but going by the date that I ended up in the cove, I think now, it had to have been sometime the night before Daniel found me."

Elizabeth was grateful; Marie and Susan continued to hold her hands, willing her their strength. She needed to go on, to face this.

"I think he realized he had gone too far," Elizabeth continued almost panting now. "So he started to untie me. At first, there was no feeling in my arms or legs. He was offering the water to me slower, almost gently, and I could tell by his actions, he felt as though he was doing me some kind of favor. He felt like a hero. He began to rub my arms and legs and as the blood started flowing again, the pain became an all-consuming, searing burn.

"I sat that way for a long time, trying hard to keep from vomiting or giving him the satisfaction of hearing my pain. As the pain began to ebb, it made room for other thoughts to seep in. I took in my surroundings. In the distance, farther than I had anticipated my body would take me, was what appeared to be a farmhouse. I focused on that structure for over an hour, seeing it as my only chance.

"He offered me more water and even chips that he said he had picked up from the gas station he had stopped at while I had slept. It must have been the same place he had gotten the beer he was downing, one after the other. The whole time he was carrying on a conversation as if everything was normal and we were just two people, out on a picnic. He talked about his job and where he lived. I slowly began adding polite conversation, hoping he would start trusting me and I would find my opportunity to escape him.

"He became friendlier and friendlier and finally my break came, when he announced he had to use a bathroom. I watched as he looked around and concluded what his only choice would be. I started rubbing my legs, hoping he would believe I was still unable to use them. For all I knew, that was the truth, but God help me, I knew I was going to try to run.

"My heart pounded as I watched him enter the tree line. Immediately I stood up, gasping silently as the prickling pain shot up and down my legs. I started to move. I knew I was moving forward, but it felt like I was running in place. I'd hoped my lack of speed would be compensated for by the darkness that had fallen. I was heading for the light lying directly across the field, the farmhouse I had seen earlier.

"A sharp snap of a cornstalk to my left sent my spirits plummeting once again. I could see the outline of a large piece of farm machinery, so I headed for it. As I hid silently behind one of the huge tires, I began to feel surrounded. My hands made contact with a loose bar that had been resting on the machine. I silently wrapped my fingers around it and when I heard him whisper my name from behind me, I swung around, wielding the metal piece. My arms vibrated from making contact with some part of his upper body.

"He started swearing and yelling. I dropped my weapon and tried to run again, but my legs would no longer listen to my mind. I knew he was right behind me, but I forced myself not to look back. In mere seconds, he had me tackled to the ground and as he kicked me, rolling me over, I saw the very same metal piece I had used on him, come crashing toward my face.

"The stunning blow gave him the opportunity to retie my wrists, and I was stumbling and being dragged back toward the car. We covered the distance in what seemed like no time at all. I felt humiliated at myself that my great escape had only amounted to maybe a few hundred yards. I expected the beating that came next, but when he started ripping at my clothes and thighs, something inside of me snapped. I forced my mind to leave, as he forcefully and savagely raped my broken body. I wouldn't allow myself to admit it was my blood mixing with the dirt on the ground, or that it was my body, lying limp and lifeless.

"I think this must have angered him even more, because when he stood to pull his pants up, without a word, he reached for the pipe and started hitting me again. I felt his hands go to my neck then and I didn't even fight at the loss of air. I was glad it would all be over soon. I was thankful when everything became that empty darkness.

"Then somewhere in that silent emptiness, I became cold. So cold that my mind began to fight the darkness. I felt my body floating in a dream, but I didn't want to wake up. I wanted to stay where I was, away from the pain, but the coldness would force me to gasp for air. The next wakeful memory I have is being in the bedroom of your house, Marie."

Elizabeth was crying and shaking her head. "How could I not have remembered all of that before?"

"Dear," soothed Marie, holding tightly to Elizabeth's hand, "there are a number of reasons why you might have shut down. What you have to understand is, none of those reasons are because you did anything wrong."

"I should have fought harder, or just let him kill me right away."

"Look at me." Marie gently took Elizabeth's face in her hands. "You did fight hard, you have the scars to prove it. As for letting him kill you, well, I know you well enough to know, you would never want that because of your children."

"But look what they've gone through."

"Look what you've gone through," sighed Marie. "You've survived and I have to believe any children of yours would share that same strength. I'm not saying there's not wounds that won't need healing, but they will heal, Elizabeth. With love and patience, they will heal."

There was a knock at the door and Daniel entered.

"Where is my husband?" asked Elizabeth, nervously.

"Actually, he's been asking about you," replied Daniel. "I was just checking to see if it was all right for him to come in."

"I need to talk to him," Elizabeth said, keeping her head bent. "I just don't know how. What if he doesn't understand?"

"Then he's a fool," bellowed Erik, entering the room.

"Erik, why don't we give you a once over," said Doc, steering Erik back toward the door. "It appears your fever has returned."

"Erik, I'm so sorry," Elizabeth began, but her words hung on her lips. She was sorry she had been so mad at him only this morning, sorry that he had to risk his own life to save hers, but most of all, she was sorry for . . . She felt her emotions trying to get the best of her and she blinked rapidly trying to stop the flow of tears.

"I know," accepted Erik, as he silently and knowingly left the room.

Chapter Twenty-seven

The pieces of the puzzle were all present and accounted for. After the detectives had finished talking to Elizabeth and then Erik, Doc had ordered both of his patients on two full days of bed rest. Elizabeth was better at following orders, because by the afternoon of the second day, Erik was up and dressed. Not even Dennis's persistent nagging could keep Erik from walking over to see Elizabeth.

"I saw her briefly this morning," stated Dennis, walking the path next to Erik. "She's doing as well as can be expected. Doc's going to have my head on a platter though, when he sees you're out of bed."

"I just want to check on her myself," commented Erik, feeling the need to see Elizabeth with his own eyes.

"You know Elizabeth's husband hasn't left her side once?"

"Now is a really good time for him to be attentive," muttered Erik sarcastically, releasing some of his pent-up anger. "He sure doesn't know how to be there when she really needs him."

"You know that's not an entirely fair statement," defended Dennis. "He's actually a pretty decent guy."

Erik snorted and kept walking.

"We've all had our share of mistakes and misplaced promises." Dennis gripped Erik's arm, forcing him to stop. "We've all had our short comings, things we wished we could change or do over again. It's easy to criticize and condemn, but believe me, Terry knows he will have to live with this mistake the rest of his life, just as we've had to live with ours."

Erik knew Dennis didn't mean to blame or hurt him, but still, it brought up the shattered images of Erik's wife and daughter. A bucket of cold water couldn't have shocked him more into understanding as he and Dennis continued to walk.

"Elizabeth's sister flew in early this morning," explained Dennis. "They seem very close."

As Erik and Dennis approached the cottage, Doc came rushing out of the door.

"Can't you count?" asked Doc angrily.

"I can," grinned Erik. "But to see you angry is better than any bed rest, any day."

"You're impossible."

"I've learned from the best," winked Erik. "How's Elizabeth doing?"

"Physically she's doing well and emotionally she seems pretty strong also. I had my doubts at first about her husband, but he's proven to be a good support for her. Now that her sister's here—"

"Erik," greeted Susan, sounding surprised, as she stuck her head out the door. "Why don't you come in? Marie and I were just straightening up. The detectives gave us the go ahead this morning."

"Is Elizabeth alone?" Erik asked, suddenly feeling like a stranger.

"She's still with her sister and husband," replied Susan almost sadly.

"I'll wait out here on the bench then, the fresh air feels good."

"I gotta get back to the office," announced Dennis, giving

Susan a kiss on the cheek. "I'll check on the kids on my way over. Hopefully, they haven't driven the babysitter crazy yet."

"Tell them I'll be over soon," waved Erik. "We can compare chicken pox stories."

Susan shut the door, but Doc remained outside with Erik. Both men sat down on the bench.

"How are you doing?" questioned Doc, turning toward Erik.

"You know, still a little weak, but I feel pretty good."

"That's not entirely what I meant."

"I know," admitted Erik. "But I'm not even sure if there should be answers to those questions."

"Everything has an answer," stated Doc, patting Erik's knee, as he rose from the bench to go inside. "We just need to find them."

Erik sat for a while, looking at the outside of the cottage, remembering when he had first laid eyes on it. He had watched as Anna chopped, pulled, painted, and scrubbed this place until it presented itself as the rare jewel it really was, much like Anna herself.

Now that Elizabeth knew who she was, however, Erik knew in his heart that he would want her to continue to shine, to move on. As Elizabeth's friend, Erik would make sure that would happen, no matter what the cost to him. She deserved a life free of turmoil and confusion.

Looking around, Erik spotted a weed growing in Elizabeth's well-kept garden. He got down on his knees and began, as Marie would call it, gardening. It was such a small thing to be doing for Elizabeth, but it kept his hands busy. His thoughts, however, were not as easily distracted and the sinking loneliness of the last couple of days were never far from the surface.

He had been Elizabeth's protector, confidant, friend, and without him even realizing it, she had been the same for him. Erik understood that if the time came to say good-bye, the feeling of loss would be great. He wasn't sure if he could survive another loss.

Doc had said to find the answers, but as far as Erik could see, the answers only complicated one part of Elizabeth's life, leaving more questions unanswered in the other. A shadow crossed, then overlapped his own. As Erik began to look up, a woman's voice, not unlike Elizabeth's, but with a great deal more confidence, began an introduction.

"Hi," said the woman. "I'm Sam. I understand from Susan we owe you a great deal of gratitude for taking care of my sister."

"It's my job," replied Erik, feeling angry that the last several months had come down to this. It had been so much more than a job to him; it had been his life. The Elizabeth he knew had taught him patience, kindness, how to give, and how to be accepted. She had shown Erik an inner strength equal to none he had experienced before, forcing him to quit wallowing in his own self-pity.

"Is this part of the job?" smiled Sam.

Erik threw the handful of weeds into a bucket and with a glower on his face, stood up next to Sam. Suddenly, guilt overcame him as he watched the single tear, glistening in the sun, begin to slide down Elizabeth's sister's face. He knew instinctively Sam was feeling every pain, every hurt, and every loneliness he himself had felt for Elizabeth.

"As much as I want to place complete blame for Elizabeth's ordeal on the animal who attacked her, I'd be lying if I didn't admit she wasn't wronged also by those who claimed to love her. Lizzie is a special person," continued Sam, almost more to herself than Erik. "Unfortunately, it took this tragedy and her absence for all of us to realize just how special."

Erik noted the sorrow echoing in Sam's voice. He gently took her elbow and guided her to the bench he and Doc had occupied only moments ago, and then he set back and let Sam begin.

"It wasn't until around Christmas that I learned Lizzie had gone. We live rather far apart and I had been out of the country on business for a couple of months. I was becoming increasingly worried though, when my phone calls were always picked up by the answering machine. Living far apart didn't mean we didn't stay in touch, so when no one was returning my messages, I began to worry.

"By December, I left a message saying I was coming as usual for Christmas. Terry immediately called me back, sounding sick and worn out. He had said it really wasn't a good time right now and when I asked to talk to Lizzie, he hung up. I was on the next flight out to my sister's house.

"When the taxi pulled up, I knew before I even stepped out, Lizzie wasn't there. She loved Christmas and decorated from top to bottom, inside and out, starting the day after Thanksgiving. Her yard was always meticulously manicured, the envy of the entire block. Now, however, every fall leaf was mixed with the melting snow, giving the house a gray, almost dingy look. The sidewalks left unshoveled, were trodden with icy footprints. The place was a disaster and that's why I knew Lizzie wasn't there."

Erik nodded in agreement; apparently, Elizabeth shared some of the same traits in both lives.

"Before I could knock on the front door," Sam went on, "Callie, Lizzie's daughter, silently opened it, letting me in. When I stepped into the house, Zach and Ken joined us in the hallway. Past visits always had the kids running and jumping around me, but this eerie calm was more than I could bear. Ken, the youngest, approached me crying and collapsing in my arms.

"I asked where their mother was and saw the wavering look that passed between Zach and Callie. Then Zach spoke up and told me she had gone away for a while after his grandmother's death. The kids were in too much pain to press further, but I was determined to get answers from Terry when he returned home from work that night.

"Terry came home looking beaten and old, but not at all surprised to see me. He tried using the well-rehearsed explanation he had fed to the kids, but when I wouldn't buy it, he gave in and showed me the letter."

"Ah yes," Erik mumbled angrily. "The infamous letter."

"I read and reread that letter over a dozen times," explained Sam. "No matter how hard I tried, it just didn't make sense. It wasn't Lizzie. She was the stability of all of us. Looking back now, I realize that was where Terry and I should have both left it, thinking like Elizabeth, but instead, we made the grave mistake of thinking like ourselves—selfish. We began to really see for the first time what Lizzie's life was like. She had always been there for all of us. She had simplified our lives, while in return, we were good at complicating hers, and she never once complained."

Again, Erik caught himself nodding in agreement. How many times had Elizabeth done this for him as well? Erik could only hope he had given as much in return and never took for granted any of her kindness.

"Lizzie's thirty-eight and I'm two years older, but all of our lives our roles have been reversed. Our parents divorced in a time when divorce was still taboo. I was old enough to get out and go away from all of it, and believe me, I did.

"At that time, Lizzie was only sixteen and still in high school. She was waiting tables in the mornings before school, and would return after school for the dinner shift. Every night at ten, after work, Lizzie would come home to an empty apartment.

"When our parents divorced, Lizzie had gone to live with our mother, who immediately found her new freedom exhilarating.

"I knew Lizzie at sixteen was being the adult as best as she could, just as I knew the price she was paying for it emotionally. I let her deal with all of the worries and humiliation that most adults couldn't have dealt with. I left her to deal with all of this on her own."

Erik's heart cried for a lonely, scared sixteen-year-old Elizabeth, but he felt Sam was remiss in excluding herself from this emotional pain as well. He could tell Sam would continue to force herself to live with the sorrow of making the wrong decision all those years ago.

"You were only eighteen yourself," Erik said, gently taking Sam's hand. "You couldn't have controlled the situation any better than Elizabeth did."

"It's just that," Sam stammered, wiping her eyes, "lately I've realized what it's done to Lizzie. She takes care of everything. She fixes everything. For years now, we've all kept her in that role. She's never had a chance to be more than that. She's been a daughter, sister, wife, and mother, and to each of those roles, she's given one hundred percent. When I was forced to realize it, I knew we had kept her so busy in our worlds that she never had time for her own. She paints, Erik. I never knew. She paints beautifully."

"Yes she does," Erik smiled. "Her work is in a gallery here and in the city."

"I know," confessed Sam making eye contact with Erik. "A friend of mine thought she had run into Lizzie in the city one night.

"It took my friend some time to call me though because she was confused by the name Lizzie's paintings were under in the gallery. In fact, her mention of it was more of an afterthought in our conversation because no one even knew Lizzie was gone. For me though, it was the first real lead we'd had.

"I finally convinced Terry that no matter what Lizzie was feeling about him or her life in general, she would never have left the kids. They were her life.

"Anyway, we both thought it best if Terry flew up there, to at least check it out. We weren't holding out too much hope, given the fact that the woman he was checking on was an artist, but as I said, it was the best piece of information we'd had. The rest of the story, well you know it better than I."

Erik shook his head in understanding.

"Thank God, Terry was willing to swallow some of his pride, or who knows when we would have found Lizzie," admitted Sam, standing up.

Erik also stood, following Sam to the cottage door.

"Do you want to come in?" Sam offered, as Erik turned the knob and opened the door.

Erik turned red from embarrassment. He had been about to enter the cottage as he had so many times before. He couldn't even remember the last time it had been by invitation.

"No," Erik said awkwardly. "I'll let Elizabeth spend time catching up with you."

"She's been asking about you. She wants to know how you are feeling. I see you've had a bout with the chicken pox."

"Could you tell her for me, the chicken pox are fine."

As for how he was feeling, Erik himself wasn't exactly sure. How was he supposed to be feeling?

"I'll tell her," promised Sam.

"Also, please tell her I hope she's feeling better, and I'm glad things are working out for her."

"I will."

Erik caught a glimpse of concern or maybe confusion in Sam's eyes as he turned to walk back to his cottage. Only for a moment he felt guilty he had let his feelings be so open, because almost immediately, the loneliness began to wear him down and once again, he became numb.

Chapter Twenty-eight

Late the next afternoon, Erik stood at his window and watched as Michael and his family arrived. Watching Garth and Megan head down the lane to Elizabeth's cottage left Erik again wondering where Elizabeth's own children were. Since Elizabeth's husband had fallen from the sky, Erik felt as if he had been, once again, excluded from the circle of friends. In all fairness, he had no one but himself to blame, for he had stepped out of that circle all on his own. He was the outsider looking in.

"Erik!" Doc was shouting coming through his doorway.

Erik turned from the window, giving little thought to the fact that his face was scruffy from a full day's worth of growth and he still had on the same T-shirt and baggy sweat pants from the other day.

"I've been knocking like crazy out there. I thought you had another relapse."

Erik watched as Doc inspected him from head to toe. He knew that even with the chicken pox he hadn't looked this ill, but then he hadn't felt this ill either. The fear of losing something so precious again gripped his stomach worse than any illness ever could.

"What are you doing all locked up in here?"

Erik saw Doc's attention turn from him to the condition of his cottage. Clothes were thrown over chairs and on the floor. Dishes were stacked precariously high in the sink. Erik's usually clean and well-organized home looked as if a tornado had just ripped through it. Well hell, Erik thought to himself, why shouldn't it reflect his life?

"I'm following your orders and getting rest," snapped Erik, sinking down on the couch, suddenly feeling defeated.

"My orders? Since when have you ever followed my orders?"

Erik just sat there, mentally too weak to argue.

"Get your robe on and a blanket, we're going outside for some sunshine."

"I don't want to," grumbled Erik, not moving from the couch.

"I didn't ask you if you wanted to," snapped Doc. "I want to. The air is too thick in here for me."

"You're treating me like a two-year-old child."

"You know what they say," laughed Doc. "If the booty fits."

Before he knew how it happened, Erik was outside watching the sunset and memories of when he first moved in began to fill his mind. The beauty of this time of day used to enthrall him, giving him a sense of peace he had never known existed. Now it only seemed to mock him, as the beauty of the orange glow gave way to the cold, drab darkness that seemed to surround his soul and crush the life right out of him.

"Her children are coming in a few days," Doc began tentatively.

"I was wondering where they were."

"Terry thought it was a good idea to wait until Elizabeth's injuries were a little less shocking," continued Doc.

"Do you agree with that?"

"It's not really my place to say," said Doc, shaking his head. "It's between Terry and Elizabeth to decide what's best."

"What's best for Elizabeth, though?"

"To pick up the pieces and try to fit into her family again. Right now, she's worried how her life will come together with her children's. I have to give Terry a lot of credit. He's been a huge support for her."

Just as Doc was speaking, Erik looked over to Elizabeth's cottage and saw the silhouette of the very two people Doc had just been speaking of. Their bodies came together in an embrace that appeared both tender and passionate. The moment seemed so private, Erik immediately turned away.

"A history is there," commented Doc. "One they both need to face and deal with, for better or for worse."

"Is that supposed to be a subtle reminder of morals and responsibilities? Because Elizabeth and I were just friends."

"Even good friends are hard to let go of sometimes," replied Doc. "And when did it change to be 'were,' instead of are? If you are as good of friend as you claim to be, you wouldn't have left her wondering and worrying about you."

"I was giving her time with her family."

"We're part of her family too now. Families are love, support, crying together, and laughing together. We've had all of those things with Elizabeth; it would be cruel to pull that away from her. Don't you dare lessen her time here down to just a charity case, because for the rest of us, she is much more than that."

Erik had heard Doc's voice turn from consoling to reprimanding. Truth was, Erik knew he deserved it. When he looked up expecting to see anger in Doc's eyes, he was shaken by the amount of love and pride that reflected in them instead. Even after the way Erik had been acting, Doc could still be proud of him and that meant everything to Erik.

"I'll go to see her tomorrow," uttered Erik softly.

"I think you've made a good decision, son," Doc agreed,

putting his hand on Erik's shoulder. "Come on, Marie sent supper over with me."

Erik rose before the sun the next morning, having experienced a fitful night of sleep. The source of his sleeplessness was the question on how to approach Elizabeth. He didn't even know where to begin. He looked up and down the cove, noting not a single house light was on.

"Of course not," Erik grumbled to himself. "Who would be crazy enough to be up at this hour?"

Erik decided to go for a run. He headed in toward town and then back again, feeling somewhat stronger and revived after the lingering weakness left by his illness. Reaching his cottage, Erik continued on to Doc's house to maybe bum a cup of coffee and some courage. Passing the cove, Erik heard faint crying. When he looked down the rocky edge, Elizabeth was standing alone on the beach, facing out toward the water. Fear knotted in his stomach at the thought of her hurt again. He raced down the hill, heading straight for her.

"Elizabeth!" Erik called, half running, half sliding down the incline. Her head turned toward Erik and he saw the fresh tears flowing down her face.

"What's the matter?" He demanded, taking her hands, while visually assessing her for any injuries.

"Nothing, I was just watching the sunrise."

Erik looked around, as memories washed over him of the countless times Elizabeth had tried to conquer this cove. Of the cold December day, when she had put a child's needs before her own, risking her very sanity. Elizabeth's sister's words rang through Erik's head—she does take care of everyone, but for one small moment in time, she had allowed others to take care of her, making her life whole. She was complete now and that thought was what finally put Erik's mind at ease.

"Doc tells me you're feeling better," Elizabeth was saying, sounding like a hurt child.

"I know I should have come by. It's just that . . ."

"You thought I needed some time to adjust," offered Elizabeth.

"Something like that."

"It's funny," continued Elizabeth, staring back out toward the water. "I met Terry right after I finished high school and for years we would run into each other on and off. Then one of our meetings came on the heels of both of us ending destructive relationships and from that point on, we were inseparable.

"I was completely in love with Terry and I could tell whenever he looked at me, he felt the same. It was as if we had a cocoon around ourselves and our growing family. Then, in one moment, we changed. Realistically it had been creeping up on us for years, but we were too busy to notice, until words were never shared between us and the love-filled glances became fewer and fewer."

Erik began to fidget with his hands uncomfortably. For some reason, this seemed to snap Elizabeth out of her memory-induced trance. He watched as she blushed, realizing she had been thinking aloud. As much as Erik didn't like Terry, he knew Elizabeth needed to hear the truth.

"I never got the chance to tell you," started Erik, groping for the right words. "Terry was the one who saved your life last week."

Elizabeth looked confused, so Erik continued.

"He heard you struggling over the receiver. When I ran out of the door, Terry wasn't far behind, even though I had left him handcuffed to the wooden pillar in my cottage. He was right there, Elizabeth, and nothing was going to stop him from getting to you."

"He never told me."

"He loves you, Elizabeth," Erik said with a heavy heart. "I saw it then, even though I didn't want to admit it."

"And I love him," replied Elizabeth. "He and my children are the world to me. Terry and I have had many chances to talk these last couple of days and we both agree that the things that had been pulling us apart before seem so insignificant now. Everyday problems seem laughable compared to what we've been through these last months. Soon after the kids come, we'll be going home."

Erik tried to hide the hurt he was feeling.

"I need to go home, Erik," said Elizabeth, almost as a plea.

Erik had been trying to prepare himself for this exact moment, but even so, the words seemed to shove him down with brutal force. His knees gave way and he landed on the cool sand of the cove.

"I will miss all of you so much," Elizabeth was saying, kneeling down next to him.

Erik couldn't seem to make his eyes meet Elizabeth's. The pain was just too much to mask.

"I'll miss you," cried Elizabeth, taking Erik's face in her hands. "You've been a good . . ."

There was a long breath, a long sigh.

"Friend," Erik supplied, as he had watched Elizabeth struggle for words. "I understand," he continued. "You've been one for me too."

"I'm sorry I doubted your methods of protecting me. I wish I could erase my angry outburst the morning I found the receiver."

"I should have told you," Erik said, wishing he too could go back in time. "You lost your trust in me that morning; I saw it in your eyes. I'm sorry for that."

"I said a lot of things because I was confused, but I truly never lost my trust in you. You've saved my life, Erik, in many ways. I have all the proof I need to know my trust was never misplaced."

"I'll always be here for you," Erik said, taking Elizabeth's hand and pressing it to his face. "Whatever you need, I'll always be here."

"I know," choked out Elizabeth through tear-filled eyes.

Erik rose and with Elizabeth's hand in his own, he slowly headed up the incline. Each step took them painfully back to the world and lives so intricately entwined and yet, so clearly separate.

Glancing upward toward her future, Erik watched as Elizabeth saw her sister and began to wave.

"I understand you've met Sam," said Elizabeth, drying her eyes with the back of her free hand.

"She's a lot like you," Erik commented as they continued to walk up.

"Don't ever tell her that. She's made it her life's work to be just the opposite. She refuses to settle down and instead, works and competes with the big boys. I understand though, contrary to all of her proclamations of not being the motherly type, she was all that and more to my children when they needed her the most."

"Will she be going back with you?"

"She insists she wants to, at least for a little while, but I know she's itching to get back to work."

"Maybe that's just the way you're used to things being," commented Erik. "Sometimes things change. Sometimes life changes the way we act, think, or even how we choose to prioritize. You know that better than anyone."

Before Elizabeth could respond, Sam had walked down the last few feet to meet them, linking arms with Elizabeth.

"It's good to see you again, Erik," Sam smiled. "I believe last time you caught me at my worst."

"I suppose the same could be said about me," replied Erik,

feeling awkward. "I need to get to work before Dennis gives my badge to some rookie."

"I don't think you'll ever have to worry about that," said Elizabeth. "Not after the great lengths he took to get you here."

"What?" Erik asked, suspiciously.

"Nothing," replied Elizabeth, snatching Sam's hand and heading toward the cottage.

"Marie wants us all to get together for dinner tonight," explained Sam, turning back toward Erik. "You'll be there, right?"

"What time?" Erik was gathering up the courage to turn her down.

"Seven."

"I'll see what I can do," replied Erik. He had felt better after talking with Elizabeth, but to have her other life thrust in front of his face, well, Erik wasn't sure if he was ready for that yet.

"I hope you're feeling lucky tonight?" chuckled Sam, lightly. "I'm helping out with the cooking."

"Then I'll be sure to bring the Tums," laughed Erik, before he realized what he had just done. He had just as much said he would be there now.

"You're on," Sam smiled, turning back toward Elizabeth.

Erik felt like kicking himself the entire walk back to his cottage. He was still angry as he stepped out of the shower and got dressed. A persistent knocking at his door only seemed to bring his anger to its climax.

"Who is it?" Erik shouted, crossing the room and none to gently, swinging open the door.

"Perhaps I should have called first." Terry was standing on Erik's doorstep.

"I was just getting ready for work."

"I'd hate to be the person breaking the law in Dodge

today," Terry said sarcastically. "Oh wait, I've already been there."

"Look," Erik said, feeling a little guilty. "I never got the chance to apologize about that."

"No need," accepted Terry, waving his hand in the air. "I'm not saying I wasn't furious, but after things settled down that morning and I put myself in your shoes, I realized what a jerk I must seem like to you."

Erik felt awkward talking to Elizabeth's husband like this. It was as though Terry had been reading Erik's mind, and that was definitely the last place Erik wanted Terry to be.

"I can't pass judgment on you," Erik said uncomfortably. "I don't even know you."

"Then I'll do it for both of us. I wish I could change my actions and correct the past, but I can't. No matter how distant Elizabeth and I were or how wide our differences were, I shouldn't have let my hurt and anger cloud my common sense. Because of me, Elizabeth was lost and alone for so long. Her life was completely torn away from her and I helped to prolong that."

"She was never alone while she was here," Erik said, defending all of those who loved her. "Marie, Daniel, and Doc took good care of her. They were her comfort and support. Dennis and Susan, well . . . she and Susan are best of friends, and Elizabeth adores Brandon and Katie. Then there's Michael and his family. I think Garth would have been lost without her."

"I know I have all of you to thank," said Terry wearily. "Especially you, Erik, for everything you've done. Believe me, that's hard for me to say. I won't claim to understand the relationship you've had with my wife, because frankly, even a friendship makes me green with jealousy, but if I've learned anything from all of this, it's to put the anger and misunderstandings away. They can only cause damage. So instead,

Erik, once again, I thank you for taking care of my wife and I appreciate your chivalry and honor that has allowed my family to stay together."

"You're welcome," Erik said, accepting Terry's outstretched hand. Erik appreciated Terry's honesty and as much as he wanted to keep finding fault with Terry, he was actually seeing the reasons everyone else seemed to like him.

"I hear we're all having dinner together tonight," commented Terry, breaking the silence.

"So I was told by Sam."

"So you've met our loveable, headstrong Sam."

"Why does she go by Sam?"

"She claims that's what gets her into board meetings and men's locker rooms," winked Terry. "And according to Sam, that's where the biggest business decisions are made."

"Locker rooms!" Erik raised an eyebrow.

"I don't really think she has," laughed Terry. "But I certainly wouldn't put it past her."

Chapter Twenty-nine

The next two days seemed endless for Elizabeth. She knew Terry had been right about letting her injuries heal before the children saw her, but her arms ached to hold them. Such a big portion of their lives had been stolen from her and each second that ticked by was pure torture.

To keep from going insane, Elizabeth worked on orders from the gallery. Peg had told her not to worry about them, but to get her life back in order. The truth was though, Elizabeth found solace in her painting; it still centered and calmed her.

"What are you working on?" Garth asked as he entered the room.

"Garth!" Elizabeth put down her paintbrush. "What are you up to?"

"I asked first."

"I had some orders I needed to finish up for the gallery."

"Are you still going to paint? I mean, when you go back, do you think you'll continue to do this?"

"I guess I never really thought about that yet. So many more important things have been happening that—"

"This seems insignificant," interrupted Garth.

"Something like that. So are you ready to make the big move?"

Elizabeth thought of all of the countless conversations she and Garth had in the past about moving and fitting in. Suddenly the irony of this situation was not lost on her as Garth put voice to her very thoughts.

"I'll be moving in," uttered Garth thoughtfully, "and you'll be moving out."

"We're both moving to familiar places that scare us half to death," Elizabeth stated, putting her arm around Garth's shoulder.

"You are afraid to go back?"

"I shouldn't be," admitted Elizabeth. "I love my family, I have friends there, and it is my home, yet . . ."

"It's different, not the same," offered Garth. "All of those factors have stayed constant and you will be the element of change. You'll feel as if everyone will be watching you, waiting to see if you fit."

Elizabeth studied Garth and knew he was talking of his own move, just as much as hers. It was odd that a seventeen-year-old boy could share the same fears, but apparently, uncertainty has no age limits or boundaries.

"If you didn't have such great parents already," joked Elizabeth, "I would willingly adopt you. As it is, it will be very hard leaving you and Megan."

Elizabeth saw the sadness return to Garth's eyes.

"Just think, though, my family and I will be spending the entire summer here. That's really not that far away."

"I like your husband, he seems like a nice man," commented Garth.

"He is," smiled Elizabeth. "And my kids are going to love having you and Megan around this summer."

"What are they like?"

"Actually, a lot like you and Megan. They're polite and

kind. They do well in school and love all kinds of sports. However, one day I turned around and I realized they weren't children anymore, but young adults and I was proud, really proud that I was their mother."

"They sound great."

"They are, which is why I think you will all get along perfectly."

On the morning of Elizabeth's children's arrival, she cleaned the cottage two times over and tended the gardens, until everything was perfect.

She was on her fifth clothing change when a thought struck her. The entire time she had lived here, clothes had been just a necessity, one she had never given much thought to. But now standing here, her appearance seemed so important. She wasn't sure if it was to fit into who she had been or keep secretly locked away who she had become. On the sixth trip back to her closet, the knock at the door froze her in midstep. Terry and Sam had gone to the airport to pick up her kids. Terry had said he wanted to talk to them and prepare them. Elizabeth had outwardly agreed, but in reality, watching Terry and Sam take off this morning for her children, reinforced in her, that she was the outsider.

Even given the truth of the circumstances, Elizabeth worried her children would feel abandoned by her. She would be forever grateful to her sister for helping Terry take care of the kids through this horrible nightmare, but a sharp pain had stabbed in her chest this morning when Sam had driven off in the car instead of Elizabeth herself.

The second knock brought Elizabeth's mind back into the cottage room and as her whole body shook with excitement, she ran to the door.

"Elizabeth," said Doc, standing in the threshold. "You're as white as a ghost."

Elizabeth let out the breath she had been holding.

"Come on." Doc ushered her back inside to a chair.

"I thought you were Terry and the kids."

"They won't be back for a while yet. I knew I should have come over here sooner."

"I should get ready then." Elizabeth absentmindedly ran her hands through her hair.

"You are ready," Doc said gently, taking her hands. "You've been ready since the moment of their birth. You are their mother, Elizabeth. I've watched you weep for losing them, struggle to find them, and die inside waiting for them."

Elizabeth looked at Doc and felt love.

"You try to hide so much from the world, Elizabeth. Your pain, your thoughts, so many things, but your love has always shown through. Anyone can see the love you have for your children. You are a good mother. You couldn't have changed what has happened to you, nor did you have any control over it. You have to let go of the guilt you feel and focus on the love. Don't let other thoughts and feelings intrude on that."

"How did you get to be so wise?" Elizabeth asked as she reached over to hug Doc.

"They say with age comes wisdom," said Daniel, coming through the door with Marie. "For as old as he is, he must be full of it."

"Then what's your excuse?"

"Would you two grow up?" laughed Marie, walking over to Elizabeth. "How are you feeling, dear?"

"I'm fine now," Elizabeth said, feeling engulfed by the love of these three very special people.

"Of course you are, dear," agreed Marie. "Of course you are."

Just then, the grinding of gravel alerted them all to a car driving up the lane. Elizabeth flew to the window. It was Terry and Sam in the rental car, and in the back seat sat Elizabeth's children. Their faces showed worry and uncertainty, not at all the innocent, happy faces Elizabeth recalled in her dreams.

Elizabeth ran from the cottage toward the car her children seemed to be cautiously emerging from. Doc was right; she had been close to her children and her love had always been open and evident. She refused to let time or circumstances try to snatch that away.

Seeing them all standing in front of her, Elizabeth could no longer control her tears of joy.

"Zach, Callie, Kenny," whispered Elizabeth; as if saying their names would validate that they really were here. Elizabeth stretched her arms out and quickly closed the space between them.

The four distinct bodies became one and the laughing and crying continued, even as they all tumbled to the ground. Terry joined the mass of outstretched limbs and a family was reunited.

"Now that's love," said Doc smiling.

"Yes it is," agreed Marie.

"Come on." Daniel took Marie's hand. "We can meet them all later. For now, let's give them time to be a family again."

Chapter Thirty

Elizabeth's children did have the chance to meet everyone and just like Terry and Sam, they seemed to blend into Elizabeth's extended family. The children never let Elizabeth out of their sights, but the feeling had been mutual.

The few things Elizabeth had considered to be really hers took only an afternoon to pack up and by the morning of the third day since the arrival of her children, the realization that she was leaving this place and her friends began to sink in. It was a bittersweet time for Elizabeth as she walked around the rooms of the cottage, remembering the sweat and hard work she had put into refurbishing it.

She had no regrets, though, for the cottage was a special place that she could escape to in her dreams. She quietly opened the door, so as not to wake anyone up. She wanted to view her gardens one last time as the sun rose up over the water.

As she walked toward the cliff, she turned and noticed Erik out on his back deck. She knew he also loved watching the sun rise and set. She met him halfway on the path and they quietly held hands, watching as a new day dawned.

"We leave tomorrow morning," Elizabeth said, breaking the silence. "I just wanted one more glimpse of all of this to store in my memory."

"But Marie tells me you'll be coming back to visit this summer."

"We are," agreed Elizabeth, tears burning in her eyes. "I just can't imagine waking up without this every morning. I need to remember."

"I know," Erik said, squeezing Elizabeth's hand.

There was another shared pause before Erik continued.

"I see a contentment in you that was never quite there before. You are happy?"

"I am."

"Then I'm happy for you," admitted Erik, gently letting go of Elizabeth's hand.

The next day came all too quickly. Terry had the car packed and now came the difficult task of saying good-bye. Elizabeth smiled as she overheard Megan and Garth talking to her own children about the things they could all do together over the summer. Brandon and Katie were running in and out of the older kids' legs, playing tag.

"What will I ever do without you?" Susan asked, smiling through tears. "Who will be in charge of my sanity?"

"They grow so fast," explained Elizabeth, looking over at her own children. "Sanity will take on many different phases, plus it's highly overrated. Besides, that's what telephones are for. I can talk you through a nervous breakdown anytime."

"I'll miss you."

"You'll see me in a few months." Elizabeth tried to hold her composure.

"I'm really so very happy for you," sobbed Susan.

"You look it," Dennis said sarcastically as he hugged Elizabeth and shook Terry's hand. "We'll see you guys in a few months then."

"We'll be living here by then," stated Michael, walking over with Cheryl.

"Good," said Doc. "Maybe now I can finally retire and get on to the really important things in my life."

"Like golf?" asked Erik.

Elizabeth looked behind her as Erik came walking around the corner. Since he hadn't been a part of this farewell party, she had assumed he had meant for his good-byes to have been yesterday morning.

"What would you know about golf?" grumbled Doc. "You can't golf your way out of a paper bag."

"That sounds like a challenge to me," laughed Terry.

"Next time you're here, you'll have to come out with us." Erik extended his hand toward Terry's. "We'll see if we can't put his money where his mouth is."

"It's a deal," Terry said, opening his car door. "I hate to say this, but we really should get on the road."

After saying their last good-byes, Terry, Sam, and the kids got into the car and waited for Elizabeth.

"Marie tells me she's going to teach you about gardening," Elizabeth said, turning toward Erik.

"Yeah," replied Erik awkwardly. "It's a lot for them to take care of on their own."

"It's a big change of pace for you," smiled Elizabeth.

"It's a pace I find I like though. I don't regret any of it. In fact, I find I like taking care of things."

"You do it well," confirmed Elizabeth, leaning up to kiss Erik's cheek.

"I hope you have one of those for me," Doc was saying, with his arms stretched wide.

"Always," smiled Elizabeth. "Always."

Marie came up next, holding a large basket.

"There's cookies in there for the kids," she said through tiny sniffles. "And a little something wrapped up for you."

"We're only driving to the airport," said Elizabeth, through her own tears.

"But you never know dear," answered Marie. "You never know what the day may bring."

"I love you," Elizabeth said, tightly holding on to the older woman. "Thank you."

"No dear, thank you. You've brought something very special back to me that I'd thought I'd lost. Thank you . . . Anna."

Elizabeth smiled at the comfort she felt from the name she had used for so many months. No one had used it since her real name had been discovered, but coming from Marie, it was a moment Elizabeth would hold on to for the rest of her life.

"You better get in the car," Daniel said, taking Elizabeth by her shoulders.

"Daniel . . ." Elizabeth looked into the eyes that had pulled her from the icy water so many months ago.

"You're like a daughter to me, Elizabeth," Daniel said as his voice began to break up. "If you ever need anything, anything at all . . ."

"I know," cried Elizabeth, holding on tightly to Daniel and feeling rescued all over again. "I've always known."

Getting into the car had been harder than Elizabeth had thought it would be. When she no longer could see the cottage, she turned to her husband and children and smiled at her future.

As they were boarding the plane for home, Sam pulled out the brightly wrapped package from the basket Marie had said would be there.

"Aren't you going to open it?" asked Sam, handing Elizabeth the package.

Elizabeth carefully unwrapped it and smiled.

Sam read softly aloud, the intricately penned phrase that had been placed on the beautifully painted plaque. "May angels hold you while you sleep."

"I have met angels," Elizabeth said wistfully, as she gently traced the words with the tips of her fingers. "And they held me. I'll always remember how they held me."

To order a signed book by the author or for more information, including the second book in this series entitled, *Found Through a Cottage Window*, visit:

<u>www.marycaroll.com</u>

or write to:

Trace Books Publishing
P.O. Box 2193
Loves Park, Illinois   61130-0193